18

A NOVEL OF GOLF
AND LIFE

John Barnes

ISBN: 9781733419772

Cover/Interior Design by: Romolo Tavani

The Unapologetic Voice House, LLC

ACKNOWLEDGMENTS

Heartfelt thanks and acknowledgment to Carrie Severson and everyone at The Unapologetic Voice Publishing House. Thanks for guiding, directing, and believing. Huge gratitude to my editors: Marsha Butler—you came, you saw, you organized; N. Amma Twum-baah—thank you for polishing my rough prose into its shining state.

To PSI Seminars for the journey. You offered the opportunity and the tools, and TSW!! This book would not have come to be without you.

Thanks so much for the bravery and candor of Terri Renella and Susan Richards. You helped shape a character that will hopefully inspire other women to heal.

To Teri Wilbur; pushing me to the "edge" got me started, and your incredible insight and compassion inspired me in untold ways. To Dan Gibbons—from the start you embody shifting the cycle of revenge in your life and the lives of so many others. To Rob Rohe, thank you for lovingly holding up the mirror. And to Kathy Quinlan, thanks for your admonishment to stop taking s*** personally.

Paul Thede, it all started with you, my friend. Your wisdom, your humor, and your heart will never be forgotten. Like Seth Reede, you didn't need to, and yet you did.

Finally, to all of those who played and coached our great game with me. My love for these fictional characters mirrors my love for all of you: your stories, your laughter, and your tears. Know always that

"I AM AN AUTHENTIC, INTIMATE, AND POWERFUL MAN, CREATING LOVE AND LIBERTY IN MY LIFE NOW."

JB

November 2019

THE NUMBER 18

In the Bible, a foreign king oppressed the children of
Israel
For 18 years.

This was the time that God's children were in bondage; it
also marks
Their freedom from bondage.

*

The Hebrew word for "life" is "chi"; the two letters that
make up the word
Are "chet" and "uid."

These are the 8th and 10th letters in the Hebrew alphabet,
respectively;
Added together they make 18.

*

There are 18 letters in the Scottish Gaelic Alphabet.

*

Three of the five divisors of 18
(3, 6, and 9) add up to 18,
Making 18 "a semi-perfect number."

*

There are 18 shots in a fifth of Scotch.

*

In numerology, the number 18 resonates with humanitarianism, independence, And building something of lasting value.

*

In China, 18 is an auspicious number.

*

The essence of 18 is the welfare of humanity.

*

There are 18 holes in a round of golf.

PREFACE

The U.S. Open Golf Championship ("U.S. Open") is the pinnacle of the game, and one of the four major professional golf tournaments in the world. It has been held over four days (seventy-two holes) in late June of each year, since the late 1800s. The weather is typically hot, and the course brutal. The United States Golf Association ("USGA") picks a new venue every year to host this tournament. The venue is usually chosen several years earlier, based on its high level of difficulty and character. The golf course is then conditioned to be even more difficult—rough grown, deeper and thicker, fairways narrowed, and greens rolled and mowed to be as fast and firm as concrete. In the months leading up to the tournament, qualifying tournaments that attract five thousand to six thousand entrants with a handicap of two or less, are held to form the field of 140 survivors. Many winners from the PGA and European tours must qualify for the U.S. Open, despite being exempt from qualifying on other major golf tours. It is the most democratic golf championship in existence.

If the best golfers in the world were polled, the overwhelming majority would name the U.S. Open as the most difficult tournament in the world. Many of the best golfers in the world have been humbled, if not embarrassed, by

U.S. Open courses, even as the USGA insists that it does not toughen U.S. Open courses to humiliate the best golfers in the world but to identify them.

More esoteric questions than "What's the U.S. Open?" or "How does one qualify for it?" are "Can a round of golf reflect a man's life? Can it change his life?"

Golf, in all its torturous complexity, brings all sorts of emotions and experiences into play—joy and despair, hope and disappointment, judgment and acceptance. Competitive golfers know this. Competition brings all this into play. The great irony of golf is that the more the golfer lets go, the easier the game becomes. The more he or she lets go of control, of desire, of personal attachment to the golf score, the more the great mysteries of golf reveal themselves. The harder the player strives, grasps, broods, and rages, the harder and crueler the game becomes. Great players will say that the secret is to care and not care at the same time. How in God's name is this possible?

Golf is a lot like life.

Most golfers start young. In their youth, their minds yield to instinct. Young golfers just play. Their youthful minds are authentic, creative, and boundless. They dive in and take what comes. They move on easily from ecstasy or disaster. In their youth, their instincts allow them to be completely present, neither celebrating nor lamenting the past and totally unconcerned about the future. As children, golfers just *are*.

Then, somewhere along the line, they want to become more skilled. They are told they must "work on their game." Unfortunately, along with the technical instructions they receive on playing the game, they are also taught that they must toil at these instructions in order to succeed at the game. This conviction often brings with it the adult dullness that dampens their childlike approach. Continual, sometimes exhaustive, practice becomes paramount, and with it comes constant evaluation and judgment. Setbacks become disappointments—emotional and psychic baggage that is literally dragged around with them. Enough of this harsh judgment can cause a golfer to abandon the game he loved as a youth. If he can't excel beyond his present level, why go on? He can feel cheated and victimized and denied success.

Ah, but some move beyond this stage. They move forward by going back. They advance by allowing themselves to remember and feel their original passion. To accept who they are as people, to accept who they are as golfers, and to just play on. Play—that authentic, spontaneous, free, and wondrous true expression of self. Play—that which leads not to excellence, but to the Divine.

This is the story of such a golfer.

PROLOGUE

If I could read the secret history of all my friends and enemies, there would be enough pain and suffering to disarm all of my hostility.

—Seth Reede

1978

"Mom, we have to go!"

The boy said it again louder this time. His mother looked up at him with a dazed look in her eyes. She was bleeding from her nose and her mouth, the left side of her face badly swollen.

That makes sense; Dad is right-handed. The boy pulled on his mother's hand, urging her up, but she stayed seated on the living room floor with one leg bent underneath her.

Helen looked up at her only son with an expression of sadness and resignation. Despite being too tired and bruised, in both body and spirit, to speak, she was still able to convey her surprise at how much he had matured. Her son was only twelve, but he had defended her like a man. Although his father had backhanded him across the room, that had not stopped the boy. He had pushed against his father's much larger and heavier frame, again and again, trying to protect her. The boy's efforts had not been enough to stop his father, but at least they had distracted him enough that he had not killed her. She had observed all this through a haze that would later be diagnosed as a concussion.

Helen was more than dazed from this most recent assault from her husband. She had moved through the stages common to an abused soul—from terror to anger to guilt to resignation and finally despair. She had done her best to understand why the abuse continued, and she could find no reason for it. Her emotional and physical deterioration had brought her to the brink of surrender. For a time, her mother's instinct had told her to fight for her son's sake, and she had, but recently her son had become her defender. He was determined that his dad would no longer hurt her. While he was outmatched by his father's rage and size, he would not back down. But he could not win. He was a boy. The combination of her husband's strength and her own weariness with life had brought Helen to this place—a place of resignation. Death by her husband's hand would be best for both her and her son.

She put her hand on her son's face and wiped his tears. She could hear her husband James outside the house—out by the tool shed—yelling at the top of his lungs, "I'm gonna kill you, woman."

Helen had accepted her fate and was waiting for him to return. She would fight no more, but she wanted her son to understand and to leave before his father returned.

"NO! Mom, he's not going to find the gun. I hid it. Come on!"

He pulled Helen to her feet and led her to the back of the old house. He pulled open the door that led to the storm cellar. The door was old and flimsy, but the boy had spent several days over the last six months reinforcing it. Now he led his mother down the steps, pulled the door shut behind them, and locked it with a chain from the inside. He braced the chain with a steel rod he had brought from the shed, then sat his mother down against the side of the concrete cellar wall and covered her with a blanket.

"We'll be okay," he whispered, taking his grandfather's 12-gauge from a corner of the cellar where he'd hidden it.

James returned to the house in a rage. "Where the hell is my shotgun, son?" He stumbled through the house, toppling chairs and lamps, shouting, "Helen, where are you? You can't hide from me."

The house was empty. From below, the boy and his mother could feel the floor shake as James stomped through the kitchen toward the cellar. They hadn't used the cellar in years, but apparently, he had remembered it. James yanked on the handle of the cellar door. It did not budge. He backed off and came at it again, this time slamming it with his boot. Still, it did not yield.

"Open this door, boy! You don't, I'll show you what a beatin' is!"

There was no reply.

"Shit, kid, you really think with a shed full of tools I can't get in there? Open up!"

In the momentary silence came the unmistakable sound of a shotgun cocking.

"You come in here, and I'm gonna blow you to hell."

Helen and her son looked at each other, frozen by a new kind of fear. He sounded exactly like his father.

PART ONE

Craig

You might not know this, but there are things that gnaw on a man worse than dyin'.

—Charlie Waite in Open Range

CHAPTER ONE

2015

The Colorado Golf Club in Parker was a relatively new, but nonetheless worthy, venue for the U.S. Open. A witty commentator described the course this way: "She's like a Diva Super Model, gorgeous and nothing but trouble." Set among the rolling hills of scrub oak and rock formations south of Denver, the course offered spectacular views of the front range of the Rocky Mountains. The galleries and players shared the course with deer, coyote, fox, and antelope while the blimp covering the tournament flew with red-tailed hawks and falcons. The golfers had to reconcile the beauty of the course with its stern quirks that tested the limits of the best players in the world.

"FROM JOPLIN, MISSOURI, PLEASE WELCOME CRAIG CANTWELL!"

The announcer's voice interrupted Cantwell's thoughts as he walked up the eighteenth fairway approaching the last green. Grandstands lined either side of the fairway and wrapped around the back of the green, creating an amphitheater. From the stands, he could hear applause. As he

3

walked, the applause grew louder, which surprised Craig. He had been introduced at the start of this last round some four and a half hours ago. The reaction from the crowd had been far more subdued then.

"I wonder who they're clapping for?" quipped Craig's caddy, Roy Wasson.

"Probably you."

"Oh, yeah, I'm sure that's it. They saw my shot on 14."

Being a veteran of professional golf, Craig had played in many U.S. Opens, but this time he had returned from golf purgatory, a non-exempt status on any Tour. He was previously a tour winner but had been suspended from the PGA Tour. His resurgence, when no one believed he could even compete, was one possible reason the crowd was acknowledging him so warmly. His performance in this tournament had put him in a position to win this championship. But that was only part of the reason.

For just a second, amid the applause for the leader of the U.S. Open, Craig reflected on his journey back to this point. Parts of that journey were being discussed publicly; others were known only to him. He preferred that it would stay that way. He did not know how this journey back would end. He just knew it had been quite a ride so far.

CHAPTER TWO

2013

Craig Cantwell drove through the Northern California countryside, following his car's navigation system to a place called Spiritual Ground Zero, popularly known as SGZ. He had programmed in the directions based on information contained in the retreat's information packet. It was a gorgeous, cloudless day. Had he not been so conflicted about how to get to where he was going, and why he was going, he might have been better able to appreciate the natural beauty of the countryside.

The man who got out of his rented car did not look like one to invite conversation. Craig looked nothing like a professional golfer, millionaire, or, for that matter, a person who previously could find a smile on a sunny day. His nearly shoulder-length hair looked as though it hadn't been combed in a week, and a long, unruly beard covered his face. All his hair drew a lot of attention, which was just as well because they distracted from his green, sunken, desperate-looking eyes. His once athletic frame now carried an extra twenty pounds, a weight that would have strained his dirty gray T-shirt if he had bothered to tuck it into his well-worn jeans. His bare feet were covered by battered running shoes.

Pro golfer? No way. Vagrant, ex-con, drug addict, or all of the above fit the picture better.

He stopped for gas in a town called Clear Lake, partly because he was early and partly because of the small town's beauty. He filled the tank at a convenience store, then found a snack and waited in line to pay. Several people were ahead of him, and it soon became apparent that no one, especially the clerk, was in a hurry. The girl talked with each customer as she rang up their purchases. Craig was not in much of a hurry, but he still found this annoying. Annoyance and impatience prevented Craig from appreciating how she connected with each person and how each of the store patrons left smiling with a bounce in their step.

Finally, it was his turn at the counter.

"Hi, how are ya?" quipped the bubbly clerk.

"OK, how you doin'?" Craig put his purchases on the counter without even looking up.

"Oh, don't you be lying to me. Hope your day gets better," she said with a smile.

He looked at her now. Mixed race, dark brown hair, and brown eyes that flashed with more than casual courtesy. It was a knowing, a recognition, and a compassion that made no sense. She knew nothing about him.

"Where you headed?"

For some reason, he allowed truth to this stranger. "Truthfully, I have no idea."

"Need directions? I know the area pretty well." It was obvious she knew Craig was not referring to his lack of a physical destination.

"No, thanks. I'll figure it out."

She looked at him unblinkingly for a long beat, totally out of whack for a convenience store encounter. She gave him a smile that held a hint of sadness. "Yup, I believe you will."

Craig walked out, his mouth open, wondering if he had ingested a hallucinogen earlier in the day. He got in his car shaking his head as he shut the door. *California, right?*

He drove out of the lot and, on a whim, turned into town instead of getting back onto the two-lane highway. He found a lakeside park, parked the car, and found a bench facing the water. Pine-forested mountains provided a gorgeous backdrop. In a gap in the mountains on the far shoreline, the blue of the lake and the sky seemed to merge and stretch into infinity. It was beautiful, but instead of appreciating the beauty, the illusion of limitlessness only caused Craig to agonize over the emptiness of his own heart.

"I'll figure it out."

"Yup, I believe you will."

God, I wish I believed that. His life was a tangled mess of mistakes, missed opportunities, and wasted chances. Not the least of these was the career he had thrown away.

I need help. I have no fucking idea how to figure my life out on my own.

A couple walked by with their daughter. The young girl had a dog on a leash and the couple held hands, talking and laughing as they went by. They nodded to Craig as they passed. He had a sudden need to get back to his car. It was twenty yards across the grass and a parking lot. Would he make it? He moved as though he were rushing to the bathroom. The short walk seemed to take forever. He slid into the driver's seat and shut the door.

Only then did Craig realize he had been holding his breath. He exhaled, and a sob broke from his chest like a pitch hitting a catcher's mitt. His head dropped as his body wracked with sobs, the dam holding his emotions finally breaking. The sobs came again and again, beyond his control. He let go of caring what he looked like as his anguish flowed from his eyes, his nose, his mouth. His hands and arms went limp in surrender. Sob after sob shook his body, the tears flowing like water from a faucet.

The tidal wave of his heartbreak finally receded. Exhausted, Craig wiped his eyes and blew his nose, doing his best to compose himself. He raised his eyes to look out at the lake again. People were still walking by, dog owners exercising their pets, runners running. The beauty of the day and those enjoying it seemed to mock him. He thought of Kelly. *Would she be better off with my life insurance proceeds?*

Just as Craig leaned across the front seat and opened the glove box, a passerby knocked on the driver's side window.

"Hey, buddy, you got a light?"

"No, I don't smoke."

"Could I use your cigarette lighter there?" He pointed to the dashboard.

"Doesn't work."

"Oh, okay. Thanks anyway."

Craig leaned back in the driver's seat and let out a sigh of relief as the guy walked away. Maybe he should just walk into the lake and keep walking.

He looked again at the gap in the horizon between the peaks, this infinity of water and sky. It looked like a far journey, and one he was unsure of taking, but he knew he would go. He checked the safety on the gun and put it back in the glove box. Then he took a couple of deep breaths trying to clear his head. Maybe oxygen was what his brain needed. He would find the courage to follow where he was led, even though he had no idea how or where.

While Craig had decided to undertake this journey, he was still in the dark as to what it would be like. The practical, analytical side of him could not accept that a week in the Northern California wilderness would bring all the broken pieces of his life together. He believed that he was a mess, that he had irrevocably and completely screwed up his life, and that there was no undoing that, but there was a small intuitive pull that made him turn his car toward SGZ rather than away from it.

"Spiritual Ground Zero." *What a name!* Craig's journey had started just like all the other travelers who had gone before him. He had attended a three-day class that someone close to him had recommended. It had been enlightening, even intoxicating, and he had decided to try the "advanced" seminar.

Five thousand dollars was a lot of money for him to lay out these days. In fact, it was damn near all the money he had in the bank. His millionaire golf pro days were long gone, so a number of things danced through his head. One—had he been duped into coming by the excitement the facilitators had created in the three-day class about this retreat? Two—hadn't he made enough discoveries in that short class that he really didn't need this one? What ultimately won out was the fact that since he'd paid five grand for whatever this was, he damn well was going to see what it was about.

As he drove further north on the two-lane highway from Clear Lake, he thought about the volunteer staffer he had asked about the Spiritual Ground Zero retreat. What the man said had stuck with him.

"So you know what it costs to go—five thousand dollars and a week of your time. Here's what you don't know: what it will cost you if you don't go."

That memory and an intuitive tug that he couldn't seem to shake that his life was not yet over kept him from turning around.

Craig wondered how he'd missed the "Reede Seminars Retreat" sign. He'd programmed the directions into his rental car's GPS. He must have tuned out its robotic voice directing him to the retreat while he pondered why he'd laid out five thousand dollars to come to this godforsaken place.

He slowed the car as he spotted a grizzled old rancher out in his pasture, throwing hay to the cows out of the bed of his pick-up.

"Excuse me," he said. "I'm looking for a place called Spiritual Ground Zero. Think I missed my turn."

The old man threw a couple more pitchforks full of hay before he acknowledged Craig's presence. "You looking for that cult Reede runs?"

The old man snorted a laugh and tossed his head in the direction Craig had just come from. "You need to turn around and go back where you came from. And this time, pay attention."

Craig thought this might be the story of his life. "How far?" he asked.

"'Til you get there."

Craig was not amused, but apparently, the old man was.

"What's an old hippie like you want with that yuppie crowd?"

Hippie? Does this old man think anybody with hair below the top of his ears is a hippie? Maybe, considering the old man's age.

"I'm not sure they'll allow a scruffy-looking fellow like you in." He chuckled and waved Craig on his way.

What a geezer! Craig muttered beneath his breath. Or maybe there really was something in what the old man said? He'd find out soon enough.

He found the "Turn Here" sign for "Reede Seminars Retreat" right where it should have been. He turned onto a dirt road that wound roughly a mile through rock formations and clusters of oak that dotted the foothills to his left. To his right, old cottonwoods marked what looked like irrigation ditches. Another mile in, he came to the main gate with a wrought iron sign above it—the letters SGZ with an iron circle around them. It looked like a cattle brand. The irony of the moment didn't escape him. *What am I getting myself into?*

On the other side of the gate stood a small compound of buildings.

This must be the place.

CHAPTER THREE

R oughly, about forty people were seated in a barn that
had been finished on the inside to form an informal
auditorium. He had met some of these folks before, and
they all reflected varying degrees of excitement, nervousness, hopefulness, and resistance. Craig saw some people
excited to jump in and take whatever came, eager to go on
this personal development journey. There were others who
looked wounded, even desperate, as though this experience
was the last chance they had to correct a wayward life. Still,
others were a bit bewildered both at the uncertainty of what
the retreat was about and at just what had led them there.
Craig fell in the latter group.

As one of the counselors rambled on about house rules
for the week, Craig's eyes wandered to a man about six feet
tall, quite slender with dark hair and eyes. Craig had no idea
who he was, but the man radiated power and energy even
though he wore a neutral expression. Craig couldn't tell if
he was bored or excited.

At one point, Craig had looked over, and for just an
instant, the man's eyes met his. Across the distance of the
room, there was the briefest of acknowledgments between
them. Almost as though the man recognized him, though
Craig was sure they had never met.

There was just a hint of danger in this man. Even though he was slightly built, he had large hands and moved with a sinewy strength. What was most striking about him was his awareness. It seemed that he would not have been surprised by anything that happened in the room. It was as if he would know immediately the right response to anything.

The counselor's voice intruded on Craig's thoughts: "It is my pleasure to introduce one of the co-founders of Spiritual Ground Zero and our main facilitator, Seth Reede."

Craig's attention grew as he watched the man he had previously noticed, from across the room full of people, stand up and walk to the center of the room. The man shook the counselor's hand, drawing him into a brief manly embrace. As he did so, he smiled. At that point, it was as if the sun had peeked through dark clouds. Seth Reede had large, perfect teeth, and his smile radiated warmth.

Seth started his lecture with a joke but quickly segued into the heart of the matter at SGZ.

"Our experiences shape our beliefs," he explained in a way that Craig had to admit made perfect sense, despite his chronic skepticism. According to Seth, this premise was the key to our survival.

"It goes back to our early human days, back before we had cell phones and cars. Actually, back before we even had the power of sophisticated communication. Imagine that you are OG, the caveman. You're out hunting, and you and your partner are waiting by the water hole to take down a deer. As you make your move, a saber-toothed tiger makes a meal out of your partner. You remember the tiger sprang out of a particular brush. From then on, you *never* hunt close to that brush again; you learned from that experience.

"While this may seem elementary, it illustrates how our minds and emotions work together to hardwire our beliefs. Our brains *reinforce* the thought pattern between Event X and Outcome Y; this is how habits are formed. Habits then become programs in our subconscious, things we do in certain situations without thinking about it. So, looking at this objectively, this process is vital in many ways. It is how we learn to do different things, how we train ourselves, right?

"The flip side of this process is that it also hardwires into our subconscious things that are not so useful. We, humans, create erroneous stories around events in our lives all too often. I'll call them lies, lies that we tell ourselves. We have an event. We have an emotional response to that event and then often draw a conclusion about ourselves as a result of that event. Often the conclusion we draw makes no earthly sense. However, when we repeat this lie over and over in our subconscious, we begin to believe the lie. We accept it as fact."

Seth's remarks were followed by an exercise in which each person was to journal about significant events in their lives, as a way to become aware of the lies each of them unconsciously tells themselves. Then they were to share their lies with each other.

Thirty minutes later, Craig sat alone outside the main classroom. He had not paired off with another student, had not shared his thoughts with a facilitator. In fact, he had not made his list of lies that he told himself. He was sitting on a bench looking out at a small group of cows three hundred yards away when Seth Reede joined him.

"How you doing, Craig?"

Craig smiled. "I'm fine."

Seth looked at him, broke into a smile, and chuckled briefly. "Craig, I've been doing this a while—long enough to spot the bullshit when somebody tells me they're *fine*. So let's talk about your list."

"I don't have a list; I don't lie to myself."

Seth continued to look at him. It was difficult for Craig to fathom what feelings Seth's presence evoked in him. Suffice it to say that Seth's directness was unnerving. Craig sensed that there was a lot to this man and knew that there was no judgment or gall in his gaze.

Finally, Seth nodded. "Okay, I'll word my question a bit differently: What is a belief you have about yourself that you would want to examine?"

Craig laughed, attempting to deflect his discomfort.

"Well, let's see . . . I would like to believe I was Brad Pitt with a short game. I'd like to believe I had Donald Trump's bank account and not his hair. I'd like to believe Salma Hayek thought I held the patent on the penis."

Seth just looked at him, a trace of annoyance at Craig's deflection of his question. Mainly, he waited for a real answer.

"Look, I don't know what you want from me. I don't know."

Seth had taken a seat across from him. He smiled slightly as he stood up.

"You *do* know, and we'll likely tackle that later. Meanwhile, I'll take a shot, if you don't mind."

"Take your best shot . . . I guess." Craig looked away again, uncomfortably looking at this frank, strange man with his uncomfortable questions. He hoped his looking off would be taken as a dismissal, but Seth did not move. After a few moments, Craig turned again and looked at Seth.

He looked into his dark eyes. He again sensed danger in this man, for reasons he could not explain. His gaze held truth and a history that was as heavy as an anvil and yet was still warm.

"A lie you tell yourself is that you will never be any better than your father."

Without another word, Seth put his hands in his front jean pockets and walked back in the direction of the classroom. His words hung like a heavy mist in the sunshine. Craig wanted to laugh them off, dismiss them. He could not. The unvarnished truth had finally come out of hiding and now confronted him as boldly as Seth's physical body had a moment before.

Seth's words had sparked a long-ago memory that Craig had buried deep.

CHAPTER FOUR

A s the memory receded, Craig thought about what he
may have decided about himself because he was his father's son. Did he think that he had inherited his father's
rage and used it when he felt things were out of his control?
Had he used it when he felt impotent like his father had?
While he might have been great at some things, he was a
failure at dealing with the worst injustices of his life.

For instance, two years ago, Craig had been in the
locker room at the conclusion of the PGA Championship
at Winged Foot. He had not given the obligatory interview
after the final round in a major tournament. This led the
press to speculate. Some said it was because he was angry
and frustrated "at another near-miss for Craig Cantwell in
a major tournament." Craig stood in front of his locker. A
short distance away, the day's winner, Zeke Monroe, was
being interviewed on camera by ESPN.

Terror, frustration, and confusion coursed through
Craig's system. And guilt. He felt so much guilt over an
event he thought he *should* have prevented, even though he
knew there was nothing he could have done to prevent it.
What was done could not be undone. It had happened, and
it would have future ramifications that would spin off new
nightmares.

Craig's longtime friend and caddy, Roy Wasson, was there talking to him, confused that Craig was in the state in which he was. This wasn't like him; what had snapped that Craig Cantwell could not bounce back from a lackluster last round of golf? Sure, they had been close to winning a major again and had been turned away again, but life went on. Craig's resiliency and perspective were big reasons why Roy thought he had the best bag on the Tour. He was confused about what had happened, about which part of Craig's spirit had given way. Roy was talking, trying to get through, but Craig was obviously not hearing his best friend.

Finally, Roy stepped away and towards a small cluster of players and caddies milling around. Jim Furyk, Craig's playing partner for the last round, approached him.

"Is Canty okay?" Furyk was a great guy and expressed concern despite just missing his own run at a second major.

Roy gave the only answer he had. "I don't know. Ain't never seen him like this."

Just then, Craig overheard part of the interview with Monroe, which was wrapping up.

"Curtis, I just had a great week of preparation, even right up until last evening." He smiled a cocky smile for the camera, seeming pleased with himself.

Craig's confusion and terror changed to white-hot rage. *His preparation last evening?! "You motherfucker!"*

Zeke Monroe was concluding his interview when Craig lunged. He saw Monroe's bodyguard a couple of steps behind but knew he wouldn't be able to stop him.

He stepped forward with his left foot, pushed off his right foot, and threw a right cross with every ounce of strength in his body and every vestige of rage in his soul.

The punch landed just below Monroe's left eye, the force of it sending him crashing into the lockers behind him, then to the floor. Craig followed him, rushing forward with more violent intent. He had lunged forward with both knees heading for Monroe's helpless torso when Monroe's bodyguard forearmed Craig Cantwell away, and Craig did his own rebound off the lockers. The blow did nothing to stem the tide of Craig's rage. He got up and lunged again, only to be taken down by the bodyguard and two others.

The entire incident had been caught on an ESPN camera, up to and including Roy Wasson helping restrain his friend and employer and furtively yelling, "Jesus Christ, Canty, what the fuck is wrong with you?"

The incident in the locker room after the PGA Championship was unprecedented in golf. Fights in other sports were not that uncommon. Baseball has its brawls following brushback pitches and hit batsmen; football has fights on the field; even race car drivers have been known to get into altercations in the pit, but golf? Golf is a "gentleman's game," in which vanquished opponents doff their caps, look the winner in the eye, shake his hand, and say, "Well-played." What Craig Cantwell had just done was not something that *ever* happened in golf.

The public, the pundits, and the Tour players themselves were stunned, not only by the incident but also by the perpetrator. Craig Cantwell was a Tour veteran, a tournament winner, and a well-liked and respected member of the Tour. He'd had some close calls in the majors, and his divorce had been a bit messy, but his life was still one that most would envy. He was a millionaire several times over, someone who could be grateful to play a great game and get paid well to do it. How had he snapped and done something as unexpectedly crazy as this?

Carl Husted was the commissioner of the Tour, a man charged with running the big show, who did an even better job than his predecessor, Tim Finchem. Husted did not come from golf; he was a marketing genius from the business world who could appeal to and bring even bigger crowds to golf. He was able to amplify the existing slogan, "These Guys Are Good," for the benefit of golf and the Tour. That is if he did not have Tour members, who had fallen short in the day's tournament, resorting to fisticuffs in front of sports news cameras.

Two days after the incident, Mr. Husted met with Craig Cantwell and witnesses to the altercation, hopeful that Craig could offer some explanation for what had happened. Craig was contrite, apologetic, and even regretful; however, he could not or would not offer anything that the Tour could use to spin the incident in its favor.

Husted did not know Craig well but still felt something might be going unsaid, some grievance unaired. Cantwell explained that he had been fatigued and frustrated by his failure to close the deal. Added to that was more frustration about a break Monroe had gotten late in the round, a bounce off a marshal and the subsequent ruling. Still, a golfer as experienced as Craig Cantwell understood that breaks were a part of golf.

The bottom line was that Craig was unable to offer a valid excuse for his actions, and Husted had no choice but to suspend him indefinitely from the PGA Tour.

In a press conference the Wednesday after the incident, Carl Husted announced that Craig Cantwell would be ineligible to play in any future Tour events. Further, the USGA had banned Craig from its events. He was also charged with assault and would have to deal with the legal ramifications as well. He was now a professional golfer with no place to compete.

CHAPTER FIVE

It was his second night at SGZ, and Craig sat around a campfire outside the main housing unit. He was part of a small group listening to Tom and Rita, the only married couple at the retreat. The couple had been married for fifteen years and were talking honestly to several young people about their life together. As they described it, it was not a fairytale marriage; it had had its ups and downs. The main point they made to the group was that the struggles their relationship survived had made them stronger.

Craig knew something about the challenges of marriage, and he appreciated the couple's candor. He also admired and envied the way they looked at each other. He could see that they had truly survived married life together, making them stronger as a result.

In an instant, Craig temporarily forgot his vow of resistance to the SGZ process and expressed his gratitude to Tom and Rita for sharing their story. Rita smiled at him.

"I was wondering when you might join in. I'm glad you finally did." It was what a number of people in the group had been thinking over the last two days.

Everyone around the campfire nodded and smiled, and suddenly Craig found himself the center of attention, something he had tried to avoid at all costs, until now. Even through his resistance, he noticed an unusual lack of judgment in the eyes of these strangers around the fire, and it felt good.

"Thanks," he said to Rita.

"How about you?"

"What about me?"

"Are you married?"

The Craig of forty-eight hours ago would have taken this as a cue to clam up, make a joke, or just walk away. But this couple had just been open and honest and vulnerable with him and the others, and he found value in that. So, despite his discomfort, he joined in.

"No. I was married before. Umm, kinda thought I was gonna be again, but . . . "

This revelation was followed by a long silence.

"Would you care to share with us?" Rita persisted.

What a new age, seminar thing to say. It was real that she and the others wanted to know, but it made him feel like getting up and running away, but something kept him in his seat.

Maybe this is one of those "growth is uncomfortable" moments that Seth Reede keeps mentioning.

So with six strangers listening around a campfire, Craig began to tell a story that, in truth, had brought him to this moment.

In 1990, I was just out of college and Tour-qualifying school and a newly minted rookie on the PGA Tour. I'd made a few cuts and a little money, feeling my way along as a pro.

After playing a horrible first round in the Atlanta tournament on a Thursday, I'd made a valiant run at the cut. I'd shot a 65 on a brutally hot Friday, and when I signed my card, I was sure I'd made it to the weekend. Then the leader posted a 62, took a 5-shot lead, and knocked out a number of players near the cut line. I was one of the casualties.

I'd slammed down a few medicinal shots in the hotel bar when a willowy blonde asked if she could move the chair next to me to another table. I nodded absently, still lost in my self-pity over not making the cut. She picked up the chair with one hand and moved it across the room. As she walked away, I noticed her legs and wished I'd struck a better bargain for the chair she'd borrowed. Missed another cut.

The reprieve came when she invited me to join their group. I did several celebrity impressions to cover up my nervousness, and that broke up the table. After that, I screwed up enough courage to ask her name.

She laughed and said she'd wondered when I might want to know. Then she told me her name was Rachelle Keys.

"Craig Cantwell," I said.

Craig paused for a moment, wondering if his story was getting longer than it was interesting. "Am I boring you?"

"No, no, go on," Rita said. "I have a feeling you're just getting to the good part." The others laughed, and Craig resumed his story.

"One of the male members of the group was a golfer and said he recognized me from Sports Center highlights that day, which led to more drinks, which led to a drunken putting lesson, which led to Rachelle showing me how to serve a volleyball, which led to a steamy night in my hotel room."

"So, did you two start dating?" asked a woman who had walked up to the campfire while Craig was talking.

He remembered when he woke the next morning he could still smell her, still feel her skin and see the spark in her eyes, but that was more than he could share even with this accepting group of people.

"No, when I woke up, the bed was empty. I called her name, but there was no reply. I looked around the room for her things. Nothing. She was gone. Briefly, I wondered if I had only made her up in my dreams. Then I saw the note she had written on the hotel mirror with my sharpie:

"I think you have a future on Tour if you avoid falling for ex-college volleyball players. Good luck and take care—R."

Silence enveloped the group around the campfire. Finally, someone asked, "Did you ever see her again?"

"Not for many years."

"Did you marry someone else?" asked another.

"I did."

"Did you just forget about Rachelle? Write her off as a one-night stand?"

Craig hesitated. He wasn't used to sharing, and the emotional drain of telling his story had left him weary. As he sat there, firelight flickering across his face, the effort showed.

"How about we save that story for another night?" Rita interjected.

Craig looked around the group. "How 'bout a rain check?"

They all smiled and nodded their agreement.

Rita touched his arm gently. "Thanks, Craig."

CHAPTER SIX

It would not be accurate to say he forgot Rachelle. In the years that followed, he would remember their night together frequently and in great detail, but after Atlanta, there was another tournament and another. It was what he did, the PGA Tour.

As he toured, there was lots of golf and lots of women. Craig easily made enough money during his first year on the Tour to keep his card. He only missed five cuts all year, and two top-five finishes in the fall put him into the conversation for Rookie of the Year.

Craig fit the steady category of PGA Tour players. He hit a lot of fairways and had enough power to play the longer courses well. His strength was in the scoring clubs—his wedges and the 7, 8, and 9 irons. He made his share of birdies and had an excellent short game. His was the type of game that made a lot of cuts—not spectacular, just fundamentally sound.

Craig's other main strength was his disposition. He was generally a happy guy, and even happier on the golf course doing what he loved. He could let go of a mistake faster than a lot of guys and could rely on a good short game to keep him in it when shots went a bit sideways. A good comparison to Craig would be Jim Furyk or Zach Johnson.

He was a good competitor, well-liked and respected by his peers.

All this ended up as a very nice career for Craig Cantwell over the next decade. Between 1990 and 2003, he won eleven Tour events and over ten million dollars in prize money. He had come close to winning in several major championships, and while he had yet to win one and join the sport's elite, by age thirty-four he was one of the *Best Players Who Have Not Won a Major.*

He was also one of the most eligible bachelors on the Tour. That was the year that he met Joan Wylie, a lovely former flight attendant, at a Tour stop in Charlotte. She was smart, gorgeous, very attracted to him, and they quickly got hot and heavy.

One day she informed Craig that she was pregnant, and he did what he had been contemplating and proposed. It seemed like the natural progression of things; he thought himself ready for a wife and kids. She saw marriage to a great guy who also happened to be a millionaire as the next step in a well-planned life.

As so often happens, things did not go as planned. Joan had a really tough pregnancy and could not travel with Craig on his tours. In August at the PGA Championship at Whistling Straights, he was grinding out a final round where it seemed everyone but Rush Limbaugh was in contention. A two-hundred-yard 5 iron to 2 feet on 18 got him into a playoff; then an obscure European pro holed out from eighty yards to win. The close loss in a Major hurt; then his cell phone gave him a message after the round that hurt even more. Joan had lost the baby.

They had gotten married, shortly after Joan got pregnant, in a small, fun ceremony in Vegas. There had been plenty of press coverage, and then the cute couple had announced their pregnancy. Craig and Joan became the latest "adorable couple" on the PGA Tour. Everyone thought they were the new happy example of marital bliss. The loss of their baby shattered that image like a shattered champagne glass.

It turned out that Joan had lost a pregnancy once before. Which made this loss even more devastating to her. So it was understandable that she lashed out at Craig. But to blame him for the loss? That was just ludicrous. She said the fact that he was gone all the time was the problem, even though she knew, before she married him, that his career involved travel on the Tour. Craig took some time off and they went to counseling, but Joan could not seem to let go of her resentment toward Craig.

For the next eighteen months, Craig played less on the Tour, and when he did, he played poorly. He stayed home a lot and wondered if it was even worth it when his wife barely spoke to him. After a time, he decided he would go back to a full schedule of tournaments, about thirty a year, since staying home to "work things out" wasn't working.

He was a lot of things during this period that he wasn't used to being: lonely, angry, guilty, and miserable. Not surprisingly, his golf suffered. He was not able to leave his baggage behind and find refuge on the course as he had done in the past. After a missed cut in Texas, he found himself drawn into conversation with a Tour groupie and found that he could add horny to his list of woes. The resulting one-night-stand could have just been harmful to his conscience and psyche, but for the fact that a diligent reporter on the Tour had recorded and reported his exit from the lady's hotel room and made it public.

Joan now had the evidence and ammunition to end her short marriage to Craig. In 2007, she found a lawyer only too happy to help her. Craig's level of guilt over the tryst and the loss of the baby caused him to roll over in the divorce. He lost their five-million-dollar home and seventy-five percent of everything else he had in the process.

CHAPTER SEVEN

For several nights, Craig avoided the campfire gathering. He would wave as he passed the main building on his way to housing but stayed just far enough to keep from making eye contact with anyone. On this particular night, Tom hailed him when he came within earshot.

"Craig, why don't you join us?"

"Ah . . . " He couldn't really think of a good excuse for not joining in. "Maybe just for a few minutes."

"We only have a few nights left here at the retreat. Would you like to finish sharing your story?" It was a good one so far.

Or be eaten by a swamp full of alligators? No, thanks. I'll take the gators.

Several in the group, who were present when Craig had told his story earlier, nodded in encouragement.

"Can I skip the marriage part and get back to Rachelle?"

Rita smiled at him. "It's your story, Craig. Share what you want."

"Suffice it to say that I met an attractive lady, and we were married for a few years. We lost a baby, and between that and me being gone all the time with the Tour, it didn't take long for our marriage to go south. I tried staying home, but that didn't work either.

"I blamed myself for the failed marriage. At the same time, I was bitter toward my ex-wife. Truth be told, neither one of us really had any idea how to be married, especially in hard times. Guilt and bitterness proved to be an unsuccessful formula for winning at golf. In the year after our divorce, I missed the cut in twelve out of the twenty-five tournaments I played in.

"I wondered if there was anything in my life I could still do well. Then one night after I had played a charity exhibition outside Atlanta, a surprise phone call led me to a bright light that in truth brought me back from hell.

"While the tournament had not been lucrative, it was fun. I had finished up and was in the locker room packing up when the attendant told me I was wanted on the phone. I had told the contact person at Atlanta Kids to contact me at the course; I assumed this was that call."

Craig remained silent for several minutes while remembering the conversation as if it had taken place just yesterday.

"Craig Cantwell speaking."

"Do you still know that volleyball is a strong rotational sport?" the caller asked.

"I'm sorry?" A tuning fork went off in his head when he heard the voice, but he still wasn't quite sure who the caller was.

"I'm just hoping my lesson from back then has stuck with you." The voice was definitely female and the accent slightly Southern.

"Is this who I think it is?"

"Depends on who you think it is."

"Rachelle?"

"Yes, Craig, it's Rachelle, Rachelle Keys. I'm sorry for just calling out of the blue like this. Do you still remember me?"

"Does the Pope remember being Catholic?"

31

She laughed. "Well, that's reassuring. Do you still do impressions?"

To which Craig replied in his best Sean Connery voice, "I distinctly remember having Margaritas with you on the sofa."

She laughed harder now, and the sound brought back all the sweetness of their night together long ago.

"It's great to hear your voice again," Rachelle said. "I saw that you were in town, and I wondered if you might have time to meet."

"Craig? Are you okay?"

Tom's voice cut through Craig's thoughts. He was not sure how long he had been silent for, but he suddenly realized that he hadn't said anything out loud.

"Oh, I'm sorry. I think I just did a little time traveling."

The group laughed.

"Well, the call wasn't from Atlanta Kids; it was from Rachelle Keys. Right out of the blue—after almost twenty years.

"We made plans to meet for lunch the next day. When I hung up the phone, my imagination went into overdrive.

"What is she like now? Does she want something from me? What is she going to think of me now?

"After Joan, I was so scared of women that I figured I would need therapy before I could even ask someone out again. Finally, I took a deep breath and settled on a nice, vivid memory of our night together so long ago and somehow managed to fall asleep."

Again, Craig went deep into his thoughts to a memorable time.

Rachelle had aged gracefully. As she moved through the restaurant toward his table, she left a trail of snapped necks on the men in the room. She still had her willowy good looks, though her hair was a little shorter and more professional than before. She still had a way of looking at him that made him believe she knew every aspect of his life. Her eyes just had a way of making him feel vulnerable.

"Thanks for meeting me," she said. "I've thought about you more than a little over the years."

"Me too. I mean, I've thought about you, not me. Well, I've thought about me, too, and you, but usually not when I'm serving a volleyball . . ."

Rachelle was laughing at the Craig Cantwell go-to strategy of trying to cover his nervousness with humor.

She let him babble on for a minute and then put her hand on his. Her look told him that there was more to this meeting than just getting reacquainted with an old flame.

"Look, I've decided to tell you something. It's important, but before I tell you I want you to know that I don't want anything from you and that I don't want to make any trouble for you. It's just important for you to know."

Know what? Is she sick? Did she do an interview with CBS about their acrobatic sex in his hotel room almost twenty years ago? Is she secretly a man? *He knew that wasn't true. It was obviously a big deal to her, and despite his overactive imagination, he was not close to prepared for what she now revealed.*

"I've, um, I have . . ." She had tears in her eyes as she struggled to find the words. Whenever Craig saw a woman crying, he always wanted to help. It was an instinct that went back to his childhood. He wanted to help any woman he met who was in pain. There was no helping the cause of Rachelle's tears, though.

Snapping out of his nostalgia, Craig continued his story.

"She was still beautiful and funny, but more nervous than I'd anticipated she would be. For some odd reason, so was I. Before we even ordered, Rachelle cut to the chase. She told me there was something important she'd decided to share with me. I couldn't fathom what."

Craig hesitated as he looked at the fireside group gathered around him. Some had their eyes fixed on him; others gazed into the glowing embers of the fire, but there was no doubt that he had everyone's attention. He could feel it as he took a deep breath. *Here goes,* he thought.

"I'll never forget the tears in her eyes and her exact words that night:

"She's too special for you not to know her. She's so amazing, and I think she needs you now."

"I was still flying blind here, so I said something like, 'I'm sorry, Rachelle. *Who* needs me?'

"She held out her phone for me to see. The screensaver was a picture of Rachelle and a very pretty young girl. They were hugging each other and smiling."

"Her name is Kelly," she said softly. *"You're her daddy."*

"That must have been quite a shock," Tom said. "Did you believe her?"

Craig thought for a moment before he answered, remembering back to that moment.

It was one of those times when the thoughts and emotions came fast and furious. Like a slideshow to a punk rock song.

"I'm a daddy?! How can she be sure? Is she shaking me down? Hell, if she wants my money, she'll have to talk to Joan; she's got it all. I'm a father?!

"Holy Shit, I can't seem to take care of myself; how can I . . . ? Maybe this is a joke."

And on it went. His head spun and his thoughts swirled. For probably a full two minutes, he couldn't take his eyes off the picture.

He finally looked at Rachelle. A tear rolled out of one of her perfect blue eyes and ran down her cheek. Craig gently wiped it away.

"Say something, Craig."

He looked back at the picture. Even though she had inherited a lot of features from her mother, he could see himself in Kelly. Right then, he had a feeling that he usually associated with golf. It was a knowing, a certainty like just before he hit a putt that he knew was going in. This was not an intellectual act, not a 'head' thing. This was a sense of knowing in his soul. He knew in his heart that this girl was his daughter, and he felt a joy that was better than all the perks of semi-fame he had enjoyed before.

"It took me a few minutes of looking at the picture and the tears in Rachelle's eyes, but, yes, I believed it. In a gut-level, all-knowing sort of way, I knew she was my daughter.

"Of course, being the emotionally retarded human that I am, Rachelle had to prompt me to express my feelings."

"What did she say?" Rita asked.

"Something like, 'Well . . .'"

A soft chuckle rippled through the group.

"Actually, I smiled and looked from the photo back to Rachelle and said the most authentic thing I'd ever said to another person:

'She's the most beautiful thing I have ever seen.'"

CHAPTER EIGHT

The group at SGZ stood around the outdoor pavilion, camping gear prepared and close. Craig guessed there were forty of them here, all with tents, sleeping bags, a supply of water, and for those not wanting to fast, a large bag of trail mix. They had been told to wait here for Seth for their instructions for the exercise. They were also told to wait in silence.

Craig had made a few connections in the past four days in this very mixed group, roughly equal parts male and female, ranging in age from late teens to one man who was over sixty. While parts of the retreat had been fun, Craig was still slipping into thoughts of just what he was doing here. There were parts of the program he had resisted, looking at them with a dubious eye. He frankly had a hard time believing something he could not see, touch, or measure. And any "growth" that happened since he arrived fit in that category. He had heard so many great things about SGZ that he was waiting for the lightning bolt to strike him. In his view, that had yet to happen.

Seth Reede walked from the barn close to the pavilion dressed in jeans, work boots, and a flannel jacket. The group was in a rough semi-circle, and Seth walked to the middle of it slowly, his usual neutral expression on his face. The group gave him their attention, immediately and totally. Craig noticed, not for the first time, that Seth radiated energy. You literally felt him when he got close. He stood still at the center of the circle, his hands in his pockets, matching the group's silence as he stood before them. After several long moments, he spoke.

"This exercise really has no time limit. You will all be going up that hill to meet someone," he said, pointing south to a wooded mountainside. "You will not be together, though you will not be far apart. You will not communicate with each other, verbally or otherwise. You will remain in an area assigned to you. You may strike your tent if you choose, but you will remain until you complete the exercise. You may wonder who you are going to meet."

At this point, Seth's gaze found Craig. "In truth, I don't know. Maybe there are demons that will come to you. Maybe angels. Maybe, for the very first time, you will meet yourself. By that, I mean who you truly are. Do not distract yourself from whatever or whoever you meet on the mountain. Accept it as fact that they, or it, are there for a reason. Examine this meeting and the reason for it. When you have some clarity, write your thoughts in your journal. Then come back down here and share it with me or someone else if you choose."

Twenty-four hours later, Craig was still waiting for his lightning bolt to strike. He had set up his camp; he had enjoyed the view. He'd relived golf tournaments he'd played in, parties he had attended, reminisced over women he had known. In short, he had done an Olympian job of distracting himself from himself.

Now he was tired and hungry. He was beyond cynical about the purpose of being alone on this hillside.

As he sat, he heard a clunk and then another. He looked around, but there was nothing. *Starting to hear things,* he thought. Then again. *Clunk, clunk,* like two pieces of wood banging together. He waited again and listened. Nothing. Then the wind rose slightly, and he heard it again. Looking up over his shoulder, he found the source of the noise. It was coming from two pine trees that were growing close together. One growing right out from under a large rock. It leaned roughly 15 degrees, making it clunk into its neighbor.

He smiled slightly, relieved to have found the source of the sound. It happened again. Now he just found it annoying. This mystery solved, he could get back to the serious business of just what the fuck he was doing here.

He looked at his journal, a leather-bound notebook with blank pages. He picked it up off the ground and wrote something quickly in large letters; then he walked back down the hill to the pavilion.

A few minutes after he arrived at the pavilion, Seth Reede walked out of the barn and toward him. His eyes pierced into Craig's, and Craig saw something he had not noticed before: a depth of kindness, empathy, and understanding. Craig's logical brain rejected this. *How can he know me?*

"How are you, Craig?"

Craig hesitated, his impatience and anger tempered by Seth's inscrutable expression.

"For once, why don't you answer truthfully and authentically, instead of running the bullshit you have been running ever since you got here?" Seth prompted.

He said it without malice, but the words evoked Craig's anger and cynicism, nevertheless.

"I'm fucking tired. I'm up on that hill starving to death and freezing, unable to wipe my ass and wondering just how fucking crazy I am to have paid $5,000 for this bullshit!"

"Well, now we're getting somewhere," Seth replied. Seth's reaction took Craig totally by surprise. "So, do you want to leave?"

"Fucking A!" Craig shot back, enraged by Seth's calm.

"Then why didn't you pack up your gear and bring it with you?"

"You can have that shit; I just want to get out of here."

"Okay." Seth shrugged, turned on his heel, and started walking back to the barn.

"Where the fuck are you going?" Craig yelled. "Is that all you have to say to me?"

Seth stopped and stood with his back to Craig. Then he turned to face Craig and asked, "What is it that you want?"

"You can start with an apology; then we'll go from there!"

"Why would I apologize to you for your choices? For things you have done, said, and felt? Are you under the impression that I have the power to change you? If you do, you're barking up the wrong tree, because I don't have that power."

Craig was once again silent. And suddenly weary.

"So, what is it you want? Why did you come here?"

"I don't fucking know," Craig said, feeling more fatigued than ever.

Seth finally allowed his exasperation with this man to show. "I am so goddam tired of your bullshit. Every time I hear 'I don't know' from you, I want to slap you. Let's pretend you *do* know. Again, why did you come here? What are you looking for?"

"For answers!" Craig blurted out. "I came here because I thought you had some goddamn answers for me."

Seth looked at Craig again. Slowly and slightly, he nodded comprehension. He knew this before Craig spoke, of course, but "answers" for this man was a heading over a long list of things.

"I don't have your answers, my friend. That's the bad news. The good news is, you have them. So go back up the hill and allow yourself to see them."

Craig just looked at him, breathed out, and did not move.

"Craig, if you were leaving, you wouldn't be standing here. You would be gone. Go on back up the hill."

Craig looked at him again. Seth stood there casually, that same inscrutable look on his face, his hands in the pockets of his jacket. That same infinite compassion in his eyes. Craig drew in a deep breath, and the feeling that he had days before by the lake returned. The feeling was not entirely welcome, but with it came the realization that he would be walking back up the hill.

Craig absently opened his journal and showed Seth what he had written.

"I guess I don't have to give you this."

Seth smiled and said, "Oh, I'll take it."

Craig ripped out the sheet and looked at it. He had written "FUCK THIS" in large block letters. He handed it to Seth, expecting that he might wad it up and throw it back in his face. Instead, Seth carefully carried the note back into the barn, as if he were transporting a piece of sage, priceless wisdom. As Seth reached the barn, Craig Cantwell began his walk back up the mountain, still in search of answers.

CHAPTER NINE

The walk back up the mountain was short but exhausting for Craig. It wasn't so much from lack of sleep or food, but from resistance and frustration. These two energy suckers had forced him to stop twice on the quarter-mile walk back to his tent.

I really do need to get back in shape.

By the time he reached his campsite, he was panting, unable to move. Craig raised his eyes and looked out over the valley. He was facing west, and the sun was already setting. For some odd reason, he saw the scene fully for the first time. More than that, he was able to experience his surroundings.

For the first time in a long time, Craig breathed in through his nostrils and smelled pine and earth and water. The smells seemed to open his other senses so that he heard, as well as saw, the gentle flow of the creek one hundred yards below him. Just to his right, and twenty yards away, two wild turkeys waddled past. He felt a small breeze against his left cheek, just a small shift of air that would have gone unnoticed had he not been so still. As the sun sank, shafts of sunlight and shadow merged before him. Bright green pines on one slope merged with dark shadows as the sun's light slowly abated. The hillside was observing, respectful and waiting on the sunset, paying homage to the light of life it brought. It was as if the mountain wanted to make sure the sun knew its love and appreciation, maybe for the fear that this would be the last it saw of the sun. Respect without regret: if I never see you again, I am glad for your warmth.

Finally, the great sun went behind the last mountain, leaving brilliant pre-twilight blue. Leaving the mountains and all the inhabitants to wait for dawn or waking for the night.

Craig blinked and with that movement became conscious again. Or the reverse, the simple act of blinking putting him back to sleep, caught up in the physical and once again oblivious to beauty and reality. He looked at his watch and realized that he had not moved nor had a conscious thought, for nearly an hour. All he could remember in that hour was breathing. He wanted the feeling of oneness, the stillness of his mind to be preserved. At the very least he wanted to achieve it again. He could not recall a time when he had relaxed more fully.

Eagerly now, Craig opened his journal and began to write. The rambling expulsion of his words ran on, from describing his latest sunset to other parts of his life. He had a sense that he was just skimming the surface of topics, that something in him wanted to stay on the surface rather than risk the pain of deep remembrance of all those events. He was pondering that when he came upon his last memory of his first golf teacher, the man who shaped his golf game as well as his early life.

Just two months before his trip to SGZ, Craig had journeyed back to his hometown. Joplin, Missouri, wasn't quite the town that time forgot, but it was close. His memories of growing up there fit into two basic categories: family and golf. He had come back to explore some of the golf memories—these were the fond ones, after all. Maybe the family memories had been one reason he lost touch with his first teacher. The one that had first taught him, a guy that most modern golfers would dismiss as a hopeless crackpot.

Hank Ames was the son of an Irish/Scottish man who had come to America to get away from home. He knew golf, and that's what he did, in almost all capacities. Hank had told Craig that his father, Seamus, had at various times worked as a teaching pro, greenskeeper, caddy, and had an undistinguished career as a playing professional. His son Hank had taken up the game against his father's advice and wishes.

Craig had met Hank when he was eleven years old, one early morning on a practice green at Joplin Gerard, one of the two municipal golf courses in town. Craig didn't know why or how he could hit a golf ball, only that he could. At that age, he didn't want to do anything else. Hank had seen his talent and did his best not to get in its way. Nurturing and suggesting without forcing a "system" on young Craig, they grew together. Since Craig's father was out of his life by this time, Hank became a father figure to him. The teacher became a friend and a mentor in more than golf. Hank cared about Craig as a person, never wanting to take credit for his protégé's success. When Craig got to high school, Hank even referred him to a respected swing teacher, telling the boy that he had reached a point where he needed more than Hank had the ability to give.

Years had passed since Craig had sought out Hank. It wasn't that they were estranged, but Craig had been busy enough that their contacts had been rare. After his Tour suspension, after Rachelle, after Kelly, Craig went back to Hank. Why? He was not sure.

After inquiring about Hank in the pro shop, he had walked to the back of the greens maintenance area. In the back of a Quonset hut, there was a large open overhead door. Craig walked to the opening and stopped. Hank was standing in front of a workbench, in the process of re-gripping a set of irons. Intent on pushing a new grip on to a 9-iron fixed in a vice, he didn't look up.

"Thought I might get a lesson," Craig said loudly. "I heard the best teacher in Missouri works here."

Hank wore his glasses perched on the end of his nose. He looked over them with a scowl; then his eyes went wide with recognition. Craig had wondered if his old friend might resent the long absence, maybe be bitter or angry. Instead, Hank had wiped his hands off, walked over to Craig with a wide smile, and wrapped his old pupil in a bear hug. He laughed while they embraced, and Craig was embarrassed by the emotion of the moment. Both his and Hank's.

"I knew you'd come back to see me sometime, Punch," said Hank, using a nickname Craig had not heard in twenty years. "God, it's good to see you."

They didn't go out to a bar or even to the crappy restaurant connected to the pro shop. Instead, Craig was given the honor of a seat on a smelly mower in the Quonset hut. He and Hank twisted open bottles of Pabst Blue Ribbon that Hank brought from a battered fridge.

"I could ask how you are, but I guess I know a little about that. Why don't you tell me anyway?"

"Well, you know, I'm all right," Craig answered. "It ain't been the best year of my life, I guess."

"Punch, we've known each other too long to bullshit. I can look at you and know you don't have your old action. Were you serious about the lesson?"

"I'm not playing anymore," Craig said. "Just wanted to see how you were doing."

Hank's smile disappeared. His expression was as if Craig had told him he had a disease. "Not playing no more? Well, that ain't right."

"It is what it is, I guess. I've just had enough."

"Why? Too many bogeys?"

"More like too many triple bogeys. More like too many fucking drives, OB."

Hank looked at him for a long moment. Then he looked out the back door of the hut. They could see roughly half the practice putting green that way, the same green that they had met on when Craig was eleven years old. A young boy was there now, working on his putting.

Hank nodded. "I remember when that was you. I taught a lot of kids, but I never saw joy like yours when you was playing golf."

"That was then," Craig said, an edge to his voice.

"What's different?"

"Maybe I grew up," Craig snapped, surprised at his anger.

"Maybe you just forgot."

"Forgot what?"

"Forgot your joy. We golfers are always forgetting, you know. One day we got it all figured out, the game is easy; we can make that ball talk. Then we change something, or something gets our attention, and we get away from those things that made the game great."

Craig sighed. He had hoped he wouldn't have to endure Hank's folksy philosophy on golf. Hank could not know what Craig had endured on Tour, in his life.

What the hell does this old man know of my life?

"Yeah, I know all that," Craig said. "What you don't know is what it's like out there. You don't know about the last couple of years."

"True, I guess I don't," said Hank. "Hey, I forgot, I got something for you. I didn't know how long it would take, but I been holding on to it for a while."

Craig followed him to a battered roll-top desk across the hut. Hank rolled up the top and took a small box from one of the compartments. He opened it up and flipped what looked like a coin to Craig. Craig caught it and turned the trinket over in his hand. The top read, "Winners Medal-Joplin City Golf Championship." On the bottom, it showed the year, 1982.

"Where the hell did this come from?"

"Your first title, you gave it to me, remember? Now I'm giving it back."

Craig smiled. He had given Hank the medal after his repeated championship win two years in a row. He knew it would never have happened without coaching from his teacher.

Craig looked up. "That's some desk."

"You want it? It's probably the biggest piece of shit in here."

Craig saw a box sitting in the middle of all the unnamed clutter. It was full of medals and badges. Curious, he picked one up. It was the kind that clipped to a hat or belt. This one said "Participant, 1974, Texas Open." Below that was the PGA Tour insignia. Craig looked at several other badges in the box, stopping when he got to one that said "1975 PGA Championship."

"Whose are these?" he asked Hank.

"Hell, they're yours if you want 'em. Though I expect you got plenty of your own by now." Hank walked away and got another two beers from the fridge, sitting back down on the mower.

Craig joined him. "You never told me you played the Tour."

"Long time ago," Hank said. "Not much to my career, at least not as a player."

"When did you play?"

"1968–1976, eight years. I chased it for a long time."

"What happened? Why did you quit?"

Hank looked at Craig, and for the first time, he saw a deep sadness in his teacher's eyes. "I'd had enough, so I thought. Like you."

"Why?"

"Because I forgot."

"Forgot what?"

Hank sighed. He hoped he could give Craig one last thing, and he wasn't sure it was going to be enough.

"Forgot my joy. Forgot how I felt when I stood on the course first thing in the morning and saw the fog rising from the marsh. Forgot to enjoy how it feels to hit a white ball into a blue sky. Forgot how great it feels to hit a bunker shot that skips and grabs and stops by the flag. I forgot how truly lucky I was to play the hardest game in the world well enough to get paid to do it."

Craig nodded. "I can relate to that. At least, you gave it a shot."

"No, Punch, I didn't give it a shot. I gave it everything I had. At least I thought so. I practiced until my hands hurt. I played 'til dark. Hell, I even played 'til the wife left. I put in the time, the sweat, made the sacrifices. And when the game didn't pay me back the way I thought I was owed, I got pissed. I thought I proved my old man right, that eventually this stupid game was gonna break my heart."

"But you stayed in the game. You stayed here; you kept teaching."

"Yup, I did. Why do you think I did that?"

Craig just looked at him.

Hank smiled and for a second looked like he did when Craig first met him. "Hell, son. I love this game. I'm no dummy, and I know a lot of people. I could do other things. But I love the game. I didn't want another life. I've had a life in golf, and I don't regret a day of it 'cept maybe the day I gave up on playing."

Craig looked out over the practice green. After a long silence, he spoke.

"Look, I appreciate what you're doing, I really do. I owe you a lot. I just can't go back now. Too much has happened. Too much has gone wrong."

Hank looked at him with a sardonic smile and shook his head slowly.

"Yeah, sounds familiar. Sounds like the same thing I used to tell myself. For years, I told myself that. And those same years and many since have helped me put a name to that story. Bullshit."

"What?"

"Yeah, it's really compelling and dramatic, and maybe even justified, but it's compelling, dramatic, and justified BULLSHIT."

This was said with a knowing smile and not a trace of malice or judgment.

Despite himself, Craig smiled too. Because if there was anything he could be certain of, it was that Hank cared about him. He had thought unjustly, for a moment, that his old teacher wanted credit for bringing Craig Cantwell back from the dead. And yet, he also knew that this man had never asked for anything from him.

"Even if I wanted to start over, I have no earthly idea where to start," Craig said.

"How about at the beginning?"

"A little tough when you are as old as I am."

Hank looked at Craig for a long minute. "Yeah, well, you ain't that old. And you ain't dead, either, even though you're doing a right fancy imitation of it. You can still give it something."

"I figure maybe I've given it enough." Craig's bitterness literally tasted bad. He spat it out as if to rid himself of it.

Hank came to face him and looked up at Craig and into his eyes. He put his right hand over Craig's heart.

"That's where you're wrong. You can still give as before."

Back on the hillside, Craig looked up from his journal. It was full dark now. He was writing by the light of a small fire he had made. He looked into that fire, seeing only Hank's face and feeling his touch.

"Give as before."

He had dismissed those words as he drove away from Joplin and from Hank. He had scarcely even heard them. Now, here on this hillside, the words came to the forefront of his mind. He was so tired, yet he knew he would not sleep yet. He looked up at the three-quarter moon and stood.

When he moved away from the fire, he realized there was enough moonlight to see the valley floor. He looked up suddenly.

"He's saying I need to forgive," Craig said to the night. Give as before. *Forgive who? Forgive what?*

He thought about the word "forgiveness." He reflected on what it had always meant to him. Until this point in his life, it had meant weakness. It had meant giving a transgressor a pass. It had meant giving up. It just was not what a tough man did. Changing the order of the word to "give as before" shifted his perspective. That change signified moving on, continuing a journey, no matter the setback. No matter how severe the injustice. Somehow, this seemed more like strength. Just two days ago, Seth had said to the group, "Forgiveness is a gift you give to yourself." Craig had chosen that moment to excuse himself and go to the bathroom. In the headspace he was in, *that* was pure bullshit.

He sighed as he allowed the thought of forgiveness to exist. Part of him thought it was impossible. Another part of him did not want to forgive, as if his anger and bitterness had become an ally he needed. Yet another part of him wondered if he was even capable of such an act. The fatigue returned, and now Craig was sure he would sleep. Before he did, he made a series of notes in his journal:

Dad, Rachelle, Joan, Kelly, Monroe, Fate, Golf

He looked at the list and let out a breath that would have been a sob if he had the energy to cry. The last thing he wrote that night was the last name on the list:

Craig.

CHAPTER TEN

Craig was awakened by a rustling sound outside his tent. More annoyed than afraid, he exited his sleeping bag and looked outside. His fire, which had been nearly out before he fell asleep, was burning orange embers again. It wasn't wild, just well contained by the rocks around it. It was also more than enough to illuminate Seth Reede's face as he sat next to the fire looking at Craig. He was not really surprised to see Seth, though he did feel an uneasiness.

Seth smiled sympathetically. "Are you ready?"

Craig nodded, wondering what he was agreeing to be ready for.

"Let's go then." Seth got up and began walking down the hillside.

As he followed Seth, Craig was inwardly surprised at his own compliance. A few hours before, he would not have moved without lobbing a barrage of questions at Seth, but now, he followed because he knew in his soul that he must.

By the time they reached the foot of the hills, they were walking next to each other. Seth's eyes looked ahead, looking over at Craig occasionally. Craig knew his apprehension showed. He felt as if he was being pulled by an invisible current toward something dangerous. And yet, he did not understand the flow nor was he able to avoid being carried by it.

After a long walk, they came to a stone wall. It was high and seemed to stretch in both directions. They walked along the wall, and Craig reached out and touched it as he walked. It was solid stone, yet without breaks or cracks for mortar. After a time, they came to a gate. It was wooden, and heavy, and opened inward to the other side of the wall. The gate was closed. Seth lifted a latch and pushed the door, but it didn't move. He looked at Craig. Craig stepped up to the gate and pushed with one hand, then both. He knew it would open, but that it would take effort. He leaned his shoulder against it and put his weight and athlete's strength behind the push he gave it. The gate opened roughly about one foot. He looked at Seth, who merely looked back at him. Another shove granted him entry, though he had to squeeze through to the other side.

Craig had no idea what was on the other side or why he must see it.

He walked forward and initially saw only the brush and landscape of the valley, at least what he could see, given the darkness. In the distance, he could see shapes. He walked slowly toward them, noticing a blue and red tinge to the light on his left as he approached. The shapes were not inviting, but he could not resist moving toward them. The colors became brighter as he walked, his focus entirely on what lay ahead. He was startled when he kicked something on the ground. It moved away and clinked slightly. Looking more closely, he saw an empty bottle. It was an empty bottle of Jim Beam. As he continued to walk, he noticed more of the empty bottles littering the ground. He followed the trail of them and soon found a small clearing. What he saw was horrible, yet he could not turn away from it.

There had been a battle here, a firefight. Multiple bodies littered the ground, blood soaking the grass and the dirt. Several corpses were missing limbs or had been badly mutilated by gunfire or shrapnel. The smell of decay suddenly reached his nose, and he winced. His breathing became rapid as the tableau before him expanded. This was more terrible than his worst nightmare. The bodies wore uniforms—most of them American military. Helmets and weapons were strewn about. He noted several different uniforms, and the bodies were Asian. *Viet Nam?*

Just when he thought everyone in sight was dead, he saw movement. A lone soldier sitting amid the bodies on a fallen tree trunk. The soldier lifted a bottle to his mouth and drank. Against his will, Craig moved closer and looked. Soot, dirt, and blood covered the soldier even though he had no evident wounds. A battered helmet lay next to him. He looked up at Craig with an infinite emptiness in his eyes. Craig returned the gaze. Looking into the soldier's eyes was like looking down a dark well.

The soldier raised his bottle again and took a long pull. As he swallowed, he looked again at Craig and smiled a mirthless smile. A smile with no warmth, one that defiled even the nature of a smile. This was the smile Craig had learned to fear in his youth.

His father's smile.

Craig had rehearsed in his mind what he would say to the bastard if he ever saw him again. He had even fantasized about beating him like he had beaten Craig and Craig's mother. The problem was that Craig was now rooted to his spot, unable to move. Unable to feel anything but terror. Transfixed, he waited.

Slowly, his father's evil smile faded. The emptiness in his eyes filled up with an emotion Craig could only call desperation. His father's face changed and filled with fear, and it seemed for a moment that he wanted to reach out to Craig for safety, yet he stayed rooted where he sat. The fear on his face turned to regret, and then his body shook slightly. Then again. He dropped his bottle. His hands went to his face, and he began to cry. His body shook with sobs, and he wailed his agony from behind his hands. Craig's father fell off the log, wailing and flailing in emotional agony. It seemed his father's fallen comrades were the lucky ones; he had never seen a man more wounded.

Craig could now move. Instead of moving away, he moved toward his broken father. The form of a young man, younger than Craig, and far more wounded. Craig knelt beside his weeping father, put his hand on his head, and moved it gently over his scalp as though comforting a child. Suddenly Craig could speak, and he marveled at his words, knowing that they came from somewhere or someone else. He would never have believed the words coming out of his mouth nor the power that they had:

"It's all right, Dad. I love you."

His twenty-year-old father sat up slightly. The man who had left the evidence of his heartbreak on the faces of his wife and son now looked at his grown son. This man who Craig feared more than anything now smiled a real smile at him. He smiled into Craig's eyes, then touched his son's face with one hand. Slowly, he stood. Then with a small wave, he turned and walked away, looking over his shoulder and raising his chin just slightly, nodding that familiar nod that Craig knew to be his father's.

The bodies and the blood were gone.

Craig watched his father walk away into the darkness. As his form disappeared in the night, Seth appeared in his place, walking toward Craig with his hands in his jacket pockets, that same inscrutable expression on his face. Craig had found it uncomfortable to meet Seth's eyes the past few days; now he looked directly at them and found the deepest empathy, immeasurable kindness.

Craig was standing exactly where the horrible combat tableau had been only moments ago, Seth's expression questioning.

"I never saw my father cry. Never believed 'til now that he could."

CHAPTER ELEVEN

Seth nodded at Craig's acknowledgment of his father, then looked slightly away in another direction, as if he heard or saw something else. Craig turned and began walking in that direction.

In the distance, a small campfire was burning. As he drew closer, Craig saw two people sitting on opposite sides of the fire. He stopped when he was within earshot. On one side sat a man wearing a uniform, though it was not a military uniform. The captain's cap lay beside him, and Craig recognized it as that of a commercial pilot. Across the fire from him was a woman.

She would have been beautiful if not for the hurt on her face. She had long auburn tresses and eyes so green they could be seen even in the low light of the fire. She had her arms crossed around her body with her knees drawn to her chin as she rocked back and forth, a slight tremble to her movements. She was naked and ashamed.

The pilot was speaking harshly to her.

"Look, it's way better this way. We can go on with our lives; we can go on doing the work we want. I don't want to take care of a kid. I don't want to pay for one. I don't want to leave my wife. Even if I did, I wouldn't leave her for a stew, anyway."

Tears flowed out of the woman's green eyes, and she shuddered as her breath left her body.

"Hey, this is good news, honestly. We would both get in trouble at work. My wife would have my head, not to mention a shitload of cash. You've never had kids; I have. They're a pain in the ass."

She stifled a sob.

"C'mon. I'm looking at this as a good piece of luck. I advise you to do the same."

The pilot stood up, put on his cap just so, and walked away without a backward glance. The woman's look of agony was replaced briefly by a look of pure hatred. As she looked at the pilot leaving and heard him whistle a happy tune, she looked briefly like she might chase after him and do him harm. Then her expression changed to neutral, and she stood. She seemed to stand into clothing, nice clothes at that. Suddenly, she was a highly attractive woman, wearing a white blouse and skirt, with expensive sandals and her hair in a long plait that fell over one shoulder. She suddenly looked at Craig a few feet away, as if she had just now noticed him. Her head tilted to one side, a sexy smile on her lovely face.

"Hi," she said to him with a blatant invitation.

Craig gasped as he looked at Joan Wylie, his former wife. Looked at Joan as she was the day he had met her, the day that he marked at that point as the luckiest of his life. He had truly not recognized her as she sat naked by the fire. It was impossible to think this gorgeous creature was the same person as the hurt, broken woman the pilot had spoken to. Craig knew she had transformed or more accurately had buried the hurt and heartbreak of her past before she masterfully created the supermodel that stood before him the day they met. Joan had never told him the details about the first child she had lost. Craig could never have conceived how awful that experience had been. She had buried that memory, shutting it out because it was the only way she felt she could survive. The trouble was that this hurt was a hidden piece of luggage she had never opened. A wound that festered over time.

It had never occurred to Craig that Joan had taken her revenge against the pilot out on him. He could now see the possibility that when she hired the most cutthroat divorce attorney she could find, she was really seeing the pilot's plane go down in flames.

Joan still stood before him, gorgeous in her elegant clothes and smiling at him as though he were the answer to her prayers. Before he came to SGZ, Craig would have said that Joan Wylie was the last person on earth he wanted to see. He would have avoided any thought of her and rejected outright the idea that he would ever show her kindness. Just hours before, what he now did would have been inconceivable.

Craig stepped over to her and gently touched her on the shoulder. He looked into her eyes and she saw his comprehension. Then he put his hands gently on the sides of her face, holding it as if she were a child. He kissed her forehead tenderly, then looked at her again with the deepest kindness.

"Be well."

She put her hand over his heart, and in her eyes, he saw empathy and kindness, maybe for the first time.

"You too," Joan said.

Then she turned and walked away, with a small wave and a slight lift of her chin as she vanished into the darkness.

Again, Seth appeared. He looked at Craig once again, and his eyes showed respect and an even deeper kindness. It was as though Seth recognized and acknowledged Craig's act of compassion. Without words, his expression showed Craig's respect for a hard task done well. Craig smiled and shook his head slightly as if he could hardly believe what he had just done.

CHAPTER TWELVE

From a short distance away, Craig noticed a young boy, eight or nine years old, walking parallel to him. The boy carried a large golf bag full of clubs over his shoulder and walked with effort; the bag was bigger than the boy. At some point, the boy began to walk directly in Craig's path. Craig could see the look of foreboding on the boy's face and felt obligated to follow him even though he had no idea why.

A short distance later, they entered a suburban neighborhood, and the boy walked up the steps of a small house. He leaned his golf bag against the porch railing and hesitated by the front door. Then he surveyed the porch and the yard around it for a minute as if he was searching for an escape route.

Then he heard a noise coming from inside the house; it seemed someone was inside. The brief light of escape in the boy's eyes was replaced with a desperate look, betraying his hope that someone might be approaching or coming home. Then his shoulders slumped with resignation as he opened the front door and walked in.

Craig went unnoticed by the boy and unseen as he now stood inside the house.

"Well, it's about time!" a woman's voice said harshly. "I guess you hit a lot of those stupid balls."

"Hi, Mama," the boy said, a fearful plea in his voice. Craig recognized the tone; it was one he had adopted as a young boy with his father. His experience over the years had taught him that what the tone really meant was "I'm home. Please don't hurt me again. Please. I'll be good, I promise."

"Did you bring my things?" she said with a coarse look.

"What . . . I dunno . . . what things?" the boy stammered.

"Typical! Typical that you forgot to bring what I asked for. I wonder if you are ever going to grow out of this self-ishness. You can remember every little detail about hitting those golf balls, but you can't even remember to take care of your mother."

"I'll go now, Mom. What do you want? I'll go get it right now."

"No, no. It's too late. It's too late for you to get my things, but not too late for you to be taught a lesson. Get downstairs."

Craig was as terrified as the boy was at this point. He wanted nothing more than to leave. He could see the terror and resignation on the young boy's face. Against his heart, Craig followed the pair into the basement. He watched as the boy's mother ordered him to strip naked. Then, horrified, Craig watched as the woman did what a mother could never do, watched as this young boy endured an unspeakable violation by the one person he was supposed to trust above anyone else. Only Craig's bewildered horror kept him from matching the boy's tears of confusion and his grunts of pain...

Mercifully, Craig finally found himself on the steps of the porch in front of the house. He could still see the boy's eyes, full of tears of hurt and confusion. Craig wondered why he was made to bear witness to such an act and if he could ever forget it.

Then a car pulled into the driveway. A man got out, wearing creased pants and a nice golf polo shirt. On his chest, he wore a name tag that said "SAM" above the words "HEAD GOLF PROFESSIONAL."

"Hey, Dad!" said a young voice. The boy was standing next to Craig on the porch steps. A light in his eyes and a youthful smile on his face. A young boy glad to see his father home from work. No one could have noticed even a hint of the horror he had just gone through.

"How you doin', pro?" his father responded. "Did you hit 'em good today?"

"Not bad. I still gotta learn to work the ball right to left."

"Aw, you'll get it. Maybe your mom will let us go to dinner, and we can talk about it."

The boy's grin widened. "You go and ask her."

The father strode up the steps and rubbed his son's head. "I'll be right back," he said with a smile. Craig watched all this with complete confusion. How could a child live like this? Thoughts of his own childhood were welcome compared to this freak show.

"Do you want to hit me now?" Craig looked confusingly at the boy who was speaking to him for the first time.

"What did you say?" Craig asked.

"Do you want to hit me now?"

He looked in shock at the boy. The hurt and confusion had returned to his face as he looked pitifully at Craig. Craig shook his head, his mouth open, even more confused. The last thing on his mind was to inflict more pain on this kid. He watched as the boy silently moved to stand next to his golf bag, which was still leaning against the porch railing.

Craig noticed it was a pro's staff bag, with "WILSON" in big letters down the side. There was also some horizontal lettering, typical of the way the staff pro always got a bag with his name on it. Craig's incredulity deepened even further when he noticed the name.

It was originally a first initial, then the last name. The original first initial had been "S," but it had been altered to "Z." The last name was "MONROE."

Years before his major championships. Years before Craig himself had broken a bone in Zeke's face after one of Zeke's golf victories, Zeke Monroe had lived through unspeakable pain.

CHAPTER THIRTEEN

Craig continued his walk along the valley floor. The moonlight was enough for him to see and move, yet he knew he could not see everything clearly. He moved by instinct not thinking about where, just allowing his feet to carry him. A lighted area was ahead, though it was not moonlight or firelight. It seemed misty and otherworldly, and it seemed to frame a scene. He walked closer and stopped in alarm when he saw a familiar figure.

Rachelle Keys stood before him, again oblivious to his presence. She had a look of bewildered shock on her face. She was dressed as Craig had never seen her before: dark pants over black rubber-soled shoes, a blue windbreaker with "FBI" on the lapel and across the back. A badge clipped to her belt, as well as a 9 mm Glock handgun and two spare clips. He wondered if she had gained weight until he realized that she had on a Kevlar vest under the windbreaker. She also held the radio in her hand as it squawked suddenly.

"Keys, report."

"Keys here. Suspect down."

"What about the package?"

Despite her training, bottled emotions bubbled up. "She's a child, not a fucking package, and she's here."

"Condition?"

Craig saw two still forms, one was an adult man, the other a young girl. The man had several wounds and was lying face up with his eyes open and fixed. The girl was lying with her face to a wall as if she were napping, but she was too still.

"She's gone——" Rachelle began, the second word catching in her throat. Despite her training, she lost her battle with tears, as several rolled down her cheeks. This only made her angrier.

"Hmm," she cleared her throat. "She's gone. He . . . um . . . killed her before the breach."

As Craig watched, several other agents appeared. They did what they were trained to do. They verified the condition of both the kidnapper and the victim. Rachelle stood rooted with the radio in her left hand while her right hand hung by her side, trembling with anger. One of the other agents looked over at her.

"Keys, you okay?"

She had just led a breach that had turned into a gunfight. He was merely asking if she was all right physically. The look she gave him was one of such intense anger and hurt. It conveyed a deep wound that might never heal.

Her fellow agent moved a step closer. His look showed he understood. "We've got this, go ahead."

She nodded loosely and turned away. Craig watched as she walked out of the room to the end of a hallway and down several flights of stairs. It was as though he were a camera following her, yet he was rooted to his spot. Rachelle walked out of the building and across a parking lot where several more agents were standing, along with a man with a stricken look on his face.

Rachelle's expression was now wooden, blank. It was as if she had used her brief journey out of the building to purge any emotion from her being. She stopped a few steps from the man who was flanked by two other agents.

"Mr. Kent, I'm so sorry. The kidnapper apparently killed Bridget . . . killed your daughter before we arrived." This was said with all the compassion of a plumber informing a homeowner of a broken sewer line.

The father's face was uncomprehending of the loss and the flat emotionless mien of the woman he had known for nearly six months. She had not called him "Mr. Kent" since the first day they met. He was Robert or Bobby to her after just a short time. Through the process of working to find his daughter, she had gone from Agent Keys to Rachelle. It just made sense because she was living in his house.

He had no answer for why one day he had taken her hand in his. She could never explain why she let him. They would never know why they had reached for each other, if it was a balm for the pain each of them felt or if maybe, just maybe, they thought they might be able to fill the hole in each other's lives. They would never know, because, on her way out of that building, Rachelle had erected a wall between them.

A double horror was stamped on Robert Kent's face. That his daughter was gone was horrible, yet he had prepared himself as best he could for that. She had been kidnapped six months ago, and he knew there was a very real possibility that he would not see her again. The other horror was that what he thought he was building with Rachelle Keys had vanished. Her face was like stone. There was no trace of the intimacy they had shared these past six months—both emotionally and, yes, even physically.

"I'm really very sorry," she said again. Then she turned and walked away.

Craig followed her, even as rooted to his spot as he was. While he watched, the scene changed, and suddenly they were standing with a low brick wall between them. Rachelle looked directly at him for a moment, and he could see that she wanted to reach out to him. He wanted to comfort her, more than he had ever wanted to protect and help any woman before.

Her eyes projected sadness and resignation as she bent down and picked up a brick. She held it in one hand and picked up a trowel with the other. Then she gathered mortar from a wheelbarrow with the trowel and applied it to the brick, then expertly placed the new brick on top. She continued as Craig watched, adding bricks to her wall. As much as he wanted to say the words that would make her stop, he had none. He felt helpless as he watched her build her wall between them, seeming to relax a bit more with each brick that she added.

CHAPTER FOURTEEN

"Why must I see all of this?" Craig asked. "I know that it is important, yet I still don't understand." Seth was standing next to him, knowing Craig's struggle. He knew it because he had been through similar struggles. In fact, he still had similar challenges of holding on to past hurts. Seth was a teacher, and yet he would never claim a smug superiority over his pupil.

"Maybe it's easier to hold on to our victim story," Seth said.

Craig shook his head. "Why do I need to know these things about the people who have hurt me?"

"Is it easier to hold on to your pain?"

"None of it is easy," Craig replied. "But at least I thought I knew who to blame."

Seth continued to look at Craig with empathy. When he spoke, he realized that he could be addressing himself. "Craig, my experience of you is that you carry this massive weight. It's the combined weight of all your pain, all the hurts you have had in your life. You're strong, and you've gotten used to this weight, but you notice that all you can do is carry it. It's taken up such a big part of you that you think you *are* your pain, your heartbreak. You've become so attached to all of the painful stories that you are stuck in them. It's as though for you to be free to gather other things in your life you must put down the weight of your pain. But for some reason, you think that you need it. You think that it protects you, and maybe it does, but in keeping out more hurt it also keeps out any joy as well."

Craig felt desperate. "Part of me wants to let go of it. I just don't know if I can."

Seth nodded. "I know. You've forgotten how it feels to live free of this burden. Maybe you even think that you've been given it because you deserve it, that you're being punished. If that is true, it's only because you are punishing yourself."

"How does knowing the pain of people who have hurt me help me let go?"

Seth shrugged. "Maybe it's because all of them have pain as well. We all have pain in our lives. Maybe because if I could read the secret history of all my friends and enemies, there would be enough pain and suffering to disarm all my hostility."

"Does that make it all right that they have inflicted pain on me?"

"No, of course not. They have taken their revenge out on you in a way. It happens all the time; we hurt someone else because we ourselves have been hurt. The problem is that there is no such thing as revenge. In lashing out at others, we only cause ourselves more pain."

He continued his walk along the valley floor. It was still dark, and Craig had no idea what time it was. He knew it was late, or rather early. There couldn't be much left of the night before dawn. He walked up a slight incline through a light fog and spotted the outline of a small structure up ahead. As before on this amazing night, he moved urgently, without fatigue, which made no sense. He should have been exhausted.

The structure turned out to be a small shack with a low awning on the outside. There was a visible outline of a man sitting on a bench underneath the awning and a seat opposite the man, whose shape started to reveal itself as Craig walked closer. A faint light shone from the inside of the shack, like from an old kerosene lantern. The scene was familiar, yet he still had no idea who he was about to meet. He took a seat opposite the man in the shadow and waited.

The man leaned forward slightly so that the faint light spilling out of the shack illuminated his face. Craig was dumbstruck. The man had blue-green eyes, wide shoulders, and a smile he both remembered and envied.

"Hello, my friend."

Craig's mouth moved, but his vocal cords failed to produce any sound. Across from him sat Craig Cantwell. He was looking into his own face just a few feet away. He was sitting in front of himself.

"Yeah, I know it's weird. But it's about time we had a talk," Craig said.

Craig could not take his eyes off himself. There was a light in his eyes. On the other hand, the flame in his own eyes had been extinguished by life's tough events like a candle in a gentle rain. There was a youthfulness and authenticity in his eyes. Craig recognized it, longed for it, and envied it all at the same time.

"So, you're still not talking? Okay. I'll start then. I've got a lot to say," Craig began. "Hmm . . . where to begin? How about here, it's time you stopped beating yourself up and start paying attention to who you are. And who you are is pretty damn tremendous."

Craig was taken aback by this comment, mainly because he was used to a far harsher assessment of himself. This was not a lot different from the things he had heard from Seth and some other facilitators at SGZ. He had argued with them then. Now, however, he found that it was hard to argue with himself, at least at this moment.

"Yeah, you've gotta stop lying to yourself."

"What?" Craig said.

"That's right, you heard me."

"What lies?" Craig asked.

"Wow, I hope we have time. Maybe start with this one: that the talent you have in golf isn't important. That you are not 'significant' or 'powerful' because you are 'just' a golfer."

"That's not a lie; that's just how it is," Craig rebutted.

"Okay, so you say, pal. Since I am part of this equation, I would like to forcefully disagree. I'm one of the best golfers in the world, playing the hardest game there is. I'm able to do things that literally millions of other people only wish they could do. They would be thrilled to do them for free. I, of course, earn big money for doing these same things. So, pardon me, but that is a lie told to the most important man of all, you."

"Glad to hear you're so important," Craig said sarcastically.

The radiant version of himself looked hard into his eyes for a moment. "Make no mistake, buddy: I am the most important person you will *ever* talk to."

"Well, I'm not playing anymore, am I?"

"Oh, that's right; that's another lie—that you blew it. You blew up and got suspended, and, oh my, you just can't play anymore. Bullshit! First, we both know why, and it's a hell of a why. Even though it was misguided. Second, don't sell me that happy horseshit that we don't have any game. There are places to play and ways to make it back to the Tour."

"Why would it matter?"

"Jeez, you're just a ray of sunshine, huh? I could go on all night and half the day on this one. Do you think that your platform in golf might have done some good in the past? How about Emmanuel Harris? The kid in Atlanta, you taught him when he was only fourteen. He got off the streets, got a degree. Now he runs an anti-gang outreach nonprofit. Ask him if you made a difference."

Craig had forgotten about Manny Harris. Forgotten about the times he had spoken to groups of young men about their choices, just before they learned to hit their first golf shots. The same kids who wrote letters to him years later about their new jobs, new kids, and happy lives. How many of those had he forgotten?

"Next, it might matter to somebody else—somebody important," Craig said. "It might just matter to Kelly. Have you stopped to think that she needs you more than ever now?"

"I don't——" Craig started before he cut himself off.

"Yeah, yeah, you don't think you're a good father. Heard that one too. Show me any 'Father of the Year' and he'll tell you about his mistakes. Fathers never know or do all the right things. The one thing you got that many don't is that you love her. She knows that, and she wants and needs you. Now more than ever."

Craig looked over at himself. It was strange to hear the positive message from this source. There was no guile, just the right amount of sarcasm. The overriding thing he felt was love. It came as a strange sensation since he had not felt it in what seemed like an eternity. He loved himself. Enough to speak the truth. Enough to not accept the normal bullshit.

"That's right, man. I do. I love me," he told himself.

"Gotta admit, that's a new one.

"Well, as much of a gloom factory as you've been, I might be your only chance at sex."

"That's enough, asshole."

Both Craigs laughed.

"That brings us to another topic, Buddy," Craig said, sounding more serious. "You didn't fail Rachelle. She had her reasons for everything, man. You did the best you could. Even she might not really know why she chose what she did. It wasn't because of you. She had her reasons, and none of them were you."

"I miss her," they said in tandem.

"And I have more to do."

Craig just nodded. He knew. For a few moments, he just looked at himself. Those eyes that had a fiery glint. The athlete's build. The face that was real and plain and could go to mirth in a second. The certainty that he would do whatever he chose.

I like this guy.

"So, sport, there's just one more thing," his vibrant self said. "The bigger reason our golf matters."

Craig would listen to him now. He waited and fervently wished he would always hear this version of himself.

"It's what you chose. Golf. It's what lights us up. It's our passion. That light you have that is yours and yours alone. It means more than you know to others, without even trying to impress them. It inspires, enables others to rise. It makes people happy."

Just then, the top of the sun peaked over the east valley wall. It was between two peaks, and the great shafts of warm light hit them and the valley at once. It was the moment of dawn where the world stops and greets the sun.

"It makes him happy too."

CHAPTER FIFTEEN

Craig drove away from SGZ feeling lighter than he had in five years. He recalled what Seth had said at the beginning of the week, seven days ago. He smiled and shook his head at the thought because it seemed like an eternity had passed since he first came here. Seth had said that for some people it was not what they discovered while here that was the most impactful, but what they let go of. Craig felt fortunate; he had made many discoveries in the last week, and he had let go of many things as well.

He had let go of anger, fear, resentment, and guilt. He was not sure if these were gone forever. He just knew that for the last three days they were not the primary feelings he was having. He had gained clarity and had started to once again appreciate his life as he had before so many events in his past.

Craig now looked ahead with a feeling of anticipation, not dread. It was not that he was certain of what lay ahead of him; he just had a hunger to keep living. This made him smile again because he really had no idea what he would do. He only knew he had a desire to find and pursue his purpose.

He was driving his rental car back to San Francisco, where he had planned a brief stay before catching a flight home. On his way south, he stopped in Rohnert Park for something to eat. He found a local place with hand-carved wooden animals out front and sat alone, eating lunch and looking out the window. At one point, the restaurant manager stopped by his table and asked how his meal was. When Craig complimented the man, he smiled and asked if there was anything else he could do for him.

"Thanks, no," Craig said. "Great food."

"Well, I'm glad. Come back and see us again," the man said with a smile.

Just before he walked away, Craig gave in to an impulse. "Hey, there is one thing," he said, calling after the manager.

"Yes?"

"Is there a . . . " Craig could hardly believe he was following this instinct. "Is there a golf course anywhere close by?"

Craig walked out on the driving range of a small municipal golf course less than a mile away from the restaurant. He had a metal wire bucket full of range balls in one hand and a rental 7 iron in the crook of his other arm. He had bought a golf glove in the small golf shop, and he had that tucked in the back pocket of his jeans. He had on sunglasses and a T-shirt he had bought at SGZ that just said "SWITCH" above an illustration of a light switch. His beard and hair were long and unruly just as it had been when he arrived in California a week ago. A closer look, however, revealed a light in his eyes that was not there before. His worn athletic shoes completed the picture; he looked nothing like a golfer. Certainly, no one on this cheap public driving range would guess he was an experienced professional. At least not yet.

Craig put the balls down on a reasonably divot-free section of grass. He pulled out the glove and held it briefly to his face, feeling and smelling the new leather. He smiled as if he was smelling an article of clothing worn by a past love and was recalling her by her scent. He put on the glove and tentatively gripped the 7 iron, swinging it slowly in the air. It felt awkward and familiar at the same time. This was as if a friend had unexpectedly come to visit him and all past transgressions had been put aside. It was a warm meeting, one that neither was sure of just yet.

Craig had first swung a golf club when he was five years old. Over the years, the act of hitting a golf ball with a club had become as natural to him as walking. There had been times of intense instruction and learning and other times of just letting go and remembering. At his peak as a golfer, Craig had felt that he was living his purpose, hitting dimpled balls at flagsticks with golf clubs. It might seem absurd to consider that this is what Craig felt was closest to his essence, but it was true. Some people painted pictures, some wrote books, some preached sermons; Craig Cantwell painted his masterpieces with golf shots.

He realized with some shock that he had not hit a golf ball in over two years.

He was startled when he again felt his passion for this game, just by putting on a glove and picking up a club. He was coming back to the game lighter now, free of the baggage he'd left on the hillside at SGZ.

The first swings were tentative. That he missed them was expected. After all, two years was a chunk of his life, especially away from golf. Each mistake, however, had a small lesson in it that he could incorporate. His body was remembering, and his spirit was reviving. On about the twelfth swing, it happened.

Craig's mind, body, and spirit aligned together as one, and he hit the ball. The feel of it was sublime, just right. The strike of the club was powerful yet effortless. The club must use the earth in the strike; it compresses the ball in a downward arc against the ground, and the ball draws from the earth the power to rise. With this earthly launch, the ball is released, fulfilling its purpose by boring through the air to a target in the far distance. The feeling of a well-struck golf shot is the nectar, the drug that hooks golfers to come back again and again. It is this glimpse of harmony and per- fection and potential that draws them back through failure, through frustration, yes, even heartbreak. This harmonious strike vibrated up through the club into Craig's hands and into his soul—reminding him of his truth. No matter what, THIS was him expressing himself perfectly.

That twelfth ball rose and soared and lighted to the earth 185 yards away. Then Craig Cantwell gorged on his golf swing like a man starved for his own expression. Patiently, he hit one ball after another. He slipped right back into the routine of hitting golf shots, and more importantly, into the joy of the action. There was a red target three feet wide out on the range, with white writing saying "180 yards" on it. His focus narrowed to just that target, as he launched shot after shot at it. He became lost in the process as ball after ball streaked in an arc toward that sign. What is boring to the non-golfer is sublime to the golfer, as he proves over and over that he can will a ball to find his target.

Toward the end of the bucket of balls, Craig knocked down the sign at 180 yards. It was the third ball that had hit the sign, and when it fell over, he blinked as if coming out of a trance. His immediate thought was that he needed a new target; then he happened to look around. There was no other activity on the range. Roughly a dozen other golfers were watching him rather than hitting their own shots. These were golfers who just wanted to hit the ball and get it airborne and who would never dream it was possible to hit even one shot like the several dozen they'd just witnessed. Their eyes and mouths were open as if they were witnessing the impossible.

The clerk from the shop was there as well, spellbound. Craig smiled a bit sheepishly at him. "Sorry about the sign."

"Ahh, don't worry about it," the young man said. "Mister, are you a golf pro or something?"

Craig just smiled.

"'Cause I ain't never seen anybody hit golf balls like that!"

Craig gave a slight chuckle. "It's been a while for me, too."

Part Two

Rachelle and Kelly

Every man lives two lives; the second one begins when he realizes he has only one.

CHAPTER ONE

1990–2009

Rachelle Keys was an adventurous woman. To call her independent would be a gross understatement. Her life up to this point had been a series of significant events that she shrugged off as being part of her past. She was passionate, with a great deal of empathy for others. Yet she lacked the attention span to devote herself to any one thing for too long.

Rachelle was talented in many ways; she was smart and did very well in school. She also dabbled in acting in school plays and excelled in sports. She was as interested in the opposite sex as any girl but did not dream of the fairytale marriage to the prince. She bored easily with almost anything—school, sports, men. They were all challenges that once conquered she moved on from. She was not mean-spirited in her quests. In fact, she remained friends with most of her past beaus and many of her sports competitors.

After a good career in college as a volleyball player, Rachelle aspired to make the U.S. Olympic volleyball team.

However, an ankle injury cut that quest short. So, at twenty-two, she found herself temporarily at a loss until one day in Atlanta changed the course of her life.

That day, Rachelle walked into a Bank of the South branch near the Peachtree Mall. She was there to cash a two-hundred-dollar check, which she was most likely going to blow on a shopping spree. Frankly, she had little else to do that day. Maybe a shopping binge would spur some creativity about exactly what the hell she was going to do with the rest of her life.

She stood in line behind a woman and a young boy. He looked about twelve, right on the edge of young manhood—an age that would justify his lingering glance at her blonde good looks. She smiled at him briefly, thinking, *I bet he'll be trouble in a couple of years.*

BAMMM!

The loud discharge of a high-caliber handgun interrupted her thoughts and shook the bank lobby. Rachelle and everyone else in the building jumped, shocked by the noise and the ear-ringing silence that followed it. She turned around, seeking the source of the shot.

An enormous man, roughly 6 feet 4 inches in height and three hundred pounds in weight, made larger by the smoking .45 in his hand, stood in front of the teller's counter. He brandished the weapon at the tellers and the five bank patrons in line and yelled, "Git on the floor; you don't wanna get shot!"

He wore overalls that covered a yellowish-brown T-shirt. His hair was close-cropped in what could best be described as a redneck cut, and his cheeks and eyes were flushed red. "I'm a rob this goddamned bank, and I'll shoot anybody tries to stop me!"

As the shock of the gunshot waned, Rachelle looked around at the other bank customers and the tellers. They all looked petrified, their faces pale and their bodies frozen in place.

"Git down!" the man yelled again.

Rachelle made eye contact with the woman and the boy in front of her. Their shock was close to giving way to hysteria, and something in Rachelle told her that would be bad. She nodded slightly and spoke calmly to them.

"Okay, let's do what he says. It'll be okay. Let's just sit right here on the floor."

The three of them sat, and the others in the lobby followed suit. The man walked toward them, verifying their compliance with his command. Rachelle watched him as he approached, noticing that he looked like he worked hard, the dirt on his hands and his clothes giving that away. While he was clearly angry, the man appeared neither committed nor in control of himself despite his manly boast. He seemed frantic and confused. Instinct told Rachelle he had chosen this violent act out of desperation to avenge some wrong that had been done to him.

Rachelle was glad to see the bank employees and customers complying with the man's orders. That seemed to calm him a little. One of the tellers was filling a satchel from the cash drawers. She was doing well, getting him what he wanted so he would leave. As they approached the last drawer, one of the tellers' phones rang.

"What the hell?! You pull an alarm?!"

"No. No, I didn't. I swear," said the terrified teller. The phone continuing to ring.

The man looked at the phone, then grabbed the satchel from the teller. "Git down," he told her. Then he hustled toward the front door yelling, "Y'all stay on the floor 'til after I leave!"

He reached for the door, opened it, and suddenly stopped. "Shit! Goddamn it!"

Rachelle looked past him at the two police cars parked outside and the four cops crouched on the other side of them with guns drawn.

"Shit!" the robber yelled again, moving away from the door. The phone rang again. The robber looked at the teller standing closest to it and motioned for her to pick it up.

"Hello? My name's Tina Greer. I work here at the bank. All right."

She extended the phone to the man. "They want to talk to you."

He took the phone and put it to his ear. He listened for a minute, then spoke. "All you need to know is that I will shoot all these people if y'all don't let me leave. I got ten people in here, and I'll kill every one of 'em."

Rachelle watched the man's face as he held the phone. His rage and confusion seemed to ease just a little as he listened. "Well, that don't change much; I still got these people."

While Rachelle was scared, a part of her was fascinated. She watched the robber calm down as he talked to whoever was on the other end of the phone. Was she imagining it? No, he *was* calming down. She wondered why he didn't slam the phone down and start shooting. He seemed to want to keep listening to the person who was talking to him. Rachelle was also surprised at herself. She realized that she knew exactly where all the people in the bank were. She even had an internal inventory of their fear levels.

Several times as the boy next to her started to fall apart, she would look at him and calm him slightly with just a few words. She was able to keep him on the plus side of terror. At the same time, she herself was scared to death, yet she could still take note of things around her. She was hyper-aware, able to observe everything amid the chaos.

Over the course of an hour, the robber talked and listened on the phone. After a lot of back and forth, he finally seemed to agree. "Well, if you want to, all right."

Then he hung up the phone and stood behind the teller line, pointing his gun right at the young boy next to Rachelle with his eyes on the front door of the bank.

A woman wearing a dark blue windbreaker appeared at the entrance. She stood there a minute, then slowly and deliberately pulled the door open, and walked into the bank lobby. She was in her mid-thirties, slender, with her dark red hair pulled back in a bun. She was obviously a cop, but her face held no guile and no judgment as she observed the setting and walked toward the teller line.

As she got closer, Rachelle could see her note each of the people in the room, just like Rachelle had. When her eyes found Rachelle's, there was just a brief acknowledgment.

Keeping her hands visible, she stopped about ten feet from the teller line and looked directly at the robber. "Thank you, Cody."

This was the last thing anyone in the bank, including the robber, expected her to say.

"Whut?"

"You let me come in and talk to you, and you didn't hurt anybody."

"That don't mean I won't, though."

She nodded. "I know. But I don't think I have to tell you how bad an idea that would be. Do you think that's what Martha would want?"

The robber's eyes widened. "How'd you know about Martha?"

"It doesn't matter how I know. It matters what happens next."

She continued to look right at him, and her eyes held empathy. When she spoke to him again, it was in a whisper. "Martha wouldn't want this, Cody. Don't throw your life away."

Rachelle watched, still fascinated, as the robber broke. His face trembled, and he began to sob. Then as unexpectedly as anything else that had happened that day, he put his gun on the ledge of the teller line and covered his face with his hands. Quickly and without panic, the agent stepped forward and moved the gun out of his reach. Still, as he sat with his head down and sobbing, the female cop moved to his side and put her hand on his massive back.

"Okay, Cody. Okay." As she comforted this man, she briefly caught Rachelle's eye and looked toward the door of the bank. Rachelle and the others quickly moved toward the exit and to safety.

Being in the middle of that aborted bank robbery affected Rachelle profoundly, but differently than it seemed to affect the others. While she talked to them and comforted them, she herself was strangely energized by the event. Most of all, she was curious and amazed by the woman who had ended the crisis.

After a while, the agent walked the robber out of the bank in handcuffs. She walked next to him, talking to him, as a half dozen SWAT agents formed a circle around the pair. Cody looked at the SWAT team as though he might still want to take all of them on, but when he looked at the woman walking beside him, he was compliant. He even gave her a smile as she put him in the back of a vehicle and closed the door.

When she was able to, Rachelle approached her. "I want to thank you. Who are you?"

The woman smiled as she again assessed Rachelle. "Agent Rhonda Timothy, FBI. What's your name?"

"Rachelle. Rachelle Keys."

Rachelle found that she was as nervous talking to Agent Timothy as she was in the bank as a hostage. The personal power of this woman was beyond impressive. Agent Timothy was only about 5 feet 5 inches but was still in total command of this situation. All the SWAT members deferred to her, despite their greater size and strength and weapons. They had all taken their orders from her, referring to her often as "Tim."

"Agent Timothy," Rachelle said. "That's why they all call you Tim."

Agent Timothy smiled, both for Rachelle and a hulking SWAT agent listening to them.

"Most of the guys I work with are not smart enough to remember a name with more than one syllable."

The SWAT man smirked, then scratched his forehead with his middle finger.

"How do you feel, Rachelle?"

Rachelle hesitated. The adrenaline was still pumping through her veins. She took a deep breath and gave an honest answer.

"Alive."

Rhonda Timothy's eyes still took in Rachelle as she replied, "Ten people in that bank; nine of them are terrified and need help. And you feel alive?"

"Yeah. What's wrong with me?"

The agent's smile faded just a little as she answered.

"Probably the same thing that's wrong with me."

Rachelle was fascinated and a bit baffled about what she had experienced. She wasn't sure how, but she knew that this woman agent had resolved the situation. She had walked into that bank and talked that redneck maniac into giving himself up. She had used charm, smarts, toughness, guile, and talent to do what a dozen badass men with guns could not.

Rachelle was hooked. The next day she began her quest to join the FBI. Like nearly all her other quests, Rachelle achieved this one too. Female recruits were rather rare at the time and highly valued in the Bureau. Rachelle was accepted, trained, and graduated top of her recruitment class. Within eighteen months, she worked in several different departments in the Bureau, as is typical. Eventually, she was trained as a Kidnap and Ransom agent, something for which she showed an amazing aptitude. It was challenging work and very emotional. Working with victims' families in an area of crime where the outcome was always hard. Even if the victim was returned unharmed, psychological scars remained.

As a result of the difficulty of the work, few agents thrived in K and R; Rachelle was one who did. She possessed the right combination of toughness, brains, compassion, and guile to be one of the Bureau's most successful K and R agents.

There was, of course, an interruption of her early career.

She had spent a night with Craig Cantwell in her early twenties, during a break in her early FBI training. While not a prude, she was not normally one for one-night stands. Alcohol and loneliness, plus her strong attraction to the funny, good-looking, athletic golf pro had all combined to cause her to shack up with Craig. After they made love that night, after Craig had fallen asleep, Rachelle had realized that she could not have a romance with her chosen career. She knew she wanted to work in the Bureau; she felt her calling acutely. Despite her feelings for Craig, when she looked at their future together, she foresaw disaster. She was a decisive woman even then and made the choice not to draw out what she saw as an impossible situation.

She had written Craig a nice note, left it on the hotel mirror, and disappeared.

Forty-five days later, however, she had discovered that she was pregnant with Craig's child. It had never occurred to her that being a mother would stop her from succeeding in the FBI. It would postpone things, yes, but she would still go on. Another thing she did not consider was contacting Craig about the baby. She was willful, strong, and responsible. She knew she could raise her child on her own.

And so it went. Kelly was born, and Rachelle resumed her career in the FBI. Her chosen field, Kidnapping & Ransom, helped; she would often be home in Atlanta for long periods until a case came in. Kidnapping cases are all-consuming, so when she was on a case, her mother and father filled in with Kelly. Being an only child herself, her folks were only too glad to help her raise Kelly. They viewed Kelly as a great blessing, especially since Rachelle's independence and self-reliance had made them think they might never be grandparents.

Rachelle found that being a mother made her better at her job. It was a job that required her to never lose her perspective. She had to always remember that the only important thing was the safe return of the kidnap victim. Her absolute love for Kelly guided her in her cases. She was a gifted agent, her record in K & R one of the best in the Bureau's history.

CHAPTER TWO

2009

Rachelle introduced Craig to his daughter without explaining to her that she was meeting her father. Rachelle had told Kelly, a long time before, that Craig was an old friend. As such, it was not unusual that the two of them had followed Craig's career. Like her mother, Kelly had a gift for athletic pursuits; she had played volleyball and basketball in high school and had been recruited by the University of Georgia and Georgia Tech to play both sports.

Her first love, however, was golf.

Kelly had taken up the game at ten years old when she started hitting balls at a driving range they had visited with Rachelle's parents. Grandpa Keys showed her a few fundamentals, and to the amazement of her mother and others, she was soon hitting balls nearly as far as Grandpa did.

Rachelle had come back from a short shopping trip to find her father watching open-mouthed as his granddaughter hit shot after shot with his driver.

"Mama! Watch this!" Kelly squealed, right before she smashed the ball 125 yards.

Rachelle was pleased, but not surprised. After all, the apple hadn't fallen far from the tree.

By the time Craig Cantwell met his daughter, she was a nineteen-year-old sophomore at Georgia Tech and captain of the women's golf team. She was thrilled to meet a Tour winner and, after some initial shyness, grilled him thoroughly about the players, tournaments, and his experiences. She and Craig bonded quickly. He knew she had inherited his love of golf, but Kelly did not. Craig had reluctantly acquiesced to Rachelle's desire that they would not tell Kelly he was her father.

As far as Kelly knew, her father had died a long time ago. There were several reasons why Rachelle was concerned about Kelly knowing the truth. First, she felt bad for misleading Kelly about her father's existence in the first place and, second, she knew her daughter wanted her own golf career.

Both mother and daughter were strong-willed, independent women who did not want to appear to need the help of a famous father or husband. Rachelle was also protective of Craig. She simply did not want to cause him trouble.

Craig, of course, had no problem announcing to the world that he was the father of such a great young woman. He didn't care what others thought and would gladly have given all he had to help his child, but he agreed to stick to the subterfuge because Rachelle convinced him it was best for Kelly.

Nevertheless, father and daughter had to play golf. Shortly after their first meeting, Craig got them on at Atlanta Athletic Club. He had a father's secret pride in treating his daughter to a round of golf at a past U.S. Open and PGA Championship venue until she disclosed that Georgia Tech had played there many times.

Watching Kelly as they warmed up on the range, Craig noticed the easy flowing rhythm in her swing. There was something familiar in her action; he realized it was very similar to his own swing.

On the first tee, Kelly bounced a ball a couple of times on the face of her driver and nonchalantly said, "So, we gonna have a little game?"

"Sure, how many strokes are you going to give me?"

"I'm just a poor little college golfer. Does a Tour pro want strokes from me? I don't think so."

"Hey, I didn't fall off the turnip truck this morning. I know when I'm being gamed. I saw your action on the range. Just trying to protect myself here."

"Yeah, yeah, and now I'm gonna hear how you haven't played much, and you have a blister on your toe, and your cat died. This ain't my first rodeo either, Buddy."

They both burst out laughing, thoroughly enjoying the banter. *My golf swing wasn't the only thing she inherited.*

"I'll play the back tees; you play the member's tees. Give you 4 a side."

"For pizza and beer when we finish." Kelly set the wager.

"Sounds good."

"Yep, it does. Play well, just not as good as me."

She had game. The difference in tees put their drives close on most holes. There wasn't that much talk between them because there often isn't much talk going on between golfers. The conversation was between the clubs, hers and his. Neither trash-talked; when you're good, you don't need to. He got one down to her after 4; then he holed a sand shot on 6 to pull back even. He hit a gorgeous faded 7 iron at the 9th to a foot, then hit his tee shot on the par 3 10th to four feet. Both times, she said, "great shot," then did her best to match his birdies. The two-up lead held to 15 when she rolled in a 15-foot birdie putt to get to one back. After they halved 16, Kelly bunkered her approach on 17. Craig stiffed a wedge to six feet right after that. If he won the hole, he would close her out. One thing Craig knew was that to let up on her would be an insult; it never crossed his mind. Kelly was tough; she expected absolutely no quarter from him.

He was feeling that the match was his. When she entered the bunker and sized up the shot, Craig saw and felt something he had seen before in competition. It was when a player turned their focus up a notch, responding to pressure. He saw Kelly's focus narrow, saw her settle into her intention. She blasted out of the sand, her ball landed on the green, took a hop, checked just a little from the back-spin, then released, and tracked right into the hole.

"Yes!" she said with a fist pump. The resolve did not leave her face as she exited the bunker; she was fiercely competi-tive. Craig pulled the flag and tossed her ball back to her. "Great shot," he said.

"Thank you. Now knock it in," she said, just like a true golfer would say it.

He saw with pride her appreciation for the spirit of the game. At its core, golf is not about beating an opponent; it is about playing your best. She had risen to the challenge and had made a brilliant shot under pressure. She understood (as true players do) that the opponent's good play elevates her. Craig's excellence, in this case, gave her the opportu-nity to rise; she welcomed his good play, appreciated it.

Craig looked at his six-foot putt and worked as hard on reading it as he would have if it meant a major champion-ship. Being at his best for his splendid daughter was now as important as anything he could do. He grinned slightly as he felt the pressure she had put on him.

Then he drilled the putt dead center.

The eighteenth at AAC is a beast of a par 4. At 474 yards from the back tee, it requires a long and accurate drive to get to a position to approach the green, which is literally an island. Anything except a great drive dictates a layup, then a testy wedge over water to get up and down.

When Craig and Kelly reached the tee, they felt a slight increase in the breeze; it was into them and was going to make the hole harder.

Craig hit his tee shot first and did not quite hit the driver solid. Still a good shot, it found the left side, a good lie in the first cut of rough. Kelly followed with a good drive, though the strong headwind left her in a questionable spot to go for the green. When they got to their drives, Kelly saw that she was away and that her ball was lying in a divot.

"Well, rat farts," she said good-naturedly, using a line from *Caddyshack* that Craig had used numerous times to his caddy when he had a bad break on Tour and was out of earshot of the TV mikes. Craig laughed.

"At least my decision is easy," Kelly said. "I'm not getting over the water from that gnarly lie." She took out an 8 iron, put the ball in the back of her stance, and punched it up the fairway 120 yards, setting up her third shot.

Craig had a decent lie in the first cut of rough. Although it was okay, he was sure the shot would not stop on the green quickly. He had 188 yards to the hole, into a wind that would add 15 yards. It was a good 5 iron, and he knew he would not lay it up even if he were 1 up in a Ryder Cup singles match. He put a great swing on it; for a split second he thought he might have hit it too hard. It started on a low trajectory, rose just enough, and cleared the water by ten yards. The little bit of grass between his clubface and the ball robbed it of any spin. It moved past the pin about 45 feet, coming to rest just short of the back fringe of the green.

Kelly had a shot from Craig on 18. It was the hardest hole on the course, so for her to tie the match she needed to get up and down from the fairway short of the green and hope Craig did not hole his long putt for birdie. "So you're saying there's a chance," she said out loud as she sized up her approach shot.

She had 85 yards, a perfect distance for her gap wedge into the wind. Craig watched with satisfaction as she hit a crisp, low wedge right at the flag. It hit five feet short, took a brisk hop, and spun to a stop eight feet past the hole.

"Nice," Craig said. He privately marveled at her skill and how much she was right in the moment. She had been in competition before and loved it. It was obvious she welcomed a challenge but did not tie her whole world to the outcome. He was appreciating this match with Kelly as much as he would have a tight match against a fellow Tour pro.

He was away and putted first. The putt had about four feet of left to right break, and he underplayed the break a bit. He left himself 3 ½ feet, a putt that still had some break to it, and downhill. By no means a sure thing.

Kelly used her putter to slap the ball back to him, conceding the putt. "Good 4."

Craig had to stifle some emotion at her gameness. She wanted to win the hole, not have him lose it. She was not even going to give him the chance to miss his last putt. In her mind, it was not going to matter because she was going to make her putt to win the hole and tie the match. It was a gesture full of confidence and spirit.

As a golfer, Craig had done the same type of thing numerous times out of respect for his opponent and the game, so this action by his daughter was enough to bring tears of pride to his eyes.

He watched her line up the putt, along almost the same line he had. A downhill eight-footer with about six inches of left to right break. Not an easy putt, even for a Tour pro. The wind had freshened even more, and the speed of the green meant that the wind would affect the putt as well.

Kelly went through her routine, got still over the ball, and gave it a smooth and solid hit. Craig thought for a second that she had hit it too hard, but about a foot from the hole, it made a right turn and found the center of the hole.

They both looked at each other and smiled for a moment. Then Kelly giggled like a little girl. "That was so much fun!" she said, as Craig Cantwell, winner of multiple PGA Tour events, took off his cap and walked toward her to give her a hug. "Great match," she said.

He held the hug a bit too long, then said, "Yes, it was. Great playing."

She was a bit puzzled by his reaction, but then he let her go, gave her a little punch on the arm, and put his cap back on. He took a couple of steps toward the back of the green and managed to keep the emotion out his voice as he said, "So I guess we go Dutch on the pizza?"

She was putting the flag back in the hole, so he had an extra few seconds to make sure she did not see the tears on his face.

CHAPTER THREE

2010

Craig parked his car at the Peachtree Mall and walked toward a popular restaurant, Rudy's. He had agreed to meet Kelly and her mother for a pre-birthday lunch celebration. He arrived before the ladies and took a table. Rachelle's birthday was a week out, but both he and Kelly would be on the road then. He would be playing in the British Open and Kelly would be there to broadcast for the Golf Channel. Her career as the channel's "IT" girl was getting more and more exciting. As he waited, his thoughts turned to his daughter and how lucky he was to have her in his life.

To say that Craig was thrilled with his daughter's affinity for golf was a huge understatement. She had been a success in college golf and wanted to turn pro when she graduated. In Craig's view, she'd had the necessary skill and determination to make it eventually, but both he and Kelly were surprised at how quickly her golf career had developed.

Craig looked up just in time to see Rachelle walk into the restaurant. She was alone.

Wonder why Kelly's not with her.

Rachelle did not immediately notice him, but he stifled an impulse to wave to her. For a few seconds, he just wanted to watch her. As she walked into the dining area, he could see she was in casual mode. "Agent" Keys was off today.

Rachelle could have been any attractive woman looking for her party at lunch: calm, happy, and looking forward to the afternoon. As always, Craig was struck by her beauty. Rachelle was still like a lovely statue: blonde, with a healthy tan and an athletic, yet unmistakably feminine, way of moving. He was just about to get her attention when she saw him. She smiled at him from across the room, holding the look for just a few seconds before she walked over as if she knew he was enjoying watching her.

"Hi," she said and gave him a hug. That did not always happen. "Agent" Keys usually didn't hug. She smelled fantastic, and Craig let himself believe that her perfume was for him.

"Hey, how are you?" he asked as they sat.

"Oh, I'm okay, except I got a call from the kid saying she's not going to make it. Cliff Lombard has her doing an interview with Bubba Watson since he's missing the British, and I guess he could only do it today."

"Well, that stinks," Craig said in mock indignation. "Bubba Watson ranks higher than me? Maybe I ought to do more YouTube videos and put a pink shaft in my driver."

"Well, I don't think it's her choice, but she's got to do the high-profile stuff, I guess."

"It's good for her. I'll get over it."

"Looks like you'll just have to settle for lunch with me—that is if you still want to."

He was surprised but gratified that she was flirting with him. He quickly forgot about the aborted lunch with Kelly and was captivated by the softness in Rachelle's eyes, something he remembered but had not seen in a long time.

"You can rightly assume I want to," he replied. "Just like you can rightly assume that the Pope shits in the woods."

She laughed. "The Pope shits in the woods?"

"Well, no, the Pope is Catholic. A bear shits in the woods . . . except when the Pope really wants to make a point."

This got another laugh out of her and a lingering smile. "Did you know the Bureau has a whole course on mixed metaphors and what they mean in a hostage situation?"

"Is that right? So you can communicate with a kidnapper saying things like 'Does the Pope shit in the woods?'"

She played along. "No, at that point we just call in the tranquilizer guns and gorilla nets."

They passed the afternoon this way. Good food, jokes, flirts. It was reminiscent of their first meeting when they were both much younger. It was free and fun, kind of like an aimless walk through the park on a beautiful day. Each time Craig began to think about where it might be headed, he blocked the thought by coming back to the present moment. After all, the present moment was so delightful.

Around three, they noticed the lunch crowd had cleared out. Craig had been totally engrossed in his back-and-forth with Rachelle that he had ignored the waitress's numerous inquiries as to whether they needed anything else. He finally waved her over and gave up a credit card.

"So, you've had some time off?" he asked Rachelle.

"Yeah, about the last ten days, and for once I've really enjoyed it. I haven't been this relaxed in a while."

"I can tell. It's a good thing, yeah?"

"Um-hum," she said.

Craig looked out the back of the restaurant. It opened onto a lake with a walking path around it. For July in Atlanta, it was not horribly hot.

He nodded toward the lake. "Let's go for a walk. You want to?"

"Does the Pope shit in the woods?"

Two hours later, Craig had driven Rachelle home. She had taken an Uber to lunch, thinking that she and Kelly were going to spend the afternoon shopping together.

They were pulling into her driveway when Rachelle asked him to come in for a second. She wanted to show him something that Kelly had sent her from the Master's the previous year.

Inside, Rachelle brought out the "Master's Care Package" Kelly had sent her from Augusta the previous April. Numerous players, Craig included, had autographed gloves, golf balls, hats, and other items to Rachelle at Kelly's request. They laughed at the various souvenirs, and finally, Rachelle pulled out a green Master's cap that Craig had signed. On the underside of the cap's brim, he had written, "I have not been able to master the overhand serve. Let me know if you are still teaching volleyball. I could use another lesson. CC."

"She asked me about this, you know," Rachelle said.

Craig looked into her eyes from just a foot away. Their last "volleyball" lesson had led to the conception of the very girl who had sent this package of golf goodies. "What did you say?"

She looked back for a long moment before answering. "Oh, not much. Just that you knew I played volleyball."

The moment stretched into several as the silence in their gazes intensified. Craig touched her face with one hand and slowly and softly kissed her. He looked again into her blue eyes and gently held her face in both his hands as he kissed her again. Her hand went to the back of his neck as they embraced.

"I've been wanting to do that all day," he whispered.

She smiled. "What a coincidence," she whispered back as she pulled him close.

Later that evening, they lay naked next to each other in Rachelle's bed. She propped her chin in her hand and looked at him.

"So, ask," she said.

"Hmm."

"I know you want to, so ask me."

He cleared his throat. "Oh, um, okay. Do you . . . want to get ice cream?"

She pinched him hard under the sheet. Though it was hard, it was not altogether unpleasant.

"Okay, okay," he yelped. "So, what happens now?"

"Well, that is the question, isn't it? What do you want to happen?"

They had gotten to this place after an entire day. An entire day that had been unplanned. But now, they were asking questions. For better or worse, the answer was important to both of them.

He looked right at her, and as much as the words scared him, he knew they were the truth, his truth.

"I want to be with you, Rachelle. That's what I want to happen. I want us to be together."

"I know. I want that too," Rachelle said. "I finally figured out that's what I want. It's taken a long time, and there have been a lot of things in my life pointing me here. It's the greatest thing, and I know it's what I want, but it really scares me, and I don't know why."

Craig nodded. "Yeah, me too, a little."

"I've actually been talking to a therapist, a shrink. I'm close to retirement eligibility, and I say I want that. I say I don't want to have to put on Kevlar and my gun and go talk some asshole out of doing something horrible. After some of what I've seen, I know I want it to end. But I guess there's something in me that has become so used to it that in a stupid, sick way it's comfortable."

Craig was rapt because she had never opened up to him like this before. Although he was glad, he was scared as well. The protector in him wanted to take this burden from Rachelle. He was a man; he wanted to fix it, but he knew there was no way he could. This was a fight Rachelle had to win on her own.

There were tears in her eyes as she said, "I want it, though, Craig. I do. I want to move on. I want to turn the corner. I just don't know how to yet."

He took her in his arms as she cried, held her tight, and kissed her hair.

"It's all right, baby. You'll figure it out, I know you will. And I'll wait, babe, I'll wait for as long as it takes."

Chapter Four

"So are you going to tell me about St Louis?"

Anne Overstreet was very good at her job as a therapist, and even though she and Rachelle had become friends, she wasn't about to let a patient get away with avoidance.

Rachelle sighed with a smile. "I can always count on you, right, Anne?"

"Always."

Rachelle paused. She *had* been avoiding the subject and was not sure why. It was inevitable that she would talk to Anne about it.

"It wasn't that unusual. The subject had a hostage, a scared older woman, and I offered a trade. Let the lady go, and he could have me as a hostage. It doesn't work very often, but he agreed this time."

"And?"

"And –" Rachelle found at this point that she did not want to think about what came next. The "subject" had pointed his gun right at her face, inches away, and proceeded to tell her how much he looked forward to blowing her brains out. At the time, her training had been enough to allow her to function-through the fear-triggered adrenaline that flooded into her veins. She had talked to him, using the leverage from the brief conversation before he let the woman go.

She played on her instincts, and they were right. She also had the advantage of pointing out the red dot on the man's chest, made by the laser sight of an FBI sniper rifle. Rachelle got through just enough that the subject lowered his pistol just before the tactical sniper was cleared to fire. In doing her job, she saved the lives of both the hostage and the subject, not to mention her own.

"Yes?" Anne prompted.

"You read the report, so you know what happened," Rachelle said. "It was—I don't know, different this time."

"How so?"

"I was more scared than I've ever been. I still did the work, I could function. I just—for the first time I had other thoughts in my mind than just what I had in front of me."

Anne just listened. She knew the value of what Rachelle was doing.

"I saw other faces, in my mind, I guess."

"Kelly?"

"Yeah, of course. And—" The effort of looking at this incident and herself was catching up with Rachelle. "And . . . "

"And Craig," Anne said for her client and friend.

Rachelle nodded, a tear escaping down her face. Her training and years with the Bureau, with mostly tough men, had taught her that tears were not useful, but Anne Overstreet was glad for these tears. This effort was leading somewhere.

"I wondered why I had to be the one in that situation. There are others who could to the work, why don't I just fade away? And you know what my next thought was? That I am the best at this. I thought that nobody can do this like me.

"God help me, Anne, I still love it. But for the first time, I guess I want to know why."

Again, Anne let the silence linger.

"I saw Craig the other day. We had this great day and night together, and I told him I wanted to be with him, and that's what he wants. I let down my guard, and I showed him . . . this!" Rachelle said with sweeping hand motions, referring to her emotions. "It's the greatest thing that he wants us to be together, great for me, great for him, great for Kelly. And the next day I was so—so distant and mean to him. I found a reason to find fault with him. I pushed him away. Even as I was doing it, I regretted it."

This was said through more tears, and as she finished, Rachelle composed herself. With forced humor, she said to Anne, "So, Doc, am I ready for the asylum?"

Anne smiled back, recognizing Rachelle's attempt to pull back from her vulnerability. Anne was great at her job precisely because she cared about her patients and because she knew instinctively what they needed. There were some who needed empathy, but this one needed to be challenged.

"We'll hold off on the rubber room for now. I was curious about something though," Anne said, seeing that she had Rachelle's attention. "Are you courageous enough to acknowledge that you are scared to death of loving someone?"

In the brief silence that followed, Ann could tell that her patient was composing a clever reply to that question. She cut her off.

"Most people have no trouble at all acknowledging that having a gun pointed at them scares them to death. That's a logical fear, right?" Rachelle nodded. "More people than you know have a fear that's just as intense of giving their heart to another person. It's a risk, even though it isn't a risk of physical danger. Many people fear the emotional risk of loving and being loved as much as they fear anything. Even death."

Rachelle was silent as she looked at Ann. There was no denying that her doctor and friend was spot on.

"So what am I curious about? I'm curious to know if you have the courage to take that risk. You were right before; there *are* others who can do what you do in your job. But there is only one Rachelle for Craig. Nobody else can love him the way that you can. Nobody else can love you the way that you can."

Chapter Five

2011

The cell phone on the nightstand chimed at 4 a.m. It was a text message. The name of a local hotel and a room number followed by the word NOW in all caps. He searched the hotel's name on his phone. It was approximately four miles from Westchester County's renowned Winged Foot Golf Club.

Thomas Kincaid was a pragmatic man. He had always been that way, through several related careers. He got through law school and mentored under a seasoned lawyer, who represented a variety of famous white-collar criminals. Kincaid learned that if an attorney could suspend focus on right and wrong, he or she could do very well financially. Inside traders, corporate manipulators, "book cookers" were all people who may eventually face charges but are all capable of paying large fees to their chosen counsel. Tom Kincaid had learned that politicians and celebrities also needed his services, and they too were in a financial position to pay handsomely for them.

By age forty-five, Kincaid was one of the leading trouble-shooters who worked behind-the-scenes in the legal field. His specialty was not negotiation of high-dollar endorsements; frankly, in his opinion, that just did not require that much talent. His expertise focused on image control and enhancement, which gave his clients the kind of draw that could command the highest endorsement deals. His people got paid for anything they did in public, and he saw to it they got away with anything untoward they did in private.

Thomas glanced at his watch, then looked again toward the other end of the room, where his most prominent client was being interviewed by FOX sports. Gil Spence and Ron Clancy, two members of his team, were watching the closed-circuit monitors of the interview. Kincaid did not need to watch the interview; he had helped script the questions. He had also orchestrated that it be taped. He would review and approve it before it aired. It was one of the many ways he crafted the image of those he represented.

Kincaid and those he worked with were connected in nearly every police department in major cities. He was well known and, in many cases, feared by those who televised sports and news. There was little he could not accomplish for his clients—for the right price.

Thomas Kincaid had clients who did not know how he did what he did; they were the ones who did not want to know. Some made it their business not to know. This current client wanted to know. He had specifically hired Kincaid after grilling him about what he had done in the past. This client wanted to know that his attorney would be unsullied by conscience.

"There are certain things that might make me look like a prick," the client had told him in the beginning. "I don't want to look like a prick. It would cost me . . . and you . . . a shitload of money if I look like a prick. I'm gonna pay you to make me look good, ya dig?"

Thomas Kincaid did indeed *dig*. His talents turned out to be invaluable to this client. He had worked his magic many times for this one, and while it took most of his time, the fact that this client had become one of the most marketable athletes in history made it more than worth it.

CHAPTER SIX

K elly Keys awoke slowly the morning after the event that shaped her young twenty-two-year-old life. The simple act of raising her eyelids was hard. It would have been so much easier just to leave her eyes closed, yet something said they had to open. Her vision was blurred, and she had trouble clearing it. She shook her head a little and immediately regretted it. She had a massive headache. Her head . . . her whole body felt heavy and worn. Her mouth was dry and her lips sore.

"Hey, hey, wake up."

"Uh, what?" she replied. As fuzzy as she was, she still sensed something was wrong—very wrong.

"Time to get up," a voice said roughly. "You have things to do today."

She sat up slowly, discovering that she had slept in her clothes. They didn't fit right somehow. Their rumpled condition was more than if she had just slept in them. Looking closer, she saw that her blouse was on backward so that she could see the label in the front below her chin.

"What's wrong with my clothes?"

A light chuckle. "Well, you can't expect them to fit when you pass out with them on."

Kelly blinked her eyes, and they cleared a little. She was able to focus on the man speaking to her now.

He was older than she was, somewhere in his forties. He had blond hair with tinges of gray at his temples and was wearing an expensive suit, although there was no tie and his collar was open. His eyes were a piercing green, and his expression was one of a man with an urgent purpose. The telltale sign in his expression was that he didn't necessarily enjoy the task at hand, but had to do it. His demeanor was not compassionate; it was clear that his task was more important than any one person.

"I what? I passed out?" she asked. "Who are you?"

"My name is Kincaid, Kelly. I work with Mr. Monroe. He called me because he was worried about you."

Mr. Monroe? Zeke Monroe? A little more conscious now, Kelly remembered that she was Kelly Keys, Golf Channel analyst, and that she had an interview the night before with Zeke Monroe, the professional golfer. That was the extent of her memory of last night.

"Why would he be worried about me?"

"Well, let's just say he didn't expect you to act the way you did last night."

Kelly just looked at him, totally confused. The pain in her head didn't help.

"Hmm . . . so you don't remember," Kincaid said with some distaste. "I guess that's not surprising. Someone that drunk wouldn't remember. Wouldn't remember drinking shot after shot or coming on to Mr. Monroe repeatedly, despite his polite refusals. Wouldn't remember following him back to his suite, banging on the door till he let you in. Probably wouldn't even remember his kindness in letting you pass out here, rather than calling your bosses or maybe hotel security."

She heard what he was saying and yet had no such memories. The pain in her head felt like a hangover, which she had experienced before, but never had she been unable to remember a prior evening. She was confused and then very frightened. She felt different than she had ever felt. Something was very wrong, though she could not name what it was.

"What happened to me?"

"Thankfully, nothing. At least not yet."

She was conscious enough to sense two things: first that he had just lied to her and second that there was a threat in his eyes.

"All that happened was that you passed out drunk and slept here. Zeke Monroe let you do that because he did not want to embarrass you. He called me because he knew I could help. The best thing right now, for you especially, is that no one else knows about last night. I can help you with that."

She suddenly remembered what day it was. It was Sunday, the final day of the PGA Championship, and she was one of the Golf Channel personalities that would cover this major PGA Golf Championship at Winged Foot. She looked at the clock. It was 9:45 a.m., which meant she was extremely late for one of the biggest days of her professional life.

"Oh my God, I'm late. I am in so much trouble . . . "

"It's all right," Kincaid said. "I know Cliff Lombard. I've already spoken to him. We'll get you to the set in a little while, and Cliff will help us."

Kelly felt only anxiety about the job she had to do that day. That purpose and the anxiety around it pumped adrenaline into her and helped with the confusion and even a little with her headache. She stood a little unsteadily and looked at Kincaid.

"I guess I should get going."

Kincaid nodded. "I can give you a ride. We'll get you to your room to get cleaned up and then over to the Golf Channel set."

"Okay, thank you." She still didn't understand. Kincaid had first been cold and judgmental, now he wanted to help. Why?

They got in Kincaid's Escalade and drove back to the Hilton close to Winged Foot, the site of the tournament. Kelly became more fully awake as she walked to the car; she noticed different things about her body. There was a hot soreness in her thighs, her buttocks, and her genitals. She was a good girl, but not a prude. She had experienced this kind of soreness after sex before. This was different, though, because there was no pleasant aspect to the soreness she felt. Even though it was the first of many times that she would try to explain away to herself, in her heart she knew that something very wrong had happened to her the night before.

Okay, no time for this, got a job to do, she said silently and firmly to herself.

Kincaid accompanied her to her room at the Hilton, up some backstairs. He even entered her room briefly, then spoke, "I'll wait outside in the hall. We should get over to the set in about fifteen minutes."

She nodded as he left her room. She undressed quickly and turned on the shower. As she was about to take off her bra, she looked in the mirror. Her underwear was on backward. Her bra was inside out, and she noticed bruising around both of her nipples. She shook her head, still wondering if it was possible that she could have gotten that drunk last night. She removed her panties and noticed that they too were torn in two places and were on backward. There was a bruise on her inner thigh, and at the top of her pubis was some dried, flaky substance.

She was suddenly scared. She had obviously had sex last night but had absolutely no memory of it or even any memory of thinking about it. What asserted itself was that she had made a terrible mistake, maybe even lots of mistakes. These mistakes might cost her greatly, her job or even much more. She was frightened of what she had done, frightened that she did not remember. Terrified that she could not undo it and horribly worried about the consequences.

A desperate need overtook her. It was vital that no one knew that anything had happened. She herself was not sure what had happened, but she knew that whatever it was, she had to protect her secret at all costs. No one must know about last night.

CHAPTER SEVEN

Kelly Keyes tried to put the previous night out of her mind and threw herself into her Golf Channel job. It was the final day of the Winged Foot tournament and comments and film clips and interviews and tweets and posts kept her busy covering it. She was able to focus and outwardly seemed her normal self. The day was all of what she loved about her job—being close to golf at the highest level, watching the championship drama unfold, even being in the spotlight. It was exhilarating and fun.

The exhilaration waned after the tournament ended. She had watched as Zeke Monroe won his fifth major title, without really thinking about him as a person. She was focused on his role in the event. After the conclusion, after Monroe had done the normal interview for the network, he then moved into the press area for a more extensive Q & A session, as was customary. Kelly was in the press room along with other press corps members when Monroe walked in. She was on an aisle seat two rows back when he took his seat on the stage.

Just after he sat down, his eyes found hers, and for an instant, she saw a coldness there—an evil, knowing look that reeked of contempt.

Kelly felt the breath go out of her. She felt lightheaded, far dizzier than she had on waking that morning. During the day she had thought of that morning as a long-ago event; being a few feet from Monroe suddenly brought the morning back so vividly that she felt it had just happened. Seeing Monroe this close triggered the soreness and pain below her waist even more acutely than she had felt it that morning. What she felt, really for the first time in her life, was terror. A level of anxiety that made her feel that someone or something else was in control of her body.

Kelly got up and walked quickly from the room before the first question was asked of the new PGA Champion. There were many looks of surprise: the rest of the assembled press were not about to miss this. She left the press area in a hurry, finding the nearest ladies' room and taking refuge in the nearest stall. She sat for a long time on the toilet, her arms wrapped around her as her body trembled and her breath came faster. After a while, she slowed her breathing to the point that her anxiety abated. When she could finally stand, she left the stall, stopping at the sink to splash some cold water on her face.

Raising her eyes, she barely recognized the terrified woman in the mirror.

CHAPTER EIGHT

Months had passed since Zeke Monroe's assault on Kelly. She was moving in a better direction with her life, albeit slowly, or so she thought.

Then one morning, as she sat drinking coffee and contemplating a message from her mom, one that she had ignored until now, it occurred to her that this was the morning she needed to face her mother, not necessarily to give a full account of recent events but realizing that she had the best friend in the world in Rachelle. Rachelle had expressed concern to Kelly more than a few times recently, and when Kelly had ducked opportunities to talk, her mom had gotten forceful about them getting together.

She was about to dial her mother's cell phone when her doorbell rang. Two men stood outside her door when she opened it. One she did not know; the other was Rick Hauptman, a friend and colleague of Rachelle's whom Kelly had met numerous times. When she saw the look on Rick's face, she really did not hear the other man, even though he spoke first.

"Ms. Keyes, I am Vince Barkley with the Bureau's Central Office. Can we come in, please?"

Kelly could not look away from Hauptman. "Rick, what's wrong? What's happened?"

Hauptman, one of the toughest, most experienced SWAT members alive, could hardly find his voice. There was a protocol for this, bureau guidelines to be followed. *Screw that,* he thought as he stepped toward Kelly. She knew. She had her mother's smarts and instincts, and he could see she was about to crumple, both emotionally and physically. He was not about to let that happen, not to this girl. He caught her as her knees started to buckle. She wailed like a wounded animal.

Rick Hauptman would hold her in his arms for as long as it would take for this first wave to break. He knew she was strong and that eventually, she would stand again on her own. Until then, though, he would hold her up.

They came in a slow, constant procession, all the FBI people who knew Rachelle, to see Kelly in the days that followed. They brought all the usual things, like food and flowers, but what they really brought was the thing Kelly needed most, comfort. Kelly had met a number of these folks, but many of them she was meeting for the first time. They told her stories about her mom, things Rachelle would never impart to her. Many were funny; some were so heroic she wondered if her mother was really the subject of them. There was something missing, though, as details of Rachelle's fatal day were foggy at best. All these offerings were meant to support Kelly, not because they knew her, but because they knew and respected her mother.

A week after her mother's memorial service, a friend of Rachelle's drove Kelly to the Bureau Office in Atlanta. She was set to meet with the head of benefits for the office, who would explain what would accrue to Kelly in a practical sense. Some of what she would be told here was a little hard to accept, especially since she was still grieving the loss of her mother. For one, because Rachelle had died in the line of duty, Kelly would receive a stipend for the rest of her life, being Rachelle's closest living relative.

It was frankly enough to keep her comfortable financially if she wasn't frivolous with her money. While she acknowledged that it was nice, she would trade it ten times over to have her mother back.

The head of benefits had been kind and proficient, and as she was wrapping up, she looked Kelly in the eye and said, handing Kelly an envelope, "There is just one more thing, Kelly. Many agents of rank put a personal note on file for their loved ones, to be given to them in the event of their death in the line of duty. This is for you."

Kelly looked at the front of the envelope for a moment, then flipped it over to the back as people so often do, a senseless gesture but somehow reassuring. She was a bit conflicted about what to do with it. She contemplated taking it home to read when she was alone, but she was starved to hear her mother's voice or feel her presence, so she opened it and began to read:

> *Kelly,*
>
> *As I write this, I wonder why I even have to. Not that there are no things to say; there are. I simply wonder why I have waited so long to say them. If you are reading this letter, it means that I died—probably in the line of duty—and this letter is proof that I lacked the courage and heart to tell you important things to your face. For this, I apologize. If you are reading this, I will likely be awarded for valor; yet I lack the fortitude to tell you some things directly. It hurts me to know that I have failed you in that way. So maybe I*

will actually buck up and really talk to you before you need to read this and we can laugh about it?

I will say again how much I love you. Though that's no secret to either of us. I could not hide that fact even if I wanted to. I am also immensely proud of everything you are, please know that. In the person you have become, I see you surpassing me in so many ways. Yes, Kelly, I look up to you. In numerous ways, you are truly the person I wish I could be.

There are things in my life I have kept from myself. There are feelings and fears that I buried. True things about me I have not faced. I have justified not facing them because I do a dangerous job that helps others. Don't get me wrong, I love my work and I know how good I am at it. But I wonder how much better my life would be if I had not buried certain things. A wise person once told me, "What you don't work on, will work on you." So, motherly advice: Don't ever be afraid to be you. Don't bury something thinking that the strong part of you can forget it. Whatever it is, work through it. Your life and your love will reward you.

All this is important, but there is something else equally important. It would be true freedom and wisdom for me to truly understand why I kept this from you. Try to forgive me, please, for telling you this in this way now.

Craig Cantwell is your father. We met a long time ago for a short time, right when I was starting with the Bureau. I pursued my career with the FBI and ran from Craig. That was my choice, not his, so know that he was blameless in the whole thing. He did not know you existed until I told him when you were nineteen. He knows you are his daughter, and it is joy itself to see how he loves you and loves being your father. I swore him to secrecy though he didn't want to keep it a secret.

As for other details, please get those from him. He will no doubt make the story far more entertaining. As to why I keep your parentage secret, let's just say I had my reasons. Probably selfish reasons—reasons that I question now. Career, image, fear. Maybe fear was the biggest reason. Not fear of being a mother, though that was there the results are amazing, so I passed that test. No, the bigger fear was what a life with a good man like Craig would have required from me. I suppose I made up that I couldn't have the career I wanted and be with Craig. This was a convenient way to justify the secret. Maybe I told myself that to be the woman I wanted to be, I had to be alone, independent, and untouchable. Perhaps I told myself that I was above all those mothers who kept house and raised kids because I was out bringing back kidnapped sons and daughters. What I have come to know is that all of that was a charade meant to protect myself. What truly frightened me was giving my heart. The irony is that I gave my heart to you. You have my heart now and always will. There is just no way to live this life without love. As much as I pushed it away, you came to me to show me what love really means. I could live a thousand lives and never be able to thank you.

I will always love you.

Mom

CHAPTER NINE

Craig and Kelly took a seat in the small auditorium of the Hoover building. It was nearly nine months since Rachelle's death, and while it was always a joy for Craig to be with Kelly, this event was one he did not know how to feel about. Kelly had called and asked him to come after the Bureau had contacted her about the ceremony honoring the agents involved in the Southland Bank tragedy. Neither Craig nor Kelly knew what to expect; they had come here knowing they could not do otherwise.

They sat in the front row of seats, before a low stage. The roughly hundred seats in the room were all filled. People stood in the back of the room. Most were FBI agents, employees, staff, and some press. Craig had been around enough of them to recognize a reporter, and the photographers were easily spotted by their cameras.

On stage, there was a row of seated dignitaries, all wearing suits. Four men and two women impeccably dressed and obviously holding important positions. To the right of them, two men sat with a third empty chair beside them. These were obviously agents, one roughly forty years old. The other man was in his twenties. Both wore uniforms of a sort—not dressed formally, but it was obvious these were men who "worked for a living." They would have appeared absurd in suits, while the dignitaries obviously dressed nicely every day. The older of the two agents was dark-haired and had dark intense eyes. His face was solemn and impassive, and one look at him gave away the fact that he was a warrior. To say he looked tough would be like saying the ocean looked wet. The younger agent looked formidable in a different way. Something about him said he was totally unflappable. He looked the type to eat a hot dog while skydiving.

A dignitary left his chair on the stage, walked down a few steps, and came over to Kelly.

"Ms. Keys, I'm Alan Weathers, assistant to the director," he said, shaking her hand. "Thank you so much for coming today. I wonder if I could ask a favor?"

"Of course," Kelly said, with her usual poise.

"We have three recipients for awards today, and one of them is your mother. Would you honor us by taking the seat next to Agents Hauptman and Feld and accept your mother's award?"

Kelly suddenly looked confused, a rare thing for her. She hadn't expected this. She felt alone until she remembered something. She looked over at her father.

Craig looked at her and nodded. He was both surprised and immensely pleased with this gesture.

Kelly turned back to Weathers. "Yes, I'd be honored." She got up and followed him to the stage. They walked to the right where Rick Hauptman and Danny Feld stood to greet her. She had met Rick before, and he gave her a hug. Danny she had heard about but had never met, and she just shook his hand.

Weathers walked to the podium. "Ladies and gentlemen, let's get started. My name is Alan Weathers, FBI Assistant

Director, and it is my honor to preside over our award ceremony today. I would like to start by introducing those on stage. Behind me is Mr. Robert Burns, head of the Bureau's swat teams. To the right of him is Ms. Rachel Burris, director of Behavioral Sciences. Next, we have Ms. Carla Pruitt, FBI director of public affairs. And finally, I would like to introduce the director of the Federal Bureau of Investigation, Mr. Carson Hunt."

There was appropriate applause as Director Hunt walked to the podium. He acknowledged the crowd and began reading a prepared statement:

"On July 19th of last year, our award recipients were essential in ending a hostage situation at the Southland Bank in Atlanta. Four individuals entered the bank forcibly at the end of the previous business day and took hostages. These individuals threatened to detonate an explosive device—one that would have been large enough in scope to result in massive property damage and loss of life. In conjunction with local police, our three honorees successfully resolved the threat to innocent citizens.

"Our first honoree is Agent Richard Hauptman. Agent Hauptman is a sixteen-year-veteran of the FBI and has commanded swat operations out of the Atlanta Field Office for six years. When a breach of the bank facility became necessary, Agent Hauptman not only planned the operation but led the assault in which all four hostiles were killed. He and his team not only saved the lives of three bank employees, who were hostages, but allowed the successful dismantling of the perpetrators' explosives.

"Which leads to our second honoree, Agent Daniel Feld. Agent Feld is a decorated veteran of the Marine Corps and has been an explosive ordnance technician with the Bureau for five years. Under extreme pressure, Agent Feld entered the bank with the SWAT breach and successfully disarmed the explosive device.

"Our third honoree . . . " Director Hunt paused here unexpectedly. Craig and the rest of the room watched as he took a moment and gathered himself. He had stopped just short of showing emotion, which in this setting, and in his position, was just not done.

"Pardon me," he said, taking just a moment. "Our third honoree is Agent Rachelle Keys. Agent Keys was a twenty-one-year veteran of the Bureau and a decorated kidnap and ransom agent. She negotiated with the hostiles her own entry into the bank, wearing undetectable sensors in her shoes that allowed our swat team to pinpoint the hostiles for the breach. With complete disregard for her own safety, and at great personal risk, she helped formulate and execute the plan for the breach. She was shot by the hostiles during the breach and shortly thereafter provided information to Hauptman, vital to the disarming of the explosive device, before dying from her gunshot wounds."

Here, the director paused as he looked out over the crowd. There was a heavy silence in this large room. Craig could only listen numbly. He was both in awe of Rachelle's heroism and dumbstruck as to how to feel. The bulk of the room had before and would again cry privately over Agent Keys' death. But in the official setting, there were a few tears.

The director broke the silence. "Agent Hauptman, would you step forward?" Rick Hauptman stood and walked stiffly to center stage. Looking closely, Craig could see Agent Hauptman's struggle. He was not happy to receive a decoration for his part in the day that brought the death of a fellow agent and friend.

"This is a commendation for extraordinary meritorious valor. The Bureau and the United States of America thank you for your gallant service."

Hunt pinned on the citation and shook Hauptman's hand, saying something only the two of them could hear. Rick looked for a long moment in the director's eyes, then nodded.

"Agent Feld, could you step forward?" said Director Hunt. "For your brilliant work under extreme pressure, you are also awarded this citation for extraordinary meritorious valor."

Danny Feld had a blank look on his face as he accepted his award. This event had happened long ago; he had expected nothing less of himself and would rather live in the now. He was not disrespectful, but he, like Hauptman, would have gladly flushed his medal had Rachelle Keys only survived.

"Here to accept Agent Keys' award is her daughter, Ms. Kelly Keys. Ms. Keys, would you please join me?"

As Kelly walked stage center, Craig marveled at his amazing daughter. She not only looked beautiful, but she also carried herself with the grace and dignity inherited from her mother. It was as if the room leaned in as she joined the director, gratified to see that Rachelle had passed on her amazing bearing to Kelly.

Director Hunt said, "For making the ultimate sacrifice, and for bravery and selfless action far beyond the call of duty, Agent Rachelle Keys is awarded the medal of honor." The director handed Kelly a frame with the medal displayed on it. "In the history of the Bureau, only seven such medals have ever been awarded. I tender this medal with my heartfelt condolences and with the highest gratitude for your mother's service."

Kelly was fighting back tears now, as many in the room were. Craig was still numb. He was surprised at this. Why didn't he feel more?

Photos were taken. Thankfully, there were no interviews. Kelly was not unknown, and some of the press vultures would have gladly pounced if not for the Bureau prohibiting it. Kelly rejoined Craig and showed him Rachelle's medal. Craig exhibited the same expression as Rick Hauptman and Danny Feld; he found the honor to be a poor substitute for Rachelle.

Rick Hauptman came over just before they were ready to leave. He exchanged some pleasantries with Kelly and Craig, looking up a couple of times to verify that the director had left the room.

"I was wondering if you two might want to have a cup of coffee?" he asked with a look that was far from casual.

An hour later, Craig watched Danny Feld and Rick Hauptman walk into the coffee shop off DuPont Circle, where they had agreed to meet. The location was a fair distance from the Hoover Building; Rick had explained that he wanted to be away from any Bureau offices for this meeting.

Rick looked at Craig with a smile. "It's great to finally meet you. Rachelle had told me you were an old friend. I guess one thing about today is that I found out you are a little more than that."

Kelly looked just a bit uncomfortable, then Rick chuckled. "Come on, kid, we agents aren't totally dense. You look mostly like your mom, but with your golf and seeing you guys today, it's not too hard to connect the dots."

Kelly smiled at that. "Okay, so, Rick, meet my Poppi."

Feld's mouth was open as he looked back and forth between Craig and Kelly. "Well, duh," he said as the light came on. "Guess I need to work on my perception skills. Good thing I'm a bomb tech. I never would have made it as a negotiator."

"That's okay, Dan," said Rick. "You just keep clipping those wires."

The banter lightened the mood after the ceremony, something they were all grateful for.

"Look, I am not supposed to do this, but frankly I am okay with at least you two knowing a bit more about what happened in Atlanta. Hell, I would tell the world if it was up to me."

"Absolutely," added Danny.

Both Kelly and Craig were nervous now. Craig sensed that a more detailed explanation of events on the day of Rachelle's death was forthcoming. He wondered if it would help.

"So," Rick began, "I guess Dan and I are both willing to risk our careers to trust you both with the truth. I hope you keep this among us, and I hope it helps."

CHAPTER TEN

Thomas Kincaid waited in the Starbucks outside of Atlanta in Peachtree, Georgia. It was not usual for him to wait for anyone, a fact he was acutely aware of. Normally people waited for him, not the other way around. He ordered his usual Grande coffee with two extra shots and had found a seat at a table in the back.

It was three forty-five in the afternoon and quiet inside the shop. It was thirty minutes past the scheduled meeting time, and he shook his head somewhat ruefully when he noticed that. He was a little annoyed, more than that surprised that he would even wait. For this meeting, though, he would.

A younger man entered the front of Starbucks. Without a change of expression, he walked straight back to where Kincaid sat. His face, which was usually readable as one that found a lot of humor in life, was now like a stone. He stood briefly next to the table, then took a seat across from Kincaid.

"Hi, Danny," Kincaid said. A hint of a smile crossed his lips. His expression was almost as if he were the one who was a half-hour late.

"Hello, sir." Danny's words were icy.

Tom began awkwardly, "I, uh, appreciate you meeting me." He had no idea what to say. This, too, was rare. Tom Kincaid always knew what to say and when and how to say it. If his companion sensed his discomfort, it didn't make a dent in his resolve to stay cold toward him.

"So, why am I here?"

"I, uh, ah, just . . . " Tom was still awkward. A thought occurred to him that led him to what seemed like more solid ground. "I heard you were at that Southland Bank thing."

"Yes."

"Well, I'm glad you're okay."

Danny didn't respond.

"Danny?"

"Yeah?" His son seemed a thousand miles away. "I mean yes, sir?"

"I just said, I'm glad you're okay."

Danny did not know what to say to that, so he didn't say anything. His mother had convinced him to come here; he certainly did not want to. Danny Feld had wanted nothing to do with his father for years. There were a lot of reasons, starting with the fact that his father had always condemned his decisions. From the sports he played to the grades he made, nothing had ever been good enough for Tom Kincaid. The capper had been when Danny had refused to study pre-law (carefully arranged by his dad) and chosen instead to enter the military.

The father had been disappointed that his son would not inherit his world, but the son's reasons were a lot deeper than simple rebellion. Like a lot of parents, Tom Kincaid was sure his son did not understand what he did for a living. After all, why should the kid care if he was so well provided for? But Danny was smart and had great instincts besides. At an early age, he had figured out that all his father's clients were very similar. They were all scumbags, people who did shitty things, and dear old dad was who they paid to keep things quiet. The moral compass that Tom Kincaid had ignored was something very strong in his only son.

"I just heard it was potentially pretty bad, and I'm glad it didn't . . . escalate," Tom said. It was strange how he wanted to acknowledge his son's work, even compliment it, and yet he could not.

"I can't talk about it," Danny said. "Even if I could, I wouldn't talk to you about it."

This jab from Danny jolted Tom from awkwardness into self-defense.

"Look, I know you don't like what I do. But it serves a purpose. My work has value to certain people, and I can do things that others can't. Bottom line is that I have worked in my career to provide for my family, to provide for you. I would hope that you would at least understand that."

Danny finally smiled, though there was no warmth in it. "In my training at the Bureau, they once showed us a taped interview of Aldrich Ames, the former CIA agent turned double KGB agent and convicted of espionage in 1994. In it, Ames justified what he had done, the betrayal of his country that resulted in the deaths of people he didn't even know. He thought he was making a compelling case. He sounded just like you."

Kincaid looked away for a few moments. The weight of all he had done in his career cast a shadow on his face. He knew his son could not be made to understand, maybe even he did not.

"Is that why you wanted to meet?" Danny asked. "To have me approve your business model?"

"No, I . . . I just wanted to see you. I was hoping we could get together in DC when you were there."

"I guess I shouldn't wonder how you knew about a private FBI ceremony."

"I wanted to go to the ceremony, but I couldn't get in. I guess I've reached the limits of my influence."

"Just as well," Danny said. "Hell, I didn't even want to go. There was only one recipient worthy of that ceremony. It wasn't me and it wasn't Rick Hauptman."

"Yes, I'm sorry about the agent who was killed. It was, um . . . Rachel Key?"

"Rachelle Keys." Danny attempted to mask the contempt in his tone. To Danny, there was something perverse about his father expressing sympathy for Rachelle when he didn't even know her name. As cool as Danny normally was, his father's phony sympathy angered him. It brought up again that the world did not know what Rachelle had done. The government could not give details beyond the issuance of a posthumous Medal of Honor because it could not acknowledge the extent of the danger that Rachelle's actions had averted.

He decided to vent because he wanted to vent at his father. What the hell? The old man was a master at secrets and cover-ups.

"Rachelle Keys," he said again. "That's a name you should know, and one you should get right. It's a name that everyone should get right, but they won't because men like you have decided what she did needs to stay a secret. It just wouldn't do for the public to know that Rachelle Keys told me with her dying words where to find a bomb. Not just any old bomb. A bomb that would have fucking gone off without that woman. Rachelle Keys is the biggest hero in this country's history, and nobody knows it. All they will know is that she was awarded a medal because the press will publish a picture of the director giving it to her daughter! To her daughter, because Rachelle is dead!"

"She had a daughter? I didn't know," Tom said remorsefully.

"Yeah, her daughter is that cute gal that used to work on the Golf Channel. Her name is Kelly."

Tom Kincaid looked directly at his son for the first time since he had sat down. "Kelly Keys?"

"Yeah, Dad, Kelly Keys. She was an anchor on the Golf Channel."

Kincaid looked shocked now. Danny noted it with satisfaction. He had never been able to shock his father before. Maybe his dad finally got why Danny did what he did. Maybe this cynical, selfish, greedy bastard might finally understand that there were things more important in this world than money.

Danny was only partly right. He could not know the full reason for the look on Tom Kincaid's face.

CHAPTER ELEVEN

Tom Kincaid had reached the pinnacle of his profession and his life. Representing Zeke Monroe had created a new summit for Kincaid and his people. Tom was no stranger to representing the wealthy and famous and to profiting handsomely as a result. His talents for 'image control" had long been sought after and paid for by the people who needed them. Zeke Monroe, however, was the most marketable of any of his past clients.

A sports superstar in a sport that had been made mainstream and "hip" by Tiger Woods, Zeke Monroe was an athlete that many high-level businesses sought out. They wanted his face, his accomplishments to speak for them to the buying public. Monroe's looks, age, and general appeal were essential to their marketing campaigns. Kincaid had carefully crafted his image to appeal to men and women of varying ages and social strata. Monroe was the kind of celebrity that could endorse a fast-food chain or a luxury car manufacturer with equal success. This star surpassed all of Kincaid's prior clients in marketability and earning power.

After Zeke Monroe's latest success, Kincaid had been able to sign him to an unprecedented mega endorsement deal. Zeke would now be the face of a new healthy fast-food chain, Joseph A Banks men's clothing, Lexus automobiles, and State Farm Insurance. The total value of these deals, just for the first five years, was $250 million.

On the finalization of the deal, Monroe had written Tom Kincaid a heartfelt note, thanking him and telling him in no uncertain terms that it would not have been possible without him. For Tom Kincaid's special talents and skills, Monroe had no problem cutting him in on 30 percent of the contract.

Tom was in his downtown Chicago condo when he opened Monroe's note, along with a confirmation of $25 million wired to his numbered Caymans account. It was the first of three equal commissions for the deal. Tom put down the letter and picked up his glass—a strong double Wild Turkey that was supposed to be a celebratory drink. He took a slug of the whiskey as he looked out over Lake Michigan.

It was a perfect day, a day that filled the lake with boats. He had his own boat a short walk away in the main marina. It would have been a simple and usual thing for him to gather a small and special crowd and take the boat out on a day like today. The "sailors" would mostly be models, though he would have a small contingent of dealmakers to massage that part of his ego. He was inwardly surprised that the impulse to celebrate on his boat held no special appeal at the moment.

Yes, this is the pinnacle, he thought as he took another hit of the expensive whiskey. He had done well before, but this deal made him untouchable. Financially, he was in a stratosphere that made anything material he wanted well within reach. Professionally, he could pick and choose who to work with. His success with Monroe had made nearly anything possible in his world.

He took another sip of his Wild Turkey. *Yes, a pinnacle.*

So why did he feel so empty?

This feeling of emptiness was not entirely new. An event from nearly eighteen months ago might have been the start of it for Kincaid. He remembered a morning back then when his usual feeling of smug success had been interrupted by a short story in the paper. A young girl had committed suicide, and her family and friends held a vigil that caught the attention of a sensitive journalist. It was the kind of story that Tom Kincaid normally would have blithely passed by, one about the normal anguish of friends and family over how such a bright girl could have been so depressed as to end her life.

That day, however, he had been ready to turn the page when he noted her name. It was then that he remembered having met her in the recent past, the morning after her "date" with Zeke Monroe. He had convinced her in his smooth way to forget getting drunk and "embarrassing" Mr. Monroe the night before. It was that name that made Tom Kincaid stop and despite his practiced nonchalance read the short story.

He beat down the pangs of conscience that day, focusing on his goals and the good things he could do when achieving them. He rationalized that he had not done anything wrong; both his client and the young lady had made their own choices. After all, he didn't know exactly what happened on Zeke Monroe's dates, did he?

What made the empty, guilty feeling return this day on his terrace was not so much the news article but a meeting some days before with his son. A son that he really did not know, a son who wanted nothing to do with him. Tom's son had lashed out at him with condemnation over a story that had made Tom both proud and horrified him. The conflict created by the story was complicated for Tom. He knew the story was true and that it made his son a true hero. That made him proud. Nothing new. He had always been proud of Danny. He'd just never let Danny know that. The truth was he had no idea how to express that pride. The result of Danny's story was worth way more than a celebration, but the biggest hero in that story was what created the hole in Kincaid's heart when he looked at $25 million in his bank account.

TEN DAYS LATER

Kincaid was a man with connections and a man of confirmation. The first attribute allowed him a visit to the Chicago office of the FBI and a seat in a private room with the Chicago station chief. Carl Stanton was his name, and he and Tom Kincaid knew each other from way back when Stanton had come up through Chicago PD.

This day, Stanton was none too happy with Kincaid's request, or the fact that he felt the need to grant it. Stanton sat down across from Tom in a private room, one that did not have any listening or viewing capabilities from outside. He had a thin file in his hand but did not immediately give it to Tom.

"I really appreciate this," Tom said. "I know it's a tough request."

"No, you don't," Stanton said, looking directly at him. "This is way beyond 'tough.' If this gets out, I'm not just fired. I'm most likely in prison. The very fact that I have this information is risky to me."

"I understand," Tom replied.

Stanton continued to look across the table at Kincaid, still considering if he could trust this man. Before he could, he had to ask one more thing.

"I need to know why you want to see this."

Kincaid considered his answer. He had a story he had concocted, one that he thought would get him a look at the file Stanton had. He also had a threat, one that he was certain to get him a look. These were two variations on how Tom Kincaid operated, and he usually got what he wanted one way or the other. He had an arsenal of such weapons, one that he had used to great effect in a long career. So, he surprised himself when he used a tactic foreign to him—the truth.

"Danny Feld, the bomb tech who was there, he . . . " Tom hesitated, borne of unfamiliarity while voicing fatherly pride, "he's my son."

"Why don't you ask him what happened?"

"I did. He's not about to talk to me about classified information, and . . . well . . . he doesn't talk to me much anyway."

Stanton looked across at the man he had known as a crafty dealmaker for twenty years. As an experienced cop, he was good at spotting lies and liars. His experience told him that Kincaid, for once, was being honest.

"I will let you read this exactly one time, while I sit here across from you. You hand it back to me, and I walk out with it. If you ever talk about it with anyone, I will not be able to protect you."

Kincaid nodded his assent.

Twenty minutes later, Tom Kincaid had finished reading the classified, unredacted, official FBI version of the events that took place at the Southland Bank. He was stunned by what he had read. The report went into far more detail than

Danny's rant had. The heroism of those agents, most particularly Rachelle Keys, was literally unprecedented. His son's expert work, performed under unbearable pressure, was awesome.

The pride and admiration Kincaid felt were far exceeded by his guilt.

CHAPTER TWELVE

Blake Manes was not the kind of reporter who was satisfied with daily mundane news, so his instincts lit up when he answered his phone that morning.

"Blake Manes."

"Blake, it's Tom Kincaid."

Hmm. In the brief silence that followed, Blake recognized the impact of the name. Thomas Kincaid was well known in most influential circles of the media. He had a reputation for being both a source and a shaper of stories. He frankly wielded a lot of power, and Blake speculated he used it to benefit his impressive list of clients. He was technically a lawyer but did a lot of things outside the purview of the law. In addition to his reputation, Blake knew him as the father of his friend Danny, the best field goal kicker in the history of their high school.

"Well, hello, Mr. K.," Blake said, using the name he'd used back in high school. "To what do I owe the pleasure?" The question was less casual than it sounded; Blake was pretty low on the media totem pole. If this was business, it was a bit strange for Kincaid to call him.

"I heard you were doing some freelance stuff for ESPN. Is that true?"

"It is indeed, though I'm just starting. Pickings for decent stuff have been a little slim so far."

"Well, maybe I can help you with that."

Blake was immediately dubious. Of all the terms he had heard used to describe Tom Kincaid, generous was not one of them. Still, he was in the business of finding things out, so he said, "I'm listening."

The next day, Blake found Kincaid sitting in front of a Starbucks in downtown Chicago. Kincaid had on the usual expensive lawyer suit, despite the late May heat that promised another sweltering Chicago summer. They shook hands, and Blake wondered if he would see the real Tom Kincaid. He had on dark shades and didn't appear to want to take them off, despite the shade over their seats.

"How have you been, Mr. Kincaid?" Blake started formally. It might have been usual to ask after Danny, but Blake knew that father and son rarely talked now.

"Oh, like usual I suppose. You?" It was quite clear that Kincaid would not chitchat long. Blake knew this to be a strictly business encounter.

"Okay, I guess. The media world has its ups and downs, as I'm sure you know."

Tom Kincaid nodded with a hint of a smile. "Indeed."

Blake let the silence linger between them. It was clear that what Kincaid wanted was not social. Blake assumed reporter mode and just waited for what he had to say. After a few moments, Kincaid spoke.

"Here's what I have. I'm going to give you the name and phone number of a woman. Follow up with her. No matter what she says, she has a big story. It involves a significant figure in sports. You agree not to divulge to her or anyone else where you got her information. When you hear her story and the stories of others she may lead you to, you may need to develop confirming information. At that point, I may—and I emphasize *may*—be able to help you with that, anonymously."

"What can you tell me about this *significant figure in sports?*"

"At this point, nothing."

"Nothing because you don't know who he is or nothing because you represent him?"

Kincaid did not reply. He simply stared at Blake from behind his shades. Blake's instincts told him what he needed to know: that this was a significant story and that it involved a client of Kincaid's. Frankly, that in and of itself made the story significant. The man did not represent nobodies.

"This woman may lead me to 'others'? Did I hear that right?"

Kincaid looked away for a moment. The dark glasses did not completely hide a look of deep thought and regret. After a couple of beats, he nodded slowly. "I need your word that I will never be anything but deep background or I walk away right now."

"You have my word," Blake said.

Kincaid nodded. He reached into his breast pocket, took out an envelope, and slid it across the table to Blake.

"Open this later. My number is in there as well," he said, standing up.

"What's this about, Tom?"

Surprisingly, Kincaid removed his dark glasses. Blake was shocked to see the look in his eyes. Blake had always remembered those eyes as steel—betraying nothing and exhibiting total control. What he saw in Tom Kincaid's eyes now was a vulnerability, the result of surrender to an impulse that for him was totally unnatural. For an instant, he looked not at all like the powerful fixer his reputation portrayed him as.

"It's important" was all he said to Blake. The shades went back on, and he walked away without looking back.

Blake left a few minutes later, walking to his car with Kincaid's envelope in his hand. He made it all the way to his car before curiosity won out, and he looked inside the envelope. Inside was a piece of paper with a name and phone number on it—nothing else. Though the name was only vaguely familiar to him, he sensed it would become more important to him in time.

"Kelly Keys."

Chapter Thirteen

The morning after his meeting with Thomas Kincaid, Blake Manes sat in his small home office. The typical skepticism he may have had in the past with some stories was not present. He was an experienced reporter who trusted his instincts. And his instincts were telling him this was big. Just how "big," he was not yet sure.

Blake began by googling "Kelly Keys." Finding basic information on her was not difficult; she had a public life after all. After playing college golf and qualifying for the LPGA Tour, Kelly had begun work for the Golf Channel. She had gained notoriety from a YouTube video she had featured in with two other friends from the ladies' Tour. It was a mock interview in which her LPGA peers played themselves and Kelly was a golf analyst. It was funny and charming and went viral on social media. More than that, it showed that Kelly knew her way around competitive golf and was comfortable in front of a camera.

Not too long after the viral video, Kelly had become a regular guest on interview shows and instructional segments. And soon, her golf experience, personality, and looks made her an appealing addition to the Golf Channel family. She was a unique talent—attractive, with a quick mind and wit— and a success at tournament golf. The beginnings of her TV career showed such great promise it had folks at the Golf Channel calling her the female version of David Feherty, an on-air personality who attracted both male and female viewers.

Despite this early promise, Kelly Keys had left the Golf Channel early this year. It was unclear why.

A little more digging told Manes that Kelly had been raised by her mother, an FBI agent who died in the line of duty the previous year. Details were sketchy. Blake doubted this story had anything to do with her mother's death. Kelly Keys was now living in her hometown of Atlanta, and Blake had no clue what she was doing.

He sat back and attempted to marry what he had found out about Kelly with the details of his talk with Kincaid. Tom had said a *significant figure in sports*. Until recently Kelly Keys had been a commentator on the Golf Channel. So, something to do with a golfer maybe? That seemed a bit of a stretch for a "big story." Golfers typically did not get into much trouble. Things like drugs and violence were not normally problems for golfers—the Tiger Woods saga being the exception.

Had Kelly dated or been involved with a married golfer? That seemed most likely but didn't match the gravity with which Kincaid had conveyed his information.

Blake searched an online roster of Golf Channel employees. He was looking for a familiar name whom he might be able to talk to about Kelly Keys. After a series of dead ends, he found a promising possibility.

Christie Wilkens was a name from the past. Some years back she had dated a good friend of Blake's. The problem was that this friend was not exactly the loyal boyfriend type, and Christie had bolted when she found out about his extracurricular activities. Blake and Christie had always gotten along; he was just not sure how she would receive him after a messy break-up with a friend of his.

Blake had not become an investigative reporter by being shy, so he called the Golf Channel and asked after Christi. He was directed to her voicemail and left an innocuous message.

It turned out that Christi was not vindictive to Blake as a result of the past faux pas of his friend. She called back two days later and was reasonably warm to Blake.

"I'm glad I am not guilty by association," he remarked after he and Christi had caught up.

"Oh no. I do my best not to put all men in the same category," she said. "I am curious though why the call out of the blue."

"Actually, business. I am working on something, and I was hoping you might be able to help."

"Well, okay, but you have to know that I can't talk about any golfers. That would get me canned fast."

"No, I understand. I am calling about a past Golf Channel employee, Kelly Keys. Do you know her?"

There was a moment of silence before Christie responded., "Yeah, I know Kelly, used to work with her. Why?"

Blake had to trust Christi, at least a little. "Look, between me and you, I have a source, someone pretty well connected who gave me Kelly's name and almost nothing else. Pretty much all I know is the public stuff about her on Golf Channel and that she left early this year. It may be nothing, but my source says otherwise. I am just looking for a starting point."

"Sorry, but I really don't know anything about Kelly that would help you."

"Okay, well, I wonder do you know why she left the Golf Channel? It seemed like she was on the rise . . . "

"No, I don't know. Listen, Blake, I'm at work and I must go. Sorry, I couldn't help. Bye." *Click.*

That took an interesting turn. One minute we're friends catching up, the next she hangs up on me.

In a way, Blake had gotten what he needed.

A short while later, he got a text message. Short and simple: "What's your mailing address?"

The number and area code were unfamiliar, but he could not ignore it after the call with Christi Wilkins. Blake answered with his PO box in Chicago.

Two days later, he received a plain envelope with no return address. The handwritten note inside was unsigned.

"I don't know why, but after the PGA Championship last year, KK was never the same. She was late for the Sunday show. The story was that she was hungover. Unlikely. Bosses took pains in telling us not to talk about it. She phoned in her job the rest of the year, distracted, irritable, detached. In January, she and the Golf Channel agreed to part ways. That's it. Don't call again."

It was obvious this came from Christi Wilkins and just as obvious was the fact that it was not proof of anything. It was a lead, though. Blake could now approach Kelly Keys.

He was not sure how long it would take to contact Kelly. Thankfully, she called him back the day after his first message.

"Kelly, thanks for calling me back, I appreciate it."

"No problem. I am curious though; are you with ESPN?"

"Technically, I am a freelance reporter, so not directly with them."

"Oh, I see. I hear that's kind of a tough gig." She was being friendly and cooperative so far. "Did you want some help with a golf story? Not sure what I can do, I've been away from the Tour for a while."

"Actually, a source gave me your name and number and told me you had something. Weird as it may sound, that is about all I know." *Gotta start somewhere.*

"Well, I don't know what I might have for you. I don't suppose you can tell me who this source is?"

"Can't do that, as you know." A little different tactic. "Hey, one thing I am curious about. I have seen some of the stuff you did on the Golf Channel. It was great. Do you mind if I ask why you left?"

Blake could feel the energy on the other end of the line change instantly. Kelly did not hesitate that long. "Oh, I don't know, nothing really tangible. I think I was a little burnt out; it had become a rat race. Why do you ask?"

"Just curious. Your star seemed on the rise. I would think they would have done a lot to accommodate your career."

Another couple of silent beats. "Well, not really. I mean, it just stopped being a fit. I wanted to move on, and so did they."

A plain vanilla answer—the same as an evasion. "That's too bad for you and them. Not to mention the audience. You got rave reviews . . . "

"Well, thanks. Hey, I just realized I am late for something. I should go."

Blake waited for the *click*, but it didn't come. He knew she wanted to tell him something but didn't trust him enough yet. He understood.

"Kelly?"

"Yeah?"

"Until you say different, nobody is going to know from me that we talked—now or ever. That's a promise."

She paused. "Okay, thank you. Bye."

This and other things led to Blake Manes traveling from Chicago to Atlanta four days later. He had told Kelly Keys he was going to be in Atlanta and hoped she would meet with him. On leaving, he was not sure she would.

In Atlanta, Blake was getting nowhere with Kelly Keys. He had left her a text and a voice message, and when forty-eight hours later he still had not heard from her, he concluded that he may have wasted a trip. Just as he was about to go back to Chicago, he received a text from Kelly. It simply read: *"Sorry, I am really busy. No time right now to meet with you. Talk to Clem Tobin at 604-572-0037."*

Who the hell is Clem Tobin? He smiled a little to himself when he realized it was up to him to find out.

It turned out Mr. Tobin was a former cop and now a private investigator. When Blake called, he was a bit surprised that Tobin would talk to him. They set a time to meet.

Blake had a large coffee and found a table outside a cluster of shops in Marietta, a suburb of Atlanta. While it was not totally private, it was outside and would enable a fairly private conversation. Blake noted this, as it was a setting he would choose for a substantive talk with a source. He hoped that's what Tobin would turn out to be.

Clem Tobin walked up and introduced himself. He looked very much like a cop, broad in the shoulders and ample at the waist, very serious, and not a guy to be messed with. He was roughly fifty, African American, with dark eyes and thinning, dark hair tinged with gray. He had a face that could have been stamped with the words "experienced" as a permanent caption.

"Thanks for meeting me," Blake began.

"Frankly, I wouldn't have if not for Kelly Keys. She suggested we talk."

Blake was surprised. "I wonder why?"

"I am in the same boat. I don't know her well, and she has not helped much with what I am working on. So I think I am as surprised as you about our meeting."

Blake's instincts made him twitch even more on hearing that. Tobin appeared to be a no-nonsense cop, not a man to waste his time. Blake was immediately curious as to what he was working on.

"Hmm, that's interesting. Can you tell me anything at all about what you are working on?"

Tobin looked directly across the table at Blake. For a moment, the younger man thought he was being questioned about a homicide. This guy could intimidate just with his stare.

"Before I do that, I am going to have to know more about you."

"That's fair enough," Blake said. Mainly because he knew almost nothing about his story and because he had nothing to hide. He also thought that what Tobin knew might help him greatly.

In broad terms, and without disclosing his source, Blake told Tobin how he had been given Kelly's name and the work he had done up to this point. Tobin listened intently, his dark eyes on Blake the entire time.

When Blake finished, Tobin nodded. "Okay, so now let's get to your why."

"My why?"

"Yeah, your why. Frankly, I don't like or trust most reporters. What I have and what I am working on might help you, but it has to be handled a certain way. If all you are looking for is a story, and you don't care who it hurts, we won't do business."

Blake smiled and nodded. He understood now.

"So, Mr. Tobin, let me tell you why I don't work for someone specifically, why I freelance. I don't have any more use for what passes as news these days, and I won't play the game anymore. I believe in my job, my role, and I believe it can have more benefit to this world of ours than circulation and ratings. I know you don't know me, but right now I think we might be able to help each other. If you could give me a shot at that without risking too much, maybe we can find out."

Tobin considered that unblinkingly for a moment. What Manes did not know was that Tobin was stuck on what he was working on. Maybe meeting Blake was the break he needed.

Tobin sighed. "I need this off the record for now, agreed?"

"Agreed."

"About nine months ago, a man came to me with an unusual request. He thought a close female friend of his, a cousin actually, had been assaulted. She wasn't ready to come forward, which is all too frequently the case, but he was, and he was quite adamant that something be done."

"Okay," Blake said. "Who is this guy?"

"A caddy on the PGA Tour."

What the hell?

"And this caddy knows—or thinks he knows—who assaulted his cousin?"

"He says he is sure of it."

"And it's a golfer?"

154

"Yes," Tobin confirmed. "A very visible golfer."

Tobin would go no further. He just looked at Blake and raised his eyebrows as if to say, "Your turn."

"My source is an agent and a lawyer, who represents some very high-profile celebrities and athletes, including some top-ranked players on the PGA Tour."

"My client—if we can call him that—is convinced this is not an isolated incident."

Blake's mind went back to his conversation with Kincaid, "others she might lead me to."

"Did I hear that right?" Blake had asked him.

The resigned look on Kincaid's face as he nodded took on a new meaning now. A darker meaning.

"Jesus."

"Yeah," Tobin said. "I don't think I will ever stop being a cop. If what I think is true is *really* true, this is not just about a fee for me. This guy has got to be stopped. This can't be a scandal, can't be played out in the media. I've got to bring a solid package to the right people, so this guy goes away."

Blake looked at Tobin and nodded. "The happy irony of that is if we help each other and he does go down, it's a pretty fucking great story. But not until then."

Tobin finally smiled, something he hadn't done since he sat down. "Well, shit, Mr. Manes. You might be the exception. Of course, if you're not, I'll pop a cap in your ass."

Chapter Fourteen

Kelly's life had changed substantially since the events that happened at the PGA Championship at Winged Foot. It seemed like a gradual thing at first, both to her and those around her. First, she had to deal with her bosses at Golf Channel for walking out at the winner's press conference. Cliff Lombard had wanted her to get another interview with Monroe, which she barely ducked. While she would not disclose why, she could not be close to Zeke Monroe. As time went on, she did fewer and fewer interviews with players and seemed to lose her enthusiasm for her job at Golf Channel. One thing led to another, and in January, she and Lombard agreed they would go their separate ways.

This was the first time since college that Kelly had been out of a job; she had started a playing career after school and then gone on to work on television right after. Both were very intensive and time-consuming careers. After leaving the Golf Channel, being idle was strange to her. She thought about going back to playing pro golf and began practicing.

Strangely, she found that she had little interest in it. In fact, she began acting out and getting angry on the golf course or in practice when she didn't perform well—something she had never done before. From her early teens, golf had been a joyful thing for her. She had always looked forward to playing and practicing, even if she played poorly. For some reason, she had lost her patience. She did not realize that she was associating golf with an event she had stuffed into her subconscious like a bag of old clothes into an attic.

Kelly had been a social drinker, even through college. Now she found herself partying more and more. She strangely took up with an old college friend whom she knew to be wilder than she was. Her name was Krystal Downs. From an early age, Krystal was two things Kelly was not: besotted and promiscuous. Kelly and Krystal began hanging out, and the results were predictable. Kelly drank more, partied more, and hooked up more—all things that she explained away. College golf and being in school had kept her so serious; it wasn't such a big deal to sow some wild oats, was it?

Kelly did what a lot of highly talented and smart people do with time on their hands: she filled that time with not so constructive things.

Her dalliances had a pattern. The young men she hooked up with were controllable and predictable—and, frankly, disposable. She knew what they wanted, and she could dictate the how, the where, and be sure there were no emotional complications. That was easy because there was little emotion in her trysts. She would wake up slightly hungover, physically satisfied, and, most importantly, distracted from anything below the surface of her conscious mind.

This pattern her life had taken was interrupted in a curious way. Kelly had joined Krystal for the usual Friday Happy Hour, extending into happy hours, followed by a ride home with the beau of the moment. The difference this time was the particular beau. His name was Joe Castor, and he was part of a group of young men who were "typical" in their mood and motivation, except he turned out not to be typical. Yes, he had met her at the bar, had watched her consume too much alcohol, and had taken her home. The difference came the next morning.

Kelly woke up in her bed alone. It was clear that she had slept alone in her bed all night. While she had the usual hangover, she didn't have the usual post-sex soreness in her body or psyche. On her nightstand was a bottle of water, two Ibuprofen, and a short note that read:

Figured you might want these this morning. As much fun as last night was, I'd like us to know each other sober. Call me if you want to, 436-754-0221.

Joe

When she was fully awake, Kelly made the mental trek through a number of responses. This was a detour around the mindless distracting sex she had come to practice. It was strange and a bit welcome for her to meet a man who wanted more than just a quick roll in the hay. The unwelcome part was the beginning of looking just a little deeper than the surface, a task she had been doing an Olympian job of avoiding. She found herself in front of her bathroom mirror, looking at herself for the first time in quite a while.

She had avoided the mirror until now because she had felt flashes of anger and shame when she looked at herself. Kelly fought that impulse now as she continued to look into her own eyes in the mirror. Gradually, she got just a little more comfortable, although she could not say that she was pleased with the view.

She had crumpled up Joe's note when she got out of bed, but now she reached down to the wastebasket and retrieved it. Intuition she'd ignored for a long time told her she just might want to keep his number.

Kelly Keyes moved around the large banquet room with a smile on her face. After the most remarkable three days of her adult life, she felt lighter, vibrant, and alive. And for the first time in a long while, Kelly knew that she would wake up excited the next morning instead of dreading the day ahead. She had just finished a three-day personal development course with sixty-two other people. She had known none of them when she walked into the room that Friday morning. Now, everywhere she turned, she saw friendly faces.

She had just finished saying good-bye to Hannah Simms, a young woman close to her age, when she bumped into Joe Castor. Joe was the one who had introduced her to the course. He'd dragged her to a presentation about the course, then encouraged her to stay the whole three days. She had spent most of the first day rolling her eyes, wondering why the hell she had come, until something the instructor said resonated deeply with her. It was then that her gratitude toward Joe for getting her there had grown exponentially.

Joe started to greet her, but she cut him off by wrapping him in the sincerest hug she had ever given another person.

"Thank you, Joe. Thank you so much for this. The last three days have honestly been the best gift I have ever been given. I don't know that I can ever repay you," she said to him through grateful tears.

"You just did."

Before she left the room, Kelly found the facilitator for the weekend. Rob Givens was a man who would forever be a treasured mentor. To her, he was an authority because he did not act like one. His humility and authenticity impressed her even more than his insight, which was otherworldly. She thanked him for everything and related the thing he had said late Friday that had gotten her attention and shifted her view of the course.

"It was a long weekend. Remind me of what it was I said."

"You were talking about the subconscious mind, and you said that what you don't work on will work on you."

"Oh, that. I would love to take credit for that bit of truth, but I borrowed it from Seth Reede."

"Who is Seth Reede?"

"He's one of the founders of Spiritual Ground Zero in California and the lead facilitator. Are you going to go?"

Kelly hesitated. "I . . . I don't know."

Rob looked her in the eye. "Kelly, this has been a great three days, but it's like an alarm clock. It just woke you up to things about yourself that you weren't previously aware of. You may have realized things in yourself that limit you, but changing them takes more than three days. I have been doing this work for five years now, and I feel like I might have 10 percent of it down. I'm a work in progress. Whatever you do, don't stop. Make this a beginning, a benchmark."

Part of the class had been to set a goal to be reached in thirty days. There were many different types of goals set; many of the class set a monetary or financial goal (X dollars earned in thirty days), some set a goal to buy something (a car or other major purchase). Some goals were career goals, finding a particular job or gaining a promotion. Kelly set a goal that was personal, and she was surprised by how important it was to her. Others in the class remarked how brave she was to set this one and that it was a really good goal for her. They knew because of how nervous she was around declaring this goal.

The goal Kelly set was to have a better relationship with her father. After Rachelle died, and Kelly read Rachelle's letter to her, disclosing that Craig Cantwell was her dad, Kelly had withdrawn. Strangely, she found herself resentful of Rachelle and Craig. Despite Rachelle's explanation that she, not Craig, had wanted this secret kept from Kelly, Kelly felt that if Craig had really cared enough about her, he would have manned up and claimed her as his own. The story that Kelly told herself was that her mother's career was more important than Kelly and that, if her father really loved her, he would have told her the secret. She had withdrawn after her mom's death. Her acting out through drinking and sex was a way of numbing herself from her grief and from a certain event that she had decided was best forgotten.

Kelly's experience in the course had revealed a lot to her. She considered that the events at Winged Foot had been the cause of her resentment of Craig. While he was blameless, her motive was numbness toward painful things. It was far easier to not feel things and flatline. The seminar had gotten her emotions working again, and even though it was uncomfortable, she came to the realization that she had only one parent left. She set the goal of resolving her relationship with Craig, even though she had no idea how to do this.

So, on a crispy Monday afternoon, not too long after she returned home from the seminar, Kelly called Craig. She asked him if he would please meet with her in Atlanta. When he arrived that Wednesday afternoon, she took him to a presentation on the same course she had just completed. He was puzzled and maybe even a bit annoyed, wondering if this was some new "business" she was into. He still went because she had called and acknowledged him, and the fact that she wanted to see him had brought him partway out of a pit he was in the process of falling into.

When the presentation was over, Kelly looked at Craig and asked him if he wanted to go to the course. The look on his face told her he was confused and unsure.

"Why did you ask me?" he asked. This was a sudden turn of things, and skepticism was just the tip of his emotional distress. He wanted to think that Kelly reached out to him with a pure motive, not some sham.

She hesitated. There were a lot of reasons she could give him, and she didn't want to sound like she had some complicated agenda. After a few moments, she hit on the why and knew it was enough.

"Because you're my dad, and I love you."

That was all Craig Cantwell needed. He went to the course because he loved and trusted Kelly. What he discovered were far greater realizations about himself that led him to SGZ, to Seth Reede, and ultimately back to the final round of the U.S. Open.

CHAPTER FIFTEEN

Tobin and Blake met again, this time in Tobin's hotel room. After he let Blake in, they sat in front of Tobin's laptop and watched a video.

"This video was made by my client. His name is David Fenton. I give you that so maybe you can verify that he has worked on the Tour. I'm not at this time able to give you the name of the woman on the video."

Blake watched as an attractive young girl with brown hair and blue eyes told a story. She described a date she had with a man in which her recollection stopped at a point that evening. She woke up the next morning feeling dizzy and unsettled. In addition, she had a massive headache and bruises she could not explain. She spoke about feeling "outside herself," "really weird." She also noticed that her clothes, even her underwear, were on inside out and backward. She described bruising, what looked like bite marks, and what she thought was dried semen on her body.

Blake was chilled by this woman's tone. At her age, he'd expect her voice to be lively and vibrant. Perhaps it had been, until this night she described. Now she resembled a brightly colored painting that had faded.

The woman on the tape went on to describe her interaction with another man the morning after, not the man she remembered being with the night before. This man was proper, cold, and addressed her as though she had acted improperly. He assured her that he would keep anyone from knowing how "badly" she had behaved on her date with his "client." The girl said she didn't even know if her "date" was this man's client. She only knew that he wanted to make sure she was "protected" from anyone knowing about her behavior the night before.

When the video ended, Blake looked at Tobin. "I notice you kept names out of what you showed me," he said.

Tobin nodded. "I have to right now, Blake." He thought a minute. "Give me a reason not to."

Blake looked right at Tobin. "I don't know if this is a reason, but I'll give you a name. Thomas Kincaid."

Tobin smiled slightly as if an instinct he had about Blake had turned out to be true.

"Then I can give you a name—off the record—Zeke Monroe."

Despite his instincts, Blake was not ready for the impact of that name. He exhaled as he realized that his estimation of his "big" story had not been near big enough.

"Holy shit."

Blake Manes and Clem Tobin talked extensively about what they needed, for Clem to go to legal authorities and for Blake to break this story. The men had agreed that going public too soon would greatly diminish the chances of Zeke Monroe facing charges. They needed as many details as they could get about the incidents that were known. Amanda Cox, the girl on the video, and hopefully others would provide them with consistency in the way they remembered the incidents. This would lead to credibility and lower the risk to the women who did come forward.

Both men were now convinced that Kelly Keys was one of Monroe's victims. Her semi-celebrity status made her participation key to their investigation.

"This guy is smart," Clem said. "Notice how his modus operandi prevents identification? He can always just claim he had a date with the victim and that she drank too much. He and his fixer really play on the mentality of an assault victim. They amplify embarrassment and shame and then become an 'ally' to help her keep it a secret. In effect, the victim starts helping the perp stay safe to protect herself."

Blake nodded. He was thinking about Kincaid's comments when they met, about the possibility that he might help anonymously.

"Man, I wonder why Kincaid talked to me," Blake said. "I think he knows a lot more than he's letting on."

"As much of a dirtbag as that guy is, he *did* come to you. As unpleasant as it might be, we need him. Can you go back to him?"

"Yes, but I want to have something really concrete before I do. What about physical evidence?"

Tobin shook his head. "There's nothing at this point. Even if we have multiple victims come forward, everything is circumstantial."

"First things first. We definitely need Kelly Keys."

"Definitely."

⚜ ⚜ ⚜

165

Kelly had been moving toward healing from her night with Zeke Monroe. Through this, one of the most important people in her healing was Hannah Simms. They were seeing the same rape facilitator who was taking them through steps that had been tested in many prior cases.

While the steps were well defined and, to an outsider, logical, they were difficult for most victims. The subconscious mind is designed to keep a person safe, and the subconscious of a rape victim works overtime to that end.

Kelly and Hannah's facilitator knew that an important life event like marriage or childbirth was often the catalyst for a victim to finally move into recovery.

The catalyst for Kelly that her counselor had noted was Rachelle's death.

Kelly had made a lot of strides in this process, yet she was still resistant to some of the things that would head her to recovery. The calls she received from Blake Manes and Clem Tobin were a factor in her process. Not only did she not know them, but she was also not ready to face what she knew intuitively was related to her rape. She did, however, take the step in talking to Susan, her facilitator about the contacts.

"Do you think they're working on this? Your case, I mean?" Susan asked.

"They haven't said as much, but I think so. Blake Manes is an investigative reporter, and Clem Tobin said he's a private investigator, an ex-cop."

"Kelly, there's a possibility that these men are working on other cases related to yours."

"I thought about that. It's just . . . it might mean going public. Is that good for me?"

Susan thought hard before answering. "Because you are my client, I'll answer that specifically. If you are looking for revenge, no, it's not good for you. If you can see this as a key step in getting clear of this, then, yes, it is good for you."

Kelly looked up at Susan, a woman she trusted and respected. Their relationship was strong as a result of Susan's help and expertise, especially because of her empathy. Susan was also a rape victim and had personally gone through a similar healing process.

"What's your advice?"

Susan looked back, knowing in her heart and mind that the possibility of this assault being aired publicly would be very hard for Kelly. Even knowing that, she knew the only right answer.

"You're going to have to, honey."

Blake Manes was taken aback when he met Kelly Keys for the first time. While he had seen clips of her work on Golf Channel, he found that she was even more attractive in person. He and Clem Tobin walked into their first meeting with her and were both struck by her looks. She was a beautiful young woman. More than that, she had strength, a strength that was partly due to her experience as an accomplished athlete. Even more than that, she had an inner strength, strength forged in the flames of adversity and loss. Her mother had died a highly decorated FBI agent.

Susan Stallings, Kelly's counselor, joined Manes, Tobin, and Kelly.

Blake was the first to speak. "Thank you for meeting with us, Kelly. We appreciate it. Let me start by saying that I think what you're doing takes a lot of guts."

"Thank you. I need to trust someone, and I have decided to trust you, as well as Susan."

"Again, thanks for that. As I told you when we first talked, nothing goes public from me until you say so. That rule still holds true," said Blake. "Clem, why don't you start?"

Tobin nodded. "Kelly and Susan, I am investigating multiple incidents of sexual assault that point to one man. The cases are unfortunately difficult to prove because of two things: lack of physical evidence and the unwillingness of victims, so far, to come forward. An anonymous source of Blake's has led us to believe that you may be a victim of this same crime. We're hoping that you will talk to us about what happened to you."

Susan broke in. "Assuming that Kelly will talk to you, what will you do with the information?"

"I'm building a case. Kelly's information will be a part of it. I want this case to be strong enough to go directly to law enforcement long before any of this is seen in the public light. I now believe this man is a serial rapist, and I want him stopped."

"What about you, Mr. Manes?"

"My motivation is the same, but with a twist. As a reporter, I will have exclusive rights to this story. Yes, it will benefit me and my career, but it will hopefully put a stop to what this criminal has been doing."

"How many other women are there?" Kelly asked.

Three different sets of eyes looked at Tobin. This was something that even Blake did not know.

Tobin's face took on the look of an experienced cop.

"Seven that I'm aware of, including you."

Kelly gasped. This knowledge was daunting, yet, in a way, it reinforced her decision to talk to these men. It also spawned in her a feeling of belonging. She had just discovered that she had six "sisters" whom she hadn't known existed. Six other women who had been sexually assaulted and were scared and ashamed and wounded. Six others who all thought they were alone in their pain. And another one whom she knew about—a victim of another sort—who was brave in a different way.

"Okay," she said, leveling her eyes at Clem Tobin. "How do I start?"

Kelly Keys' description of the night before the final round of the PGA Championship matched almost exactly the story that Amanda Cox had told on the videotape. Kelly had shown resolve in her statement to Blake Manes and Clem Tobin, something both men admired in her.

While they felt exhilarated in moving forward in this process, they knew that more was going to be needed.

"This is a big break, I admit," Clem said. "She's a brave woman who most likely can start the process of others coming forward."

"I get the feeling there's a 'but' coming."

"It's still circumstantial. We have a similar story told by multiple victims, we hope. It establishes a *modus operandi* (MO), but we still don't have any physical evidence. Given the powerful public figure that Monroe is, we can assume that he's covered himself, probably multiple ways."

"One ace in the hole we have is Kincaid. I can still go back to him. He may help us."

"That may be true, but I still have an urge to bust that guy, too. He knew what he was doing," Clem said.

"He still came forward, though. I wonder why."

Tobin shrugged. "Don't know. Let's focus on the rapist for now."

Blake nodded. "Okay, what do we need? What puts us in a position to go to law enforcement with evidence so solid that they can't ignore it?"

"I've been thinking about that. First, he drugs his victims. Where does he get the drugs? It's most likely Rufalin or something similar. I am betting somebody gets it for him. If we can trace the drugs to him, that would help a lot."

"I can go to Kincaid for that."

Tobin stared back at Blake. "Will he tell you?"

Blake didn't answer.

"If he's reluctant, maybe I'll motivate him."

"I'll keep that in mind. I bet he'll at least point us in the right direction."

"On that subject, Kincaid is key. If he were to testify, I think we've won."

Blake shook his head. "I'm almost positive he'll stop short of that."

"My offer still stands," Clem said.

"I know you're only joking, but we have to be clean with this," Blake said. "If not, it becomes a stupid media circus and Monroe walks."

"You're right. It's just emotionally satisfying to think about tuning both these guys up."

"What else?" Blake asked.

"Any kind of physical evidence will be helpful. We need hair, fiber, fingerprints, anything. DNA would be the best. Again, they are smart. In Kelly's case, Kincaid did all he could to make sure Kelly cleaned up the next morning. That just about ensures that any physical evidence is gone."

"Maybe we'll get lucky."

Tobin seemed to think of something. "Hey, this guy qualifies as a serial offender. Any psychological profiling that we have access to might help as well. It occurs to me that the FBI may be who we need in this. They might be able to help."

"They might be glad to help, given who Kelly's mom is. Was," Blake corrected.

"Sometimes these sick bastards keep a souvenir, some sort of trophy."

"Jesus," said Blake.

"Yeah, I know. Maybe it's an angle with Kincaid."

"I'll find out."

CHAPTER SIXTEEN

Blake Manes sat on a bench in view of the mirrored orb on Chicago's Michigan Avenue. It was a clear, early afternoon, and lots of foot traffic bustled through the Downtown streets. Blake could have been a tourist or an employee in one of the high-rises on a late lunch break.

Blake noticed a group crossing the street walking toward him when the light changed. Most of the group had paired up with someone except for a blond man wearing expensive sunglasses. He walked as though he was very familiar with the streets; he seemed comfortable and in control. He wore an expensive button-down shirt with an open collar and light-colored pants over expensive loafers with no socks. He moved with purpose and had a face that looked like it rarely smiled.

The man in the shades approached Manes's bench and allowed a half-smile.

"Well, Blake Manes. What a surprise," he said with an extended hand.

"Hello, Tom," Manes replied, wondering why Kincaid acted as if they had not planned to meet here.

"How have you been?" Kincaid asked him, deepening Blake's curiosity about the act.

"Busy, actually," Blake said back, glaring at Kincaid with a look that was far from casual.

"Productive, I trust," Kincaid said, keeping the casual facade. Blake was a bit annoyed at this.

"Yes," Blake bit off. His intent was to get on with things. "I'm hoping you can help."

"I'll do what I can," Kincaid said, which annoyed Blake even more. Tom Kincaid was not a gracious man, and both of them knew it.

"Rufalin." This one word negated any pretense Kincaid had adopted. He looked off a minute before replying.

"Ah, so?"

"Who gets it for him?" Blake said with a direct look at Kincaid. For once, Tom's face betrayed that he was surprised and he was in deeper water than he had planned.

"I am not sure I can help with that," he said nervously, the casual facade gone.

After his investigation, after talking with Kelly Keys and Clem Tobin, Blake Maines was not in the mood for Kincaid to backpedal. Angered by Kincaid's nonchalance, he decided to use what leverage he had.

"Tom, when we first talked, I had no idea what this was about. Now I do. Don't be under any illusions—this is going farther and is going to get very bad for the man you know. Backing out now could be very bad for you."

"We had a deal, remember?" Kincaid said. "You gave me your word."

"Yes, I remember," Blake said. "But there will be other people involved in this, and I can't promise what they will do or say if your name comes up. Your involvement is clear to them. If you want any leverage, I suggest you choose a side, quickly."

Blake stood up to leave. Tom Kincaid wondered how he wound up on this side of a conversation he'd had in the past with many others. He admired Blake, knowing the man's tactic left him little choice. Before Blake took two steps away from the bench, Kincaid stopped him.

"Manes."

Blake stopped and looked back at Kincaid. He was a bit surprised to see the trapped look on Kincaid's face. Tom nodded. "I'll see what I can do."

Blake nodded back, then turned on his heels and walked away.

The next day, Blake got a text: "Carter Travis, Houston."

CHAPTER SEVENTEEN

You just never know, the dealer thought. He could usually tell when someone wanted to score, but this man was an exception. The dude was older, maybe fifty. He sort of looked proper. However, he had also been convincing during their meeting the day before. The dealer had vetted him as well; a good client had vouched for him. Plus, it was only roofies. Some of those customers were straighter in looks than the losers who wanted ecstasy or pot, which made up most of the dealer's business.

This newest client walked in the laundromat like they set up yesterday and followed the dealer into the dirty men's room in the back.

"Good to see you, Clem. How is it going?" the dealer asked.

"I'm good, Carter. Thanks for the fast service. Are we good?"

"You know it, bro." The dealer pulled a small bottle out of his coat pocket. "Mix with a little booze, and your princess is all yours."

"100 bucks, right?"

"Yep," Carter said as Clem handed him a c-note and took the bottle.

Carter pocketed the bill. "Don't be shy about asking for some X or reefer if you want," he said as his customer headed for the door.

Clem Tobin turned back at the door and smiled at this scumbag. "I'll keep that in mind."

They had caught a break when it turned out that Monroe's Rufilin dealer was from Houston. Tobin had spent a lot of his career there as a police detective and had plenty of friends in narcotics. They weren't overly thrilled with only the prospect of busting a low-level roofie supplier until Tobin related what he was really after. Assisting in the arrest of a serial rapist had a lot more allure for these cops, and they were friends of his anyway. Getting a street informant, who bought from Travis to vouch for him, got Tobin in and arresting the dealer and sweating him for details on Monroe was not tough. When Travis understood he was not ratting out a street thug that would do him damage, he rolled over.

It turned out Kincaid had proven useful after all.

CHAPTER EIGHTEEN

"Gentlemen, I am really not sure why we are talking. Zeke Monroe is a client of mine, but I know nothing about his personal life. Even if I did, I couldn't ethically talk to you about it." Thomas Kincaid sounded professional and dismissive as he spoke to Clem Tobin, Blake Manes, and Rick Hauptman. While he had agreed to meet with these men, it was obvious that he did so for his own benefit. The lawyer in him saw the advantage of appearing to cooperate without divulging any real information. At this point, Kincaid's conscience had only pushed him far enough to give Manes the name of Kelly Keys.

While Kincaid desired control in this meeting, the men he was talking to were not about to concede anything. All three were vested in the pursuit of Zeke Monroe; all three were certain of Monroe's guilt. Blake's motivation went beyond journalism; he was finally doing work in his chosen field that meant something. Clem Tobin was a former cop who had never gotten over his addiction to putting bad people behind bars. These men had met with Rick Hauptman of the FBI through the introduction of Kelly Keys. Hauptman was more personally involved than any of them after he had talked with Kelly. After Rachelle's death, Rick felt a fierce desire to protect her only daughter.

Hauptman leveled his dark eyes directly into Kincaid's. His warrior's stare had a strong impact on most anyone, and it was obvious what he had seen and done over a long career.

"Numerous victims talk about a man who visits with them after their assault and who covers up the event. We know that man is you. What you need to understand is that you are criminally involved in these assaults." Hauptman paused, his stare persistent. "Personally, I hope you stay silent. That way, you can go down hard for your part in this."

Kincaid the lawyer was not the least bit surprised by Hauptman's tactic or comments. He knew exactly where he stood legally; if these men had a strong case against him or Monroe, he would be under arrest.

"I have no direct knowledge of an assault on anyone by Mr. Monroe. I've already told you that."

Clem Tobin reacted more to this comment from Kincaid than Hauptman. As a private investigator, he was less bound by the law than Hauptman, and he was hard-pressed to contain a desire to beat information out of this lawyer. Tobin was standing behind Rick and took several steps away after this exchange. He was fighting frustration. He knew they were close to Monroe, but not close enough. He wanted to "persuade" Kincaid and knew that the skills he had in that area would not be enough.

For his part, Blake Manes was just as passionate as Hauptman and Tobin. He did not buy that Kincaid was going to continue to stonewall them, however. He knew that something had made Kincaid come to him initially and did not believe that was just a moment of weakness.

There was something that moved Tom Kincaid to want to right a wrong he was a part of. Something that moved him out of the greedy lawyer mode he had always lived in.

"So, Counselor, we're off the record, right?" Blake said to Kincaid. Those were the terms under which Kincaid had agreed to talk.

Kincaid nodded. "That's right."

"Off the record, then, why the hell did you call me two months ago?"

Strangely, this question had more of an impact than the threats made by Hauptman. Kincaid considered the question, pursing his lips as his eyes avoided Blake's.

"I don't know."

Manes grunted. "I'm not buying it, Tom. I think you *do* know." He got up, still looking at Kincaid, then turned and left the room.

"All right then, gentlemen," Kincaid said to Hauptman and Tobin, "I guess we're done here. I regret that I can't help you further." He stood up as well and left the room, not wanting to talk to these men anymore, wanting desperately to move away from the mirror that Blake held up in front of him.

"Dealing with the pressure of a bomb disposal is not about knowledge or even experience. It's primarily about mind-set. Having any thoughts at all about *anything*, other than what you have to do in the next second, impairs your ability to do your job."

Danny Feld was at the front of a small classroom in the Atlanta field office of the FBI, addressing a small group of agents in training. The position they were training for was that of Explosive Ordinance Disposal Technician, something Danny had been for the last six years. He was not much older than his audience, yet he spoke with the authority of his experience.

"There is no single way to get in the right frame of mind," he went on. "Those of you with military experience may be able to draw on your time in combat. There are those warriors who accept right away that they are already dead, and as a result, they can perform as a combat soldier needs to. Other technicians can detach from the consequences of what they are doing like a tightrope walker can focus on the rope and not the fall. However it's done, achieving this mind-set is essential."

There was a pregnant pause as Danny looked at some of the agents briefly. Some of them nodded; others looked down at their desks and fiddled with their pens. Danny wanted the importance of what he had said to sink in. Mastering this concept could very well save one of these agents' lives someday.

Before Danny could continue, a door at the back of the classroom opened, and Danny's immediate supervisor walked in. Feld could tell by the look on the man's face that class was over for now.

"Agent Feld?" his boss said with a look that Danny knew well. This same look generated excitement that Danny joked "sends your balls up into your abdomen." If you were afraid of heights, the feeling that this moment gave you was like looking straight down from the observation deck of the Sears Tower. To most men it was terror; to Danny Feld, it was feeling alive.

"That's it for today, guys . . . duty calls." He walked quickly from the front of the classroom and led his boss out the door.

Tom Kincaid had been doing his best to avoid Blake Manes and Friends. He had been bouncing between regret over ever contacting Manes and dread of what it might lead to. In his most self-serving mood, Kincaid worried that his brief meeting with Manes would destroy all he had worked for. On the other hand, he worried about the huge hole in his life that money could never fill. The hole caused by his lack of any relationship with or approval from his son, Danny. A hole he longed to fill.

Unaccustomed to doing the right thing, Kincaid was now unsure if the information he had given Manes would result in anything positive.

Kincaid's thoughts were interrupted by his cell phone buzzing. His brow furrowed, he recognized his former wife's number, and a dreadful instinct made him answer.

"Julie?"

"Hello, Tom." Her tone of voice made it clear that the reason for this call was dreaded by both of them.

"What's wrong?" There was only one reason she would call him.

"It's Danny. He—he said he didn't want me to call you. I had to, though."

"Where is he?"

"Atlanta General, the burn ward."

Kincaid glanced at his watch. "I'll be there in three hours."

"All right . . . Tom?"

"Yes, Julie?"

"Hurry."

Tom Kincaid found the burn ward in a section of the ICU at Atlanta General Hospital. The waiting area in the ICU was large. Visits to see the critically injured are usually short. Gazing at the almost full waiting room, Tom realized that the crowd was there for his son. While none of these people wore uniforms, Kincaid could tell they were all FBI agents. One dark-haired man looked with surprise at Kincaid as he entered. It was obvious that Rick Hauptman neither expected nor welcomed this new visitor.

Danny's mother lingered at the entrance to the waiting area as though crossing the threshold might lead her to a place from which she could never return.

"Julie?" Kincaid said in a hushed voice. "What happened?"

"He was on duty. He . . . " Julie's voice choked as her emotions overwhelmed her and sobs wracked her body. Tom felt a strong hand on his shoulder as a man inserted himself between Tom and Julie. He gestured to Tom to follow him down the hall a few feet. "I'm Agent Drake Barnes, Mr. Kincaid. I understand that you are Agent Feld's father?"

"Danny got a call to a textile factory where a fired employee had shot up the place and rigged several bombs to go off. Danny was disarming one of the bombs and . . . "

Tom's chest tightened, and his throat seemed to close. He wanted to ask more questions, but his voice didn't seem to work. Finally, he managed two syllables. "How bad?"

Agent Barnes hesitated for a moment, and Kincaid glanced at Julie, standing just a few feet away. Her eyes told him, though her voice could not find the words.

"I'm afraid the news is as bad as it can be," Barnes continued. "It's something of a miracle that Agent Feld was not killed outright by the explosion. In any event, he won't . . . "

The shock of something too terrible and too real was on Tom Kincaid's face. Only a short time ago, he was concerned with so many "important" things. Only a short time ago he knew he had time to repair his relationship with his son. Caring about those other things was now suddenly dwarfed by the impending loss of Danny and that vital opportunity to repair their relationship.

Thomas Kincaid, the man who always had an answer, who always had a plan, who always had a way out, had no idea what to say or do now.

But maybe there is one chance. He turned to Julie, Danny's mother, and the only one besides him who could answer the question he had.

"Can I see him, Julie?" he asked in a whisper. He could only imagine her surprise at hearing a plea from Tom for the first and only time since she had known him. "Please."

"He's extremely sedated," the ICU nurse said as she led Kincaid back to see Danny. "Even if he is awake, I doubt he can speak to you. I can only allow you a few minutes."

Tom nodded, his face pale as they walked. It is abject cruelty for a parent ever to have to witness their child's suffering, let alone their child's death. The nurse who accompanied Tom Kincaid understood this, and yet she could not know that a part of Kincaid acknowledged this cruelty to him as a just consequence for how he had lived his life.

Kincaid could hardly reconcile that the heavily bandaged and sedated figure was his son. Danny's perpetual energy and vitality were completely disguised by bandages and drugs. Only one half of his face was visible, and it was a blackened and swollen distortion of Danny's fine visage. His whole body was swaddled in cloth designed to ease the massive pain of outward injuries, though they paled by comparison to Danny's internal injuries.

As Tom looked at the broken body of his son, the shock and dread of his soul shone on his face. A part of him wished he had not pleaded with Julie to see him, as he wondered now why he thought that doing so would help in any way. Like any parent, no matter how misguided, Tom would have willingly changed places with his son. He would take his pain if it were possible. The guilt of his inability to do so washed over him now, no more logical than love itself.

As Tom watched, Danny's right eye slowly opened. Its brilliant blue contrasted the burned flesh of his face as recognition showed. Tom's attention was immediately rapt, as he knew that Danny knew he was there. That, at least, was something.

His son's mouth moved, wanting to form words. The nurse showed her surprise at this, lightly dabbing his burnt lips.

Mmmm . . . a small sound escaped with effort. Tom watched silently, not wanting to make a sound to drown out what Danny might say.

"Mom," Danny said softly, with just a hint of a wry smile.

Tom nodded, his eyes tearing now. "Yes, even though you told her not to call me, she did. And I'm so glad she did."

"Hard," his son whispered softly.

Tom nodded again. "Yes, it will be."

"He . . . p . . . " Another sound, audible but unintelligible. Tom could not fathom what pain it cost his son to speak. The nurse moved close to him, urging him to stay quiet. Danny's reaction surprised both her and his father.

His one exposed eye blazed for a moment with the passion he had always shown for life. He had something to say, and he was by God going to say it.

Danny looked at Tom. His father had seen this look in his son's eyes before, recently, when Danny had expressed dismissal of him and just a small hope that someday Tom would act with compassion and courage.

"Help her . . . once."

For once in my life? Tom thought.

"Help her."

Danny's exposed eye closed after that, as the nurse made sure his suffering was minimized. Those would be the last words Tom Kincaid would hear from his son.

Kincaid walked out of the ICU and left the hospital, feeling unworthy of staying with others who had the love and respect of his son. He exited, realizing that he had been dropped off by a cab and had no means of transportation save his feet. He walked on in the Georgia heat in his $2,000 suit until he found a bench and sat down. He noticed none of the passersby, though a few of them wondered why a man would wear so many clothes on a hot day like today.

At this moment, Tom accepted as fair the heat of the day and denied that he was worthy of minimizing the discomfort by removing his expensive jacket. He saw the death of his son as penance for his life, for his greed and his selfishness. He wondered if the God he didn't believe in was really punishing him. If that were true, then God really was fair. As he sat sweating in the heat, Tom Kincaid saw the disapproval in his son's eyes. His son who was brave and selfless despite his father. He saw too the eyes of the innocent victims, those whose only sin was trust and a desire for connection. He saw his willingness to capitalize on their circumstances, justified in what society's rules deemed acceptable. In his son's burned and broken body, he saw the destruction he had facilitated. In the triple-digit heat and 80 percent humidity, Tom Kincaid sat in his own version of Hell.

As Kincaid sat on the bench with his eyes open, seeing nothing but his son's burned face, Rick Hauptman walked near him. The emotions the SWAT man felt at this moment could hardly be quantified. Rick was losing a trusted friend, a brave man who was a bona fide hero. He had just learned that Danny's father was the same man who had covered up Kelly Keys' rape, for the almighty dollar. Hauptman could plainly see the pain on Kincaid's face and, as a father, could empathize with him. One part of Rick wanted to beat Kincaid until he agreed to testify against Zeke Monroe, another wanted to put a friendly arm around his shoulder.

He took a seat next to Kincaid on the bench.

"Well, this is one for the books, isn't it?" Rick said.

Kincaid swiveled his head and looked at Rick, as if unaware that he was there until he spoke. The FBI agent had seen this stage of grief many times—shock and sorrow so recent that even tears are impossible. The warrior in Rick knew he could not inflict any pain that was greater than what Kincaid now felt.

Hauptman thought for a moment how unlikely it was for him and Kincaid to be sitting on this bench this day. In spite of his orderly mind, Rick wondered if there was a greater reason than coincidence.

"I have lost more than a few friends in my line of work. Kinda come to accept that it's going to happen, but it never gets any easier."

Kincaid just looked at Rick, realizing that death had probably stolen from this man many times. One big difference between them was that Kincaid had far fewer people in his life whose loss would cause him pain.

"What I know is that we in this business accept the risks. We make our peace with risk; it is what it is. I can look back without regret. I know that there was nothing unsaid or undone between me and Danny."

He looked at Kincaid now. "Or between me and Rachelle Keys. We are clean. The way it should be."

Kincaid looked back at him, with a real question. He had to know.

"What if there was something? Something undone?"

"Then I would do it. Whatever it is. I would do it to honor the dead."

Hauptman stood up and walked away, leaving Tom Kincaid sweating on his Georgia bench. Hauptman himself was satisfied that the purpose of his encounter with Kincaid was now clear.

Kincaid returned to Chicago after he had made clear to Julie that he would pay all of Danny's final expenses. That offer was mildly rebuffed, as Danny's status with the Bureau provided for his funeral.

Tom walked into his penthouse condo off Michigan Avenue and poured a large tumbler of Wild Turkey. He was grateful for his usual method of dulling the edges of his life, but for some reason, he did not drink it. He could still see Danny's face, the burns, and his one eye blazing blue out of his ravaged face.

Help her.

He couldn't rid his mind of his son's last words. They rang in his head like chapel bells calling the holy to vespers. Tom was anything but holy, but he needed to do what had been left undone if only to gain a small measure of peace. In his last interaction with Julie before he left Atlanta, she had made it clear she neither wanted nor needed any help from him. It was as if his desire to do anything that his son would respect had come too late to make a difference.

He wandered into his office, wondering if he could distract himself with work. For one of the only times in his life, he felt uncomfortable in his chair at his large desk, in front of his power wall, a shrine to his career as an agent and lawyer. On the wall, his eyes found a framed and autographed photo of him and Zeke Monroe. For some time now, looking at that photo was not something he enjoyed. For now, though, looking at the framed tribute sparked a thought that maybe Kincaid had overlooked something. Something undone.

Help her.

He opened the door to his office closet, then quickly dialed the combination to a large safe. A lot of the expected comforts were inside—close to $100,000 in cash, expensive jewelry, and a 9 mm handgun. He was not looking for any of these things. He opened a small drawer in the safe and found a sealed plastic bag. In it was an article of clothing, women's clothing. Its owner had not wanted to keep it, as it was a reminder of a day she would rather forget. He had kept it, though. Tom Kincaid was a pragmatic man, and he hedged every bet he had ever made.

Tom sat the bag on his desk and sat looking at it for a long time. He wondered if wherever he was Danny would know. He wondered if this was that undone thing that would heal his soul. He didn't know the answer, but he liked the idea. He dialed a number on his desk phone.

"Hello?"

"Manes, it's Tom Kincaid."

"Yeah, Tom?"

He suddenly realized that he felt alive for the first time in a year.

"I've got something for you."

PART THREE

The Open

The most important days in a person's life are the day they are born, and the day they discover why.

CHAPTER ONE

2015

On the morning of the final round of the U.S. Open, Craig Cantwell awoke suddenly at 6:30 a.m. and bolted upright in bed. He had dreamed about what most third-round leaders of big golf tournaments dream about in one form or another. That everything had gone wrong. In Craig's dream, he had played the final round of the U.S. Open with a ball larger than the holes he was putting into. Everything seemed normal, except for the ball he was putting when he got to the green. It was a Titleist ball, the size of a cantaloupe with a sledgehammer for a putter. The ball could not go into the hole, even when he used his sledgehammer putter to pound it in. Instead of going in, pounding on the ball created a "Gallagher" golf effect that was outrageous; the ball exploded, and he lapsed into confusion about what the appropriate penalty for this bizarre event would be. It seemed to be great comic relief to everyone there, the gallery, his playing partner, commentators; even his caddy was in a fit of laughter.

He stumbled to the bathroom and used some cold tap water to shake the image from his groggy mind. He looked in the mirror and suddenly remembered Robin Williams's old riff about golf:

"So, do you have a nice large hole on a wide-open surface?"

"Fuck noooooooooooooo!!! We make the hole wee and we hide it!"

Craig smiled. At least he could find humor in his stupid golf nightmares.

He looked again at the clock and sighed. *So much for sleeping in.* That had been his plan when he went to bed four hours ago. *Hell, even if I could go back to sleep, I'd probably dream about putting a shot put with an egg whisk or some crazy shit like that.* He smiled again when he remembered an old ritual. That was the ticket.

He looked in on his caddy, Roy Wasson, aka "Waz," and decided to let him sleep. Then he slipped on a pair of jeans and an old T-shirt, grabbed his Scotty Cameron putter and a sleeve of Titleists, and walked out the door.

They were staying across the street from the Parker Golf Center. The center had a driving range, a short par-3 course, a miniature golf course, and a good practice putting and chipping green. It was early, so there were only a handful of people out. Craig walked through the dense morning fog and onto the deserted putting green.

He dumped the balls on the green and leaned on his putter for a minute, taking in the early morning scenery. The fog was thick. He could see the outline of the condos across the street but little else beyond that. There was a substantial amount of dew on the grass, and it smelled like summer. Craig closed his eyes and breathed in the smell of morning on the green grass. This scene took him back to early mornings when he was young and had first discovered and learned to love this stupid game. He would go out to the practice area as the old men were teeing off and work on his putting and chipping while the grass was still wet.

His first teacher, Hank Ames, saw him for the first time on a practice green like this one. He had walked onto the course with a quizzical look on his face. This was where young Craig could be for hours, away from a short and tough childhood, doing something he had a natural gift for.

The thought of Hank evoked an even bigger smile, and he remembered one of his teacher's favorite putting drills. He got over one of the balls, lined up his putter toward a hole about twenty feet away, closed his eyes, and stroked the putt. "Listen close to what the putter and the ball say to each other," Hank would say. Craig could immediately feel that he hit the putt slightly off the center of the putter face. He moved another ball into place and repeated the process. When he felt that he had hit 5 putts that he knew were struck by the putter's sweet spot, he started using his eyes. Craig just wanted to feel the club in his hands and feel it lightly roll the ball. After the dream that woke him, he just needed to reassure his mind, his hands, and his spirit that they could still do this.

Craig ambled over to the three balls on the edge of the green and suddenly felt the sun on his face. The sun was well up and had just finished its job of piercing the morning fog. The fog was burning off, and the sky above it was a brilliant early morning blue.

Another smile. There might be a lot of crazy to deal with in the world, maybe more than usual today, but here, in this spot, he could find peace. He could take this memory

with him into this day in which he might not otherwise find
peace in his mind and heart. He stood about fifteen feet
from one of the practice holes and rhythmically hit three
putts in a row that rolled straight in the center and rattled in
the bottom. He put the balls back into the sleeve, the putter
in the crook of his arm, and walked back to the condo.

Skip Harris, the on-site manager of the condo complex,
was waiting for Craig as he walked back from his short practice session.

"You're up early, Canty. Don't tell me you had trouble
sleepin'."

"Nah, Skip, I been out all night putting in the dark. It's
my thing. I wouldn't let a little 'ole U.S. Open' affect my
sleep."

He grinned. Skip was a buddy from way back.

Skip looked at Craig. "Hey, buddy, don't know what it's
about, but there's somebody here looking for you. Young
gal, cute as hell. She wouldn't believe me when I told her
there was '*no Craig Cantwell staying here.*' She's hanging out
in the courtyard waiting on you."

"Well, I do appreciate a persistent groupie. She doesn't
have a gun, does she?"

"Nah, she's nice enough. She said you'd want to see her."

"Well, okay then."

"Fairways and greens today, buddy," Skip said in parting.

Craig could not remember the last time a golf groupie
had approached him. They were around, of course, and he
had enjoyed his share of female attention back in the day.
But he was forty-seven now and found it hard to believe any
of the attractive young women following the Tour had any
interest in him.

Craig entered the courtyard, and there she was. His eyes and face softened, and he experienced a rush of emotion like he had not felt in some time. It was sweet, familiar, and a little scary all at once. The girl was mid-twenties, dark blonde hair tied back, blue eyes, and the kind of athletic figure that turns a lot of male heads. Medium height with a strong presence about her. When she smiled, he saw the shadow of a hurt she had acquired some years ago. Seeing her now made Craig the happiest he had been in a year.

"Hi, Poppi."

CHAPTER TWO

"Hi, baby," Craig said as Kelly approached and hugged him. It felt better than hoisting the U.S. Open trophy. "I'm surprised to see you here. I'm really glad, but I just didn't think you would want to be around all this."

"Well, I don't know if 'want to' describes it, but it's kinda something I need to do."

Craig was confused. *What does Kelly need to do at the venue for the U.S. Open?*

"Geez, that sounds a little ominous. Are you going skydiving or something?"

"I wish. I think that would be a lot easier."

He could tell from the expression on her face that she wasn't there to skydive. "I came to tell you a few things, things you might not want to hear. However, it's important that you hear them from me before people start talking."

Craig Cantwell, king of the comeback, was speechless. He had an idea of what his daughter was planning, but he wasn't concerned about the effect of her actions on him. He knew the path she was taking would be hard on her.

"Are you sure you want to do this, Kel? Is this the right time for you?"

"It's been too long, Poppi. I am going to do this for me, but also for you. You've been carrying this burden, partly for me, I know, and it's not fair to you. You're the best man I know, and it's not okay that so many people judge you harshly, especially when they don't know the truth."

"It's only important to me that *you* know the truth, Kelly."

She smiled, and it made him think of her mother. "See? That's the man the world needs to know. It's up to you what you share; there are lots of reasons I need to speak out now. You happen to be the most important one."

He was torn by this news. Something in him had always known that Kelly would speak out about the past. He knew in his heart that she needed to do this to heal. The relief he felt was tempered heavily by his instinct to shield and protect his daughter. Like every father, he wanted to spare her the pain, even if that meant taking it on himself. It was hard for him to accept that this was a path she had to walk without him.

"When is it going to happen?"

She looked at him with a foreboding and apologetic look. He knew before she answered.

"Today."

"Today?" Craig repeated. "You *do* know that we have this little golf tournament winding up today? This little U.S. Open thing that your dear old dad is working on winning?"

Kelly looked at him as tears flooded her eyes. She reminded him so much of her mother and the day Rachelle had told him about Kelly for the very first time.

"I do know that, Poppi. We've been planning this for a while. You-know-who would probably be contending. I just didn't know my dad would be leading the damn tournament."

CHAPTER THREE

On the Sunday morning of the U.S. Open at Colorado Golf Club, a dark Chevy Suburban worked its way through the restricted entrances. At a couple of stops, the security personnel used their radios before waving the vehicle through. The occupants of the vehicle had neither players' badges nor the work permits normally required for non-members. Nonetheless, the Suburban worked its way to the Club House, where it stopped at the main entrance— quite a grand one at that—and where they were met by Bill Whitehall of the USGA.

Three men and a woman got out of the Suburban, all obviously law enforcement types of some sort. They had IDs and were armed. They also moved with the serious authority of cops on a mission.

After a brief conversation with Mr. Whitehall, he led them into the ornate Club House. The people watching all this unfold would later note that Whitehall had looked as white as a sheet and that he led them to the players' locker room where all five of the officers walked in, including the woman. Whitehall looked as though he wanted to tell her that it was for men only, but he didn't.

In the second row of expensive wooden lockers, Zeke Monroe was just finishing up lacing his Adidas golf shoes.

His assistant sat in a comfortable chair close by, reading a newspaper. As the contingent approached Zeke Monroe, his assistant stood up with a confused look on his face and watched as the woman walked up to Zeke Monroe's bench, where he stayed seated.

"Ezekiel Monroe?"

Shock and panic flashed briefly across Monroe's face; then he recovered and looked up at her with a dazzling smile. The same smile that was now selling numerous products on clever, well-conceived commercials at peak viewing times.

"Yes, that's me. I go by Zeke. I'm not used to seeing a woman in the men's locker room. I've got nothing against it, though."

Monroe noticed that his "charming" reply had not the slightest effect on the woman. If anything, the glint in her hazel eyes became more intense.

"Excuse me, you can't be here," said Gill Clancy, the retired Navy Seal whose job it was to keep Mr. Monroe safe.

"It's all right," said Whitehall, still obviously unsure of how to act in this situation. "These people are with the FBI."

Rick Hauptman leveled his eyes at Clancy, who noted that this guy also had his hand on a 9 mm Glock. Clancy was a veteran of three Tours as a seal but knew at a glance not to challenge this man.

Hauptman was a SWAT man by trade and so would not normally be here. But a chat with Kelly Keys some months ago had led them all to this spot, and he would not have missed being here for anything—even if it were his final act as an FBI agent.

"Please stay back," he said to Clancy. Both men knew what those three words really meant. "I don't want to, but if necessary, I will kill or die to stop you." Clancy stepped back and could only watch.

The woman resumed, savoring the brief interplay that Hauptman brought to the encounter. In a way, it was satisfying. *Gotta love those SWAT boys*, she thought.

"Mr. Monroe, I am agent Rachel Burris of the FBI."

"Nice to meet you, Agent Burris. What can I do for you?" Monroe said, standing with a smile that said he hoped all Agent Burris wanted was an autograph.

In the few seconds that followed, Rachel Burris looked directly at Monroe as if she was considering which effective self-defense technique to use. The effect of her stare was noticeable on Monroe's face, as his charming "star" facade faded.

"Mr. Monroe, you are under arrest for aggravated sexual assault. Please listen carefully as I read you your rights. You have the right to remain silent. If you give up the right to remain silent . . . "

The color drained from Monroe's face as he listened, the weight of his actions crashing in upon him. He began to shake and slowly collapsed onto the bench behind him. His eyes did not leave the face of Agent Burris. He was struck by how much she looked like his mother as he remembered her from his youth.

"Do you understand these rights, as I have read them to you?" His face pale, Monroe acknowledged Agent Burris's question with a trembling nod. He looked around and seemed to notice Rick Hauptman for the first time. Over six feet, over two hundred pounds, with dark hair and dark eyes that had seen way too much in their time. Even as shocked and scared as he was, Monroe could see that this was a personal thing for this man. He was professional, yet Monroe sensed what danger he would be in if he was in the least uncompliant.

Hauptman stepped toward him. "Please stand up, sir." A polite sentence that was nonetheless a threat. Monroe stood, and Rick Hauptman handcuffed his wrists in front of him, never once looking away from his eyes. Monroe felt an iron grip on his upper arm as Hauptman and the FBI marched him out of the locker room and through the ornate Club House. As they approached the front door, they could see a large throng outside, along with more than a few video cameras. Monroe recoiled, but Hauptman tightened his grip and took him out and straight to the back door of the Suburban, as the crowd parted like the Red Sea before the intensity of the agent's glare.

The crowd was strangely silent as they passed, stunned by the sight of golf's Golden Boy in handcuffs. Finding their voices, the press began shouting questions to the agents and Zeke but got no answers. The agents got in on all sides, and the Suburban moved. The crowd and the cameras could only watch as Zeke Monroe rode off in FBI custody.

CHAPTER FOUR

The first tee of any major championship is an electric place. Grandstands surround the teeing area on three sides, the stands are full, and the players, their caddies, and tournament officials enter through a tunnel. Several thousand fans seated around the tee box create a buzz that is more than slightly distracting to the players. That distracting buzz grows in intensity as the day progresses because the order of the golfers teeing off goes from those farthest from the lead to those closest to it.

Craig Cantwell and "Waz" Wasson walked through the tunnel in the stands to the first tee of the U.S. Open on Father's Day Sunday at Colorado Golf Club. There was little more than a smattering of applause for Craig. He shook hands with the officials on the tee box; he knew both men from many first tees in many tournaments.

Craig took a deep breath and looked down the first fairway. It was a ribbon of green that rolled gently to the left and downhill, framed by white sand traps and pine trees. In the distance, the front range of the Rocky Mountains rose into a blue sky. It was a gorgeous setting, well used by the experts who designed the golf course. Ironically, this pastoral beauty was anything but relaxing for Craig Cantwell.

The nerves felt by a world-class golfer in a big tournament never go away. Craig felt the adrenaline pumping through his body, felt his pulse in his fingertips and the tingle in his limbs. He reminded himself again to breathe and inhaled slowly and deeply, tightening his abdominal muscles slightly as he emptied his lungs before the next breath. He had a fleeting desire to bend over, put his hands on his knees and hyperventilate, something that would no doubt be noted by the crowd. He smiled a little at the thought, the humor of it relaxing to him.

Waz walked over and gave Craig a private, knowing smile. "Gorgeous day, ain't it?"

"You brought that barf bag, right?"

"You know, I forgot it," Waz said in the same low voice. "Just puke on the starter's shoes; it's a great Sports Center moment."

Both men smiled. They were two pros acknowledging that they were nervous and that nerves were a part of the game. Truth be told, they would rather be here than anywhere else in the world.

Jordan Spieth, Craig's playing partner, and his caddy, Michael Grellar, came through the tunnel. In contrast to Craig's entrance, the crowd erupted when they saw Jordan. He waved briefly to the crowd and walked up to Craig and Waz.

"Hey, man, good to be here," Jordan said as he shook hands. Unspoken was his nervousness; this was not something deniable by any golfer in a final round of a major. Jordan was a pro, a past winner of this event. His youthful looks and energy disguised an old soul. He was remarkably mature and grounded for a guy in his early twenties. He and Craig Cantwell knew that a golfer pretending to be calm on the first tee was acting. If you were human, you were nervous.

Just a little casual round, Craig thought as Spieth stepped away to greet the officials.

Waz looked at him in mock seriousness and spoke gravely, "Just remember one thing . . . "

"Yeah?"

"Whatever happens today, there are six hundred million Chinese who don't give a shit."

Craig let out a belly laugh while Waz tried to keep a straight face. "Folks, they don't call him the best caddy on the Tour for nothing."

The USGA official starter nodded to Craig and Jordan, then keyed his mic. "Ladies and gentlemen, we are pleased to welcome you to the 2:06 starting time. From Joplin, Missouri, please welcome Craig Cantwell."

The announcement was followed by polite clapping and more murmurs from the crowd. The public still had mixed feelings for Craig. He waved anyway and managed to get his ball to stay on the tee. Just before he started his pre-shot routine, he looked at Spieth. "Let's have a great day, Jordan."

Spieth's steely eyes caught Craig's. "Play well, Craig."

CHAPTER FIVE

The first hole at Colorado Golf Club is a 644-yard par five. The hole plays downhill, and the fairway is firm and fast, making the yardage a bit deceiving. In the modern world of pro golf, this is an opportunity to make a birdie out of the box. Craig knew this as well as any player in the field.

He narrowed his focus to a very small target on the very right edge of a bunker 352 yards from where he stood. He knew he could not reach the bunker with his tee shot, but the target he had chosen would kick the ball left into the center of the fairway.

Breathing allowed his heart to slow. He focused solely on his target and let his training, experience, and instincts take over. His downswing caught the ball solidly, and the sound of contact, and the ball's movement through the air, echoed back from the canyons of the grandstands. The ball left the clubhead at 160 miles per hour. On impact, Craig knew he had struck his first shot of the day perfectly.

However, as well as Craig hit his tee shot, Jordan Spieth outdrove him. When they got to the point in the fairway where the balls stopped, Craig noted that his playing partner's ball was twenty yards closer to the green.

"Jordan, you still using steroids?" Craig joked, the last salvo against nerves.

His partner smiled. "Not since last week."

Waz told him they had 312 yards left to the hole, 297 to the front of the green. There was no reason to lay up, no hazards between them and the target to be aware of. The slight following wind and downhill shot made getting the distance right a challenge.

"What do you like, bud?" Craig asked Waz.

"We got some wind help, maybe a half club. I like 5 wood, the better miss is short." Translation: hitting a 3 wood well might just go past the hole, leaving a tougher third shot.

"I like the five too."

Again, he caught the shot perfectly. It flew 250 yards, then settled into a downhill roll. Craig watched his ball as the cheers from the crowd grew louder. His shot was tracking right at the flag; the question was if it would stop. After buzzing the flagstick, it kept going past, finally stopping thirty-five feet long of the hole. A solid shot and a likely birdie.

Even though Craig was resigned to focusing only on his game, he could not avoid seeing Jordan's second shot; it was brilliant. Spieth hit a gorgeous 3 hybrid that tracked on the same line as Craig's 5 wood. The difference was that Jordan's shot had the exact right distance; it rolled the last forty yards and stopped within four feet of the hole. The crowd roared its approval. The intensity of the cheers increased the entire walk up to the first green.

When Jordan made his eagle putt after Craig had two-putted for birdie, Craig's lead was down to one shot. As important as it was to focus only on his own game, Craig was aware of this and felt even more pressure.

"Good start, pards," Waz said to him. "We keep doing that, we're good." Craig nodded as he walked to the second tee, his head down, serious now.

"Hey," Waz called. When Craig looked over, he saw his friend smiling. "Remember the Chinese."

Craig smiled at that, thankful again that he had Waz on his bag. *Perspective.* His caddy's humor on the first tee was both funny and useful. Craig had learned the value of shifting his perspective, and it was now something he could use.

On the way to the second hole, he passed a father with a little girl perched on his shoulders. He looked at them and smiled, remembering that it was Father's Day. His fatherhood, though secret, was a deeply set anchor he could hold on to, even in the crucible of the final round of the U.S. Open. He thought of Kelly then, something that always made him smile, even though today might be tough for his daughter. *Again, perspective.* No matter the outcome of today, he would always be there for Kelly.

CHAPTER SIX

At the PGA Championship at Winged Foot

Craig had come to really enjoy any association with the Golf Channel. Most Tour players cooperated and worked with golf's twenty-four-hours, seven-days-a-week TV outlet, simply referred to as GC, for obvious reasons. Craig was not much different. However, he had come to appreciate it more because his daughter was always a part of GC coverage at Tour events. She was nearly always on-site, and he was able to see her a lot. That alone was a great reason for him to interact with all things Golf Channel.

Craig and Kelly had developed a ritual. They almost always had breakfast together before a final round he was playing in. This worked well both ways since Craig was always inspired by his daughter and she, in turn, got insights that helped her connect with her audience on the air in more interesting ways. These pre-round Sunday breakfasts were something that Craig always looked forward to. He felt they were a great way to get in the perfect state of mind before a final round. Roy agreed and sometimes joined them.

However, pre-round breakfasts had never been the same since that day two years ago when Craig had first suspected that something terrible had happened to Kelly.

It was mid-morning, and Craig and Kelly had made plans to meet for breakfast before the final round of the PGA at Winged Foot. He was two shots off the lead and had played well all week. Craig had been close in majors before, but this time he felt good about finally breaking through. Kelly was set to do a piece on the top three contenders. She was excited about meeting him that morning, so he was surprised when she was late. He sent her a text but got no response. That was when his "Dad'" alarm went off. He knew how self-sufficient and put together Kelly was. She wasn't a "no-show, no-call" kind of person. His instincts told him something was wrong.

He was still pondering whether to go to Kelly's room to check on her when Christi Wilkins walked into the restaurant. Christi was a production assistant for the Golf Channel, and Craig knew her well. She appeared tense and worried until she saw Craig. Then she smiled and walked over.

"Hi, Craig, how are you?" Craig's anxiety ratcheted up a notch when he sensed how nervous Christi was.

"Morning, Christi. Do you know where Kelly is? We were supposed to talk over breakfast today."

"I know, and I'm so sorry. She sent me over because she couldn't make it. She woke up this morning and was just like feeling terrible. I mean, like she is starting to feel better, so she can get through the day. She said to tell you to have a great round, and hopefully, she can interview you after the win."

"Oh, okay." Something still didn't seem right to Craig. He had known Christi for three years and had always seen her as a pro. Now she had just rambled through this explanation like a ditzy seventeen-year-old trying to explain the dented fender on her dad's Lexus. Plus, Kelly had not answered his text, which was unlike her. Despite his concern, he really could not voice it to Christi. No one, not even Kelly, knew he was her father.

"She just said to wish you great luck, and she will see you soon."

"Tell her to feel better."

"Oh, I will. Good luck today, Craig," Christi gushed and hurried out of the restaurant.

He went back to eating his breakfast, still distracted by his feeling that something was wrong.

Craig left the restaurant and walked toward the locker room. Then he changed his mind and turned toward the front of the clubhouse. He had to find out what was up. This was going to bother him all day if he didn't, and he was, after all, contending in the freaking PGA Championship.

The Golf Channel set and production crew were on-site. He walked in that direction, rehearsing in his mind how to word his inquiry. He had to voice a more casual concern than he felt.

Craig saw Cliff Lombard, one of the GC producers, talking to a cluster of people who normally worked with Kelly on her commentaries. Craig casually waved, and Cliff came over his way with a big smile.

"You here to pre-tape your winner's interview?" Cliff joked.

"Uh, let's wait a while on that one. No, I was supposed to meet with Kelly this morning for breakfast, and Christi told me she was under the weather. Just thought I'd check to see if she's okay."

"She's okay." Cliff lowered his voice to a conspiratorial tone. "You know how it is; sooner or later these youngsters are gonna party just a little too much. She's just gotta learn to play hurt, that's all."

Craig shook his head and smiled back. "Well, we've all been there," he said. What he was thinking was something else entirely.

Bullshit. Kelly rarely drank and she loved her work. She wouldn't jeopardize it by partying all night. And even if she'd been up late, she would still be on it this morning. He was also convinced that nothing short of double pneumonia would have caused her to miss breakfast with him on the last day of a major championship. He could tell that Cliff was snowing him, but he didn't know why. Christi had done likewise, but if he wanted to keep his promise to Rachelle, he could not voice his fatherly concerns.

As Craig stood there wrestling with his emotions, a black Escalade pulled up, and Kelly Keys got out of the passenger side. Craig could tell with one glance that she was not okay, but she plastered a smile on to her face and walked briskly up to Cliff and Craig.

"Okay, boss, if you are willing to forgive last evening's excesses, I'm ready to do the show topless if that will get me back in your good graces."

She turned to Craig. "Sorry about breakfast. That whole TV corruption thing is real, I guess."

Before Craig could respond, Cliff interrupted, "Okay then, Sport, we've got work to do. Let's see if you can play hurt."

As they walked away, Kelly looked over her shoulder at Craig. "Have a good round."

Craig saw something in her expression that he had never seen before. Her tough facade had dropped for just an instant, and he'd seen hurt and humiliation in her eyes. He stood there for a few seconds and watched as they started miking her up for her segment. She was back on now, joking with her mates about needing a bucket to puke in.

Daddy Craig's bullshit meter was on overload, but he had a final round to prepare for. He turned back toward the players' area and glanced again at the Escalade Kelly had just arrived in. The driver was standing next to the car looking over at the GC crew. Craig realized he wasn't really a driver. It was the way he stood looking over the scene. The "driver" turned and nodded at Cliff, and Cliff went over to him and extended his hand. The "driver" took Cliff's hand in his and pulled him close. Something was being said that no one else could hear. What was clear to Craig was the threat in the man's gaze. Cliff nodded and backed away, glancing briefly at Craig.

As he got back in the Escalade, the driver looked Craig's way as well. Craig was attempting to place the dude when it hit him. This guy wasn't a driver. Craig had seen him in the wake of the newest star on Tour, the next Tiger Woods, Zeke Monroe. The last thing Craig saw was the vanity plates as the Escalade pulled away.

"FXR."

CHAPTER SEVEN

Craig Cantwell's play in the first part of the final round was very good; anyone who knew golf and was watching could see that. The fact that he had lost the two-shot lead he had started with was due entirely to the brilliant play of his fellow competitors. For the first part of the final round, Craig felt like a commuter obeying the speed limit while faster cars flew by him.

On the second hole, a picturesque 154-yard par 3, Spieth continued his onslaught. Jordan struck a solid 9 iron that flew over the top of the flagstick, caught the upslope behind, and slowly spun back to eighteen inches from the hole. Craig hit a solid iron just right of the left-placed flag, leaving just fifteen feet for his birdie. When Craig's solid putt caught the left edge of the hole and stayed out, he found he was tied with Jordan Spieth.

Craig reminded himself to be patient and focused as they headed to the third tee. *A lot of golf to play—stay present.* He had not hit a poor shot the first two holes, but his playing partner had just been brilliant.

Craig hit another solid tee shot on the third, a 3 wood aimed at the center of the fairway. At 428 yards, with a sharp dogleg left, the third is a finesse hole. He didn't even watch his ball finish rolling; he was certain he had hit it well. When he and Waz reached his drive, his patience was further tested.

Craig had indeed hit his drive well. It was in the left middle of the fairway. It had rolled far enough to be in an old divot. An inch shorter or two inches longer and his lie would have been perfect. As it was, his ball was sitting in a hole made by a golf club a good quarter inch below the grass.

"Well, rat farts," Craig said softly to Waz, borrowing a line from *Caddyshack.*

"Your honor, your honor," Waz gave back, both smiling briefly.

The uncertain thing about a shot like this, even for a pro, is how far the ball will go. The club would have to contact the earth before it contacted the ball, which creates a lack of control.

Craig knew the ball would not stop quickly when it landed on the green. There was a deep bunker between him and the flag; he would aim away from the flag and plan to have the ball hit short of the green and run up to the putting service.

He hit the shot as well as he could, the ball coming out of the hole with a large chunk of sod. Despite aiming it away from the yawning sand trap fronting the flag, the poor lie made the ball behave oddly; the flight started left, then it seemed to float like a knuckleball and veer right, heading toward the bunker. All Craig and Waz could do was watch as his shot found the front bunker.

When they reached the green and looked in the sand, the first thought Craig had was not *Caddyshack* humor. His ball had hit the face of the bunker and was half-buried. It was on the upslope about four feet below the front lip of the sand trap. The way to hit this shot was to hit the sand behind the ball hard with a sand wedge and have a small shovel full of sand fly out of the bunker, carrying the ball with it. Craig executed this trouble shot well, but with no spin, the ball scooted fifteen feet past the flag.

With Waz's help, Craig worked as hard as he could on making this par-saving putt. Doing this is both technical and intangible, feeling and visualizing the success of the stroke as well as trusting the physical technique. Craig was sure he had made it when he executed his stroke. His eyes tracked the ball's roll, heading right to the hole on his intended line. It veered just slightly as it got there, and instead of dropping in, caught the very left side of the hole and rolled around two-thirds of the edge. His ball stopped on the front right of the hole, a fraction of an inch from going in.

After tapping in for bogey, Craig had lost three shots in three holes to Jordan Spieth. He was now one shot behind the new leader.

The fourth hole at CGC is a beast of a par 4, five hundred yards into the prevailing breeze. If that were not enough, the shortest route to the green—up the left—was guarded by a natural waste area. This was a mini canyon—a gulch—that was filled with large rocks, cactus, and scrub oak. Craig was certain that you could probably find the dead bodies of golfers down there.

Craig refocused and hit a superb drive on the fourth, splitting the fairway with a low bullet that went 310 yards into a slight breeze. While he never rooted for an opponent to make a mistake, he did note that Jordan Spieth hit his drive a bit too far right and caught a fairway bunker on that side. Jordan had little choice from the bunker and punched a 7-iron out of the bunker that stopped a good sixty yards short of the green. He would have a challenging up and down opportunity to save par.

Craig hit a solid 4-iron through the wind, his shot catching the right to left slope of the green and stopping twenty-five feet below the hole. This was an excellent shot, giving him a good run at a birdie. If Spieth could not get up and down for par, Craig saw a chance to make up the ground he'd lost on the third hole.

Craig and Waz waited on the green while Jordan and his caddy worked on his pitch to the green. As they sized up the shot, there was a huge roar from the gallery up around the fifth green. Craig and Waz had heard a lot of crowd noise in their time on the Tour and knew this roar was attached to something big.

Jordan played a crisp knockdown wedge from his spot short of the fourth. It was a crowd-pleasing shot, as the ball's flight gives the illusion of the ball being hit way too hard. This shot had a lot of spin, however, and after the ball hopped briskly on the green the spin slowed it down and the ball began a gentle roll toward the hole. It seemed the ball had to stop short, yet it kept going. As the crowd noise built to a crescendo, Craig and Waz watched Spieth's ball tumble into the hole for a birdie. He was now four under par for the round and two shots ahead.

Craig Cantwell putted for a solid par on the fourth hole, and the group walked to the fifth tee. As Craig and Waz walked past the gallery ropes, a faceless heckler in the crowd called out, "Karma is a bitch, huh, Cantwell?" Waz immediately turned his head, hoping to lock eyes with the lunkhead. Craig kept walking and did not react—visibly.

Though a man of his experience knew the logic of what was going on so far, Craig Cantwell was no Mr. Spock. No golfer is. He was aware of many, many things firing off in his subconscious as a result of where he was. A variety of thoughts and feelings were arrayed before him like items in a buffet line: *Maybe the jerk is right. Maybe I don't deserve to win. I haven't missed a shot yet; how can I be behind? Why the hell don't I get the break Jordan just got? Jesus, how good do I have to play?*

As they reached the fifth tee, another loud murmur rippled through the gallery, followed by cheering. Up ahead of them, former U.S. Open champion Dustin Johnson had eagled the fifth hole by holing out from 180 yards with his second shot. Johnson and Spieth were now tied for the lead at 6 under par with Craig two shots behind.

Roy Wasson was not only an exceptional caddy but also a fierce friend. He knew that Craig needed him to get grounded again.

"Pards, we can't do nothing about anybody else. We are playing fine. We ain't close to done, and our time is coming. Focus on this next shot."

Craig looked in his friend's eyes and nodded. The last two years had been hard for a lot of reasons, but he could choose to see them as callouses that made his spirit stronger. Recent experience had taught him that he could only be his best. Despite his desire for control overall, he could only control himself. Grounding himself in his own assessment of his life, not the judgment of others, is what brought him back here. Despite a nagging voice that he had failed, he had to choose to focus now on what he had, not what he had lost.

CHAPTER EIGHT

Rachelle's Funeral

Craig stood with other mourners at Park Cemetery. The gray July sky was muggy and warm. The morning drizzle had stopped. They had all come from the service at a local funeral home for the internment here. The service was heavy with FBI presence. Colleagues and friends of Rachelle's in the Bureau had spoken about her record, about their friendships with her, shared anecdotes that were mainly funny and related to her service to the Bureau.

The director gave a short eulogy and, while he noted her heroism, he omitted many details that caused Craig to begin to wonder how she had died. It did not appear that the Bureau was at liberty to provide details. In a way, it was fitting because Rachelle would never share any specifics about her work either.

"Why was it so hard for her to be safe?" Craig wondered. "Why wasn't I enough for you to leave the Bureau and be happy? What could I have done or said to make you want to live a happy life? You told me you wanted that life. What was it about me that kept you from it?

He looked up and saw Kelly sitting between her grandparents, and his indulgence in grief was interrupted. She looked sad and shocked, it hurt his heart to see her that way. He knew then that he had to become her comfort, that there was no place for anger and grief, only room for being the father she needed now and going forward. "But wait," he thought, "no one else knows, except Rachelle, that I'm Kelly's father." He wondered, amid his confusion, if Rachelle would want the secret told now.

CHAPTER NINE

As the group moved off the five green, towards the sixth tee, they saw that they would be delayed for a while. The group ahead, Dustin Johnston and Justin Rose, was still on the tee looking at the group ahead of them on the green. The sixth is a 251-yard par 3, which is a recipe for a round delay even without the pressure of the U.S. Open.

"Got a deck of cards?" Craig asked Jordan.

"Sure, how about a little Blackjack, boys?"

Craig smiled and retrieved an energy bar and a water bottle from his bag. He and Jordan would settle in for the wait, entertaining themselves enough to stay patient but not enough to distract.

Waz stepped away for a minute. As Craig waited for him to return, one of Craig's demons—a similar delay in a major championship a couple of years back—popped up to fill in the void. Craig fought it but could not help but remember the situation in the final round of the PGA Championship at Winged Foot two years ago.

2013

Craig Cantwell was in the fourth to last group in a two-some with Jim Furyk and his long-time caddy, Mike "Fluff" Cowan. It was a good pairing for Craig and his caddy, Roy "Waz" Wasson, in several ways. First, Jim and Craig played at a similar pace and had compatible temperaments on the course. Both could be described as amiable competitors. Also, Craig and Jim knew each other and enjoyed each other's company as did their caddies. Inevitably, the conversation during delays was enjoyable yet not distracting. All the parties knew the tone that such discussions needed to take, pleasant yet not so absorbing as to inhibit re-focus when it was time to play a shot.

The group encountered a long delay at the sixth hole. The sixth is a par three, and the Cantwell/Furyk twosome was the third group on the hole. The twosome two groups ahead had just left the tee when Jim and Craig and their caddies got there. Both Craig and Jim knew that to be impatient was like poison to their chances of winning, so they settled into what was likely a twenty-minute wait.

Craig grabbed a snack and water bottle from his golf bag, and he and Furyk chatted. It was a typical small talk. Jim talked about his family and then segued into sports. Waz and Fluff were a ways away talking as well. At a lull in the conversation with Furyk, Craig ambled over to the caddies. He came over in the middle of a Fluff monologue in time to hear him say, " . . . Bull said he was surprised too, but it sounded real."

"It's a little tough to believe, isn't it?" Waz replied. "I keep hearing that, though, so you wonder. It's like if I hear one rumor, I can dismiss it. Even if I hear it twice, I can dismiss it, but after a few more times, you start to wonder."

Craig was immediately curious about the nature of the conversation but decided not to ask because he didn't want to be distracted.

Waz cut short his conversation with Fluff by asking Craig if they were getting close to teeing off.

"Still waiting for takeoff," Craig said. Curiosity won out since they were still waiting. "What was that all about?" Craig asked.

"Ah, just some strange things I'm hearing about Monroe," Waz replied. "You know Red Bull?"

"Yeah, a little, not real well," Craig said. Red Bull was a caddy, nicknamed as a result of his apparent addiction to the energy drink, who had worked for Zeke Monroe, as well as a few other players. "What about him?"

"Fluff tells me Monroe didn't fire him; he quit." Roughly six months before, Zeke Monroe had changed caddies. This was not big news. Players often went "in different directions" and fired caddies all the time. Long-tenured player/caddy relationships like that of Craig and Waz (and Furyk and Fluff) were rare; briefer caddy/player combos were more the norm.

"A caddy quitting a bag like that is pretty strange. He had to be making big money with Monroe. Is Zeke that big an asshole?"

Waz gave Craig a sardonic look over the top of his shades. "If that were the only criteria, I would have left a long time ago."

"Valid point."

After a small shared smirk, Waz went on.

"No, Fluff said Bull told him he just couldn't stomach how Monroe treats women. Said he had a friend who dated Zeke and she told him that Zeke was more than a jerk."

Craig shrugged. "A lot of times, one side of the story is no way to judge a guy." He wouldn't want someone to judge him solely on the word of his ex-wife, for example.

"Yeah, yeah, I know. But it sounds weirder than that."

"Hey, boys, we're getting close," Fluff called from the tee, and they started toward the markers.

Craig pulled his glove from his pocket and put it on. He undid and reattached the Velcro twice. He focused on hitting his shot, but, nevertheless, something nagged at him in the back of his mind about what Waz had said.

Even though he was absorbed in playing golf and felt the pressure of the final round of a major championship, Craig still found his mind wandering back to Waz's comments about Zeke Monroe. If they had been able to play faster, Craig would not have had time to think about it. The problem was that the pace of play had slowed to a crawl. They were waiting on nearly every shot, and the tendency is to become impatient. As a seasoned player, Craig knew that being impatient would hurt his chances of playing his best significantly. So, he had to distract himself some way. This knowledge and the lingering feeling about what Waz had said about Monroe, coupled with the strange incident on the Golf Channel set that morning, pulled him into a need to know more about Monroe.

At the eleventh hole, another par 3, the group encountered an even longer delay. Two groups ahead, a player had been unable to find his ball and after a long search had returned to the tee. Jim and Craig shared a glance and a brief head shake as they saw the two-group delay. Jim took a seat on a bench and looked to be meditating. Craig knew not to intrude and walked over to Fluff, who was re-stocking his caddy bib with balls and tees and making sure his man had enough water for the final holes.

"Enjoying the death march?" Fluff asked Craig in his Northeastern accent.

"You bet," Craig said sarcastically. "No choice, right?"

"That's for sure."

"Hey, Waz was telling me that he's hearing some strange stuff about Monroe. You catch any of that?" They had time, and Craig just had to find out what he could.

"Yeah, well. Who knows?" Fluff was obviously reluctant to say much. He knew Waz well, but Craig not as much. He didn't want to be the caddy that betrayed confidences and started rumors.

Craig moved to Fluff's other side, away from the gallery ropes and lowered his voice.

"Look, I'm not going to CNN about this. I would just like to know if one of our guys is dangerous."

Fluff considered Craig's words for a moment, then glanced Jim's way. Furyk was still seated and seemed to be in his own world. The caddy looked back at Craig.

"Red Bull has this cousin. They grew up close, and she was shadowing him on Tour earlier in the first part of the year. She's a real cutie, and she catches Zeke's eye, Bull being his caddy and all. Well, at Pebble, this girl, her name is Amanda, goes to Bull Saturday morning and says something's come up and she's gotta go home. Bull can tell she is really shaken up. Finally, she tells him the last thing she remembers the night before is having a drink with Zeke. She wakes up, her clothes are on backward, she feels like shit, and she's sure she had sex but doesn't remember a thing. Some lawyer comes in and tells her she got shitfaced the night before and 'embarrassed' Monroe and that he wants to see that she doesn't do it again."

"A lawyer?" Craig asked. "Did she say who it was?"

"No, she didn't. But Bull thinks Monroe roofied her, man, and then got some mouthpiece to shut her up. Bull's been looking into this. I think he might have even hired a PI, and he thinks Monroe has done this shit before."

"Jesus," Craig said. It was hard to hide the feeling that Fluff's story had produced. He remembered seeing Kelly that morning and how she said she'd missed breakfast because she was "hungover."

That was probably all there was to it, he had told himself. Except what he remembered most about that morning was Kelly's last glance at him—that hurt, scared, desperate light in her eyes.

This left him with two things to wonder about, neither of which was beneficial to him winning a major golf tournament. The first was, had Kelly scheduled an interview the night before with Zeke Monroe? The second—who was the mystery "lawyer"?

CHAPTER TEN

The sixth hole at CGC is just a "petite" 251-yard, par 3 for the pros. The course designers were good at deception, that fact no more evident than here. The yardage (a very good shot with a driver for most amateurs) was a sham—up in front of the green was a kick slope that sent shots bounding forward. A player needed only to fly a shot 215 yards to have it bound forward and find the putting surface. A little knowledge of the course (which Craig and Waz had) canceled out the long distance. That challenge negated, the real one of distance control was what the players focused on. Variables like how far their shots might bounce and roll with the slope, as well as wind conditions, caused the delays on this hole.

After having lost his lead in the final round, now two behind both Spieth and Johnson, Craig had to stifle the desire to make up ground right away. His inner demons told him to press; his golf experience (and his caddy) told him they had thirteen holes left in this final round. He had to remember that anything could happen over that stretch— both to him and his fellow competitors. He imagined there were two deals on the table: one was to go victim to his lack of breaks and his playing partner's streak of good ones. The second was to recognize that fortune always swings like a pendulum and that if he stuck to what he knew and trusted it, good things would happen.

The green had finally cleared, and Craig stood next to Waz and pulled on his glove.

"You hear anything from the Chinese?"

Waz smiled and shrugged, sensing his friend and boss had gone through their wait and had come out with a constructive state of mind.

"They still don't give a shit," he said lightly.

"Well, I still got you," Craig said. "What do you like here?"

After a short discussion, Waz handed him the 5 iron. Once the club was selected, Craig remembered a great shot with that same club—one that happened two days ago on this same hole. Friday, he had hit a 5 iron to three feet from the flag here. It was a great image for him to bring as he stepped to the shot.

The rhythm of his swing was smooth, and the ball sprang off the clubface toward his target. As planned, the ball flew 220 yards on a line to the flag. Craig had again executed his swing well, offering the shot up to the slope in front of the green, the wind, and the mercy of the golf gods. His ball took a hard bounce off the firm ground and another one just short of the green. When it hit the putting surface, the ball had no backspin and rolled through the green. It finally stopped in the long grass between the back of the green and a bunker, some forty feet from the flagstick.

When Craig and Jordan Spieth reached the sixth green, they saw that both their shots had run through the putting surface into the long grass beyond. Both thought they hit their tee shots perfectly. The wry smiles on their faces reflected their chagrin.

"Welcome to Sunday at the Open," said Jordan.

Craig nodded as he looked over his lie. The grass was three and a half inches deep here, and a golf ball in grass that deep can react differently when hit by a golf club. The blades of grass between the club and the ball will make distance control uncertain. Craig had to read his lie like a fortune-teller reading Tarot Cards. After a couple of practice swings in the turf, Craig chopped down on his ball with a sand wedge, doing his best to estimate how far it would fly and then roll. He flew it right at his first target, but the grass robbed the ball of any spin, and it scooted on the firm green rather than checking as he planned. The result left him twelve feet from the hole—a putt he needed to avoid falling further behind.

Craig drove any images of bogey from his mind and focused firmly on the putt going in. He made a decisive read of the break (the green was fast and running away so there was almost none) and narrowed his sight to the smallest possible target. He focused on one blade of grass on the back edge of the hole and used his putter to send the ball there. Craig's fixation with the vision of his putt going in the hole was so total that the crowd's acknowledgment of it going in was almost a surprise. He had his par on 6 and now could breathe and focus on the next shot.

When he got to the seventh tee, Craig saw an opportunity to be aggressive and make up some ground on the lead. At par 5 and 583 yards, the seventh hole could be a bit deceiving; the hole could be shortened by driving over a fairway bunker jutting in from the right side. Taking the risk of going over that bunker bore the reward of a chance to hit the small green in two. Success here could yield an eagle. Failure to clear the bunker had a consequence. The lip of that pit was high and steep, and landing in there meant a chip out either sideways or short, making bogey or even double bogey very possible.

When they stepped up to the tee, Craig was about to propose an aggressive driver over the bunker for his caddy's approval. When he looked to Waz, he realized no words were needed. Waz had already pulled the headcover off his driver and was handing it over.

"You like this?" Waz said in golf parlance.

"Does the pope shit in the woods?" Craig answered back in a phrase that his caddy understood completely.

Craig anchored his mind in a vision of the drive he wanted. He knew he could hit this shot, more than that he knew he would. The carry over the right side of the cross bunker was 290 yards, "the ideal line." Craig did not need 100 percent of his swing to clear that distance. He just needed to surpass the normal 80 percent that pros use regularly. There was a bit of extra power and even more extra focus on the right swing. As soon as he swung through and held his finished position, Craig knew he had caught the drive flush. His ball cleared the bunker by ten yards and settled in two a roll down the fairway. It stopped in a perfect position to go for the green into 250 yards from the flag.

As they started walking, Craig handed the driver back to Waz.

"Sure is good to see that the pope is regular today," Waz said with a grin.

Craig allowed a tight smile and realized that they were probably on camera and that commentators were at this moment speculating on the golf strategy he and his caddy were discussing.

Jordan was close enough to hear the exchange. After admiring Craig's drive, he could not help joining in.

"After that, I may convert to Catholicism," he said, getting a laugh from Craig, Waz, and his own caddy.

"Do you realize how much I would get fined if they miked me up?" Craig asked the group.

Craig and Waz shifted back on task when they reached his ball. They decided on a 4-iron, still anticipating the ability to roll the shot part of the way to the green. When Craig again hit the shot flush, they were worried he might have hit it too well. This time the ground and the golf gods smiled; his second shot rolled softly up onto the small putting surface, twenty feet from eagle.

Since Spieth had not reached the green in two and had already missed his birdie putt and settled for par, Craig had a chance to tie the lead if he made his eagle putt. Both he and Waz were in an aggressive mode now; neither one would entertain any idea that did not include this putt going in. The putt had a gradual right-to-left break, but not a severe one. If Craig could pick any line for this length putt, this was the one he would choose. He put all his intention on his vision of the putt going in. He got over the putt and put a confident firm stroke on the ball.

This putting movement was the same one he had built his lead with. The ball left the face of his putter and rolled cleanly as if it were on rails leading to the hole, machine-like in its movement. This firm putt was Craig regaining both his hold on the U.S. Open and his strength. This putt would put him back in a tie for the lead and in confident control of this last round. As the putt passed the halfway point to the hole, he knew that it was preordained that the ball would finish the journey at the bottom of the hole.

Except it missed.

Craig's confident stroke on his par-saving putt on the last green worked against him here. The putt had just a fraction too much speed, and it missed on the high side, buzzing the edge of the hole and going three feet past. He had taken a step out of his stance toward the hole when the ball was halfway there, ready to pick the ball out of the hole and acknowledge the crowd's cheer of his eagle. When it missed, he stopped dead in mid-step, his face showing his disbelief.

In just the short period of time from when he hit this eagle putt until it missed, Craig Cantwell had formed an expectation. He had gotten just that far ahead of himself in his thoughts, and when the result was different, he was stunned. Not a lot, but enough to jar him out of his present confident state. Enough for a spec of doubt, a sprinkle of the victim, to creep in. This was a brief indulgence in the unfairness of three superb efforts not yielding the eagle he needed. Justified, certainly—any golfer living can empathize with what Craig felt.

This was a state of mind that had to be discarded before another shot was struck. Unfortunately, the allure of this menagerie of victimhood can hang on; he retained just enough of it when he stepped to his short birdie putt that this one too was still above ground when it stopped.

CHAPTER ELEVEN

The Last Round at Winged Foot

The pace of play improved only slightly as the last round progressed. After the delay at the par 3 eleventh hole, Craig found himself four shots behind. He would not press; as a pro, he knew better. But a more aggressive approach was needed if he was going to close the gap and have a chance at winning. The fourteenth hole was an opportunity to make up ground, a risk/reward par 5, one that Craig had chosen to layup off the tee the first three rounds.

On Sunday, he could no longer afford caution and attempted to hit a driver to a narrow slot of fairway to the left of a cavernous bunker. The carry was nearly three hundred yards, and from the tee, the landing area looked about as wide as a bathtub. Craig pounded the driver, knowing he had hit it well enough to cover the distance. His ball cleared the hazard, and for a moment looked as if it would find the small landing area and give him a great shot at reaching the green in two and carding an eagle. At the very last second, the shot veered right and splashed in the bunker, going to the bottom with a "Winged Foot" bunker lip of twelve feet between Craig and escape. He was over-aggressive with the recovery shot, which hit the top of the bunker lip, went straight up in the air, then came down in the same bunker and to rest a few feet in front of where it was before he hit it.

The resulting double-bogey took Craig out of contention for the championship.

After holing out on the eighteenth, Craig doffed his cap and shook hands with Furyk and Fluff. Proceeding to the scoring area to sign his card, he discovered that he was in eighth place. With six players still on the course, and all of them ahead of him, the worst he could finish was eighth. While he was disappointed in the lack of a win, he could still notch another top ten finish in a major. He would like a win, but eighth wasn't bad. A payday just under $100K wasn't bad for a week's work.

Craig would be heading to the airport soon, but he wanted to see Kelly before he left, if he could. As a member of the media, she was most likely pretty busy, but after this morning, he at least wanted to verify that she was okay.

Craig ambled toward the press area. Zeke Monroe had won the PGA Championship and would be giving a post-round press conference. There were lots of people around, both inside and outside the press room, and Craig hoped to see Kelly briefly before he headed out.

When he got to the press center, he saw Monroe walk in, which meant the press conference was just starting. Still outside, he shrugged, thinking that he would miss Kelly. He would have to stay around until things concluded in the press center. That was the only way he would catch her; she would no doubt be glued to her chair as the new champion answered questions.

Some thirty feet away to Craig's right, there was another entrance to the press area. Craig looked through an open door, just as Monroe started the press conference and saw Kelly out of the corner of his eye rush out of the room, a look of sheer panic on her face. She did not see Craig as she slipped into the women's bathroom a short distance away. Craig was confused and startled by her demeanor, not to mention the fact that she had bolted from the press room just as the new PGA Champion began answering questions. On impulse, Craig walked in the direction of the ladies' room. As he stepped out into the hall, through the door Kelly had just exited, he nearly ran into a man with blond hair and intense eyes, wearing an expensive suit.

All the other people inside and outside the press room were riveted by what Zeke Monroe was saying, all except Craig and this man. He reminded Craig of a secret service agent, his expression was that intense. He met Craig's eyes for just a moment, then casually walked to the other side of the hall, looking out a window over the Winged Foot grounds.

Craig realized in a flash that this was the same man who had driven up to the Golf Channel set that morning with Kelly in the black Escalade. With sudden terror, Craig knew what had happened to his daughter the night before.

In the next forty minutes, until he broke a bone in Zeke Monroe's face with his right fist, Craig Cantwell agonizingly recounted what he knew. He knew that he was Kelly Keys' father and that no one else in the world except her mother knew that. He knew that he had pledged secrecy to Rachelle about that fact. He knew that Zeke Monroe had raped his daughter the night before. He knew that Monroe's "lawyer," whoever the hell he was, was going to make sure that the new golden boy got away with it. He somehow knew that Kelly would not or could not accuse Monroe and that, if she did, she would have little or no support for such an accusation. Most of all, he knew he had failed. He had failed in a golf tournament, again. He had failed to know his only daughter, and to have her know him. He had failed to protect her.

CHAPTER TWELVE

A round of golf for the serious and competitive golfer provides inevitable blows to the golfer's psyche. So much of success in competitive golf is the player's ability to withstand these mental and emotional body shots. The higher the pressure, the harder it is. When pressure and circumstances and failure start to cascade on a player like a wave over a small boat, certain emotional moorings can give way. What a golfer can normally shrug off can become a huge burden.

As a boxer might say, "Everyone has a plan until they get hit."

When he was poised to charge back, Craig's 3 putt on the seventh green was a body blow that staggered him. This is never outwardly visible to the casual observer. It manifests in subtle changes in how the player thinks, and this, in turn, affects how he executes shots.

Craig stepped to the short par 4 eighth tee, ready to bite through steel. He was irritated, annoyed, okay, downright pissed, at how things had been going so far. In his mind, there was no tangible reason why he had lost his lead. He was even par for the round and felt he had played well enough to be 3 or 4 under par. His anger and irritation were where he went to avoid despondency. An athlete can instinctively use anger to push through. Golf, unfortunately, is a game that rarely rewards this approach.

The eighth at CGC is a par 4 of only 311 yards, and the green can be driven with a good tee shot. The siren call of the green can make a golfer forget about the hazards surrounding the target—trees, deep swales, and bunkers waiting to devour even a small miss. Roy Wasson could sense the heat in his boss as a result of the 3 putt on 7, something that only grew on their silent walk to the eighth tee. He knew that a bit of time would cool Craig back to golf reality and silently hoped they had a delay. However, they found the hole clear, and Craig stepped up impatiently to the tee.

Waz did not want his man being aggressive in his present state, so he tried to counsel caution.

"I like a 3 hybrid to that flat spot left of center, boss."

Craig didn't glance away from the flag 310 yards away. "Nah, let's get there. Driver."

Waz hesitated. It was not the shot he didn't like; it was his player's mood. Before he could state his case, Craig grabbed the driver out of the bag, took off the headcover, and handed it to Waz. The caddy could only step back and hope his man could pull a great shot out of his still steaming ass. From the tee box, the green looked as large as an inner tube in a roiling sea. There was an intermittent breeze blowing in from the left that was almost impossible to judge. Unlike the driver Craig hit on the last hole, this landing area was not 35 yards wide; he would have to send this ball 310 yards in the air and land it in an area about the size of a Mercedes compact—and get it to stop.

Craig stepped to his teed ball, and for the first time that day, he swung from his shoes. The action back was quick, the move down even quicker. One could freeze a photo at any point in this swing and appropriately caption it "anger." The ball started left off the clubface and hooked further left. The course marshal on the tee pointed left, as did Waz. A player who hit this shot would also normally point that way, protecting the gallery. In his heated state, Craig didn't bother, either because he didn't care or because he knew he had hooked the shot even left of the gallery.

Craig and Waz found his ball left of the gallery in the trees and natural prairie growth. It lay nearly behind the trunk of a pine, between two roots of the tree. Craig had a backswing but would have to manufacture a clean contact of the club to ball with a chopping motion to advance it. He had 54 yards to the front of the green and 58 yards to the hole and would have to take care not to snap the shaft of his club on the follow-through. If that weren't enough, the shot had to go under some branches of another tree ten yards ahead.

"Well, this was a real good idea," Craig quipped, regaining at least a small part of his sense of humor.

"Do what you always do, blame the caddy," Waz said, hoping to rebalance his man.

All he could do was chop down on the ball and hope. He managed to get the club on the ball, but it clipped the front root. This turned out to be fortunate as the root took off the ball's spin, and it knuckled forward under the branches, scooting forward and ending up in the front bunker. As ugly as it was, the result was far better than many from the same position.

As Craig and Waz waited for Jordan to play his short second shot from the fairway, Craig pulled off his glove and grabbed his water bottle.

Waz looked at him over his shades. "You back?" he said wryly.

Craig allowed a small smile. "Yeah. Sorry, bud."

"No worries. Get up and down, and all is forgiven."

The silver lining on Craig's first two shots was that he left himself in an easy position to save par. He hit a textbook sand shot to four feet, then calmly rolled in his par putt, minimizing the damage.

"Not bad for a temperamental adolescent," Waz said under his breath as Craig handed back his putter.

"That's enough out of you, asshole," Craig said in the way that men frequently address their very best friends.

CHAPTER THIRTEEN

The first story of the day on the noon sports center on ESPN flashed a picture of Zeke Monroe. "To say the golf world was shocked today by the arrest of five-time major winner Zeke Monroe would be a huge understatement," the commentator began. "FBI agents arrested Monroe at the U.S. Open at Parker, Colorado, just before he was to begin his last round in the U.S. Open. While we have no word from Monroe or his people on this situation, our independent investigative reporter Blake Manes is here with more."

The shot shifted to Blake behind a desk, looking the part of a field journalist. His dark eyes and expression showed the amount of hard work he and Clem Tobin had put into getting Monroe arrested. His commentary was made all the more powerful as a result.

"Five-time major championship winner, Zeke Monroe, was arrested today by the FBI for aggravated sexual assault. Sources tell us that the Bureau has substantial evidence supporting multiple allegations against Monroe and that the alleged incidents occurred in multiple states, giving the FBI jurisdiction. I was made aware of this breaking story originally by former golf channel analyst Kelly Keys, who is herself one of Monroe's alleged victims. She came forward . . . "

The FOX commentators covering the Open immediately picked up on the story. They not only reported

Monroe's arrest, they immediately set out to find Kelly Keys, whom ESPN had reported as one of Monroe's victims to come forward. As it turned out, Kelly was not hard to find. She was on-site and had already set an interview on the story with Steve Sands from the Golf Channel.

While Kelly had done plenty of television, she had never been the one being interviewed. She was about to accuse Monroe publicly of raping her on what was now the most terrifying day of her life, an event that until six months ago she would have vehemently denied. The nerves she felt were exponentially worse than any stage fright she had previously experienced. She knew there would be a lot of judgment, and questions, and hard tasks ahead.

Kelly was scared, but she could plant her feet on solid ground. She only had to think about how her life had unraveled after her "date" with Zeke Monroe or think of her friend Hannah Simms, who had helped her find the courage to heal or think of the other women she knew about that Monroe had hurt, to gain perspective.

Finally, she could think of another secondary victim of this whole affair. A brave solitary victim whose absolution was way too long in coming.

Fox cut away from coverage of the U.S. Open for Steve Sand's interview with Kelly Keys. After speaking about her cooperation with law enforcement and withholding any details that would hurt the case against Monroe, Steve led her to an important subject, important both to the Monroe saga and to the day's events at the Open.

"Kelly, I understand that there is another important disclosure that makes today even more difficult for you."

Kelly smiled in a shy and rueful way before she began to disclose a secret that was years old to the world.

"Yeah, Steve." Kelly paused for a deep breath. *Here goes.* "After my mother passed away, I learned that my father . . . " Despite her training, her preparation, and her resolve that this day was inevitable, Kelly's emotions surfaced. It didn't take long for her to compose herself though, a gift from Rachelle. "I learned that Craig Cantwell is my father. I also learned that he knew he was my father long before I did. Somehow, he also knew what had happened with Zeke Monroe the night before the final round of the PGA Championship two years ago . . . "

The media that covered the golf world fairly jumped out of its skin with the revelation of it all. The story went hard to the conventional news sources as well. These same sources had reported Craig Cantwell's attack on Zeke Monroe and speculated that it was driven by things like drug abuse, mental imbalance, and jealousy on Craig's part. He had remained silent on the incident, which fueled the belief that he was guilty and that Monroe was a virtuous, forgiving champion. Monroe's arrest and Kelly's disclosure generated apologetic empathy for Craig. Unbeknownst to him, the media at large and the public shifted their view of him from a hot-headed, dangerous loser to a protective father.

Every parent who feared for a child's safety could empathize with Craig Cantwell.

After Zeke Monroe was taken to the Denver field office of the FBI, Agent Rachel Burris gave a short press statement.

"Today, the Bureau took Zeke Monroe into custody on multiple charges of aggravated sexual assault. At present, formal charges have been filed by seven women against Mr. Monroe. While the investigation is ongoing, the Bureau has substantial evidence to support these charges and will be pursuing this matter in federal court."

CHAPTER FOURTEEN

The last group of the fourth round of the U.S. Open mounted the ninth tee. Craig marveled momentarily that they had only completed eight holes; it seemed like there had been enough energy expended on last round-ups and downs for a full eighteen. Yet more than half the round remained. He was two shots back of the leader, Spieth, with Dustin Johnston at one shot back. He could reflect on a number of things not going his way so far, and yet he was still very much in the tournament. This thought re-energized him. He chose to think that he was due for some breaks.

The ninth at CGC is a strong hole, a 483-yard, par 4. From the tee, the players cannot see the landing area, which slopes hard to the right. This is inconvenient for the player needing a birdie, as the ideal approach to the green is from the left. Craig and Waz decided a high right to left drive would leave Craig in the best position.

Craig's impatience and irritation on the eighth tee were gone, and he focused intently on the drive at 9. It was a shot that required both power and finesse—his specialty. He played the shot to draw and produced the right outside to in swing path for that shape. The ball started for the left center of the top of the hill, then dutifully worked toward the left edge of the fairway. It disappeared over the crest of the hill, and Craig saw it bounce straight. When he and Waz walked over the crest of the hill a few minutes later, they saw his ball in a flat lie on the left edge of the fairway, 185 yards from the pin on the back left of the green.

The ninth green had the same severe left-to-right slope as the fairway, and the pin on the back left meant that going long was disastrous. The entire course was firming up; the USGA did not believe in putting water on the course during a U.S. Open. Throwing an iron (even a spinning wedge) into these firm greens and expecting it to stop quickly was an unreasonable hope.

This time Waz spoke first. "What'cha thinking, boss?"

"I like a draw again, something coming in against the slope. If we land it on the first few feet of the front, the slope will slow it down enough to stay below the hole."

Waz nodded and looked at the flagstick, then the trees to their left. He knew that they had to allow for the wind. He felt a helping breeze against his bare legs.

"I know it's normally a standard 6 or a hard 7, but with this breeze, I'm liking an 8, especially if you spank it."

Craig considered that. "It's a pretty stout 8. What's the yardage?"

"185 flag, 169 front."

Craig nodded. "If front is the target, 8 is the club."

"Yeah, the miss is short."

That decided, Craig put the image of the shot he wanted in his mind, then made practice swings to produce it, then stepped to the ball and trusted his swing.

The shot came out low for an 8 iron and started at the right edge of the green. The club had compressed the ball against the firm ground and, as a result, imparted a counterclockwise spin on it. The result was the desired right to left flight. The ball landed two yards onto the green, where the spin slowed it only slightly, mainly because of the water-stingy habits of the USGA. Instead of stopping, the ball kept rolling and didn't stop until it had run through to the four-inch grass just three feet over the back edge of the green.

Craig had again executed a good shot and had not been rewarded. In this case, however, he could shrug it off. He knew that everyone was playing the same course and that U.S. Open conditions were made to be tough—even unfair.

As he and Waz walked up the ninth green, the gallery began applauding. This was not altogether unusual, though it normally followed a brilliant shot. Neither he nor Jordan Spieth had particularly distinguished themselves here, so Craig just thought the gallery was acknowledging Jordan.

Craig sized up his chip from just in back of the green. It was the kind of shot that would give an amateur night-mares. The ball in thick grass had to be hit to a small patch of lightning-fast green. Craig sized it up in a matter-of-fact way—he'd hit this shot thousands of times before. He took his stance with the face of his wedge wide open and made a swing that would have sent a ball unencumbered by rough fifty yards. The clubhead made a *shump* through the thick grass, and the ball popped up and forward as gently as if Craig had tossed it underhand. It flew four feet and landed softly on the firm putting surface, rolled side hill to the hole, and stopped six inches away.

This was not an unusual shot for Craig Cantwell. What was strange was the reaction of the gallery around the ninth hole. The silence before he swung gave way to a building rush of sound. As his ball got closer to the hole, it was followed by a collective "ohhhh" as it stopped close. The sound of the crowd and the growing applause followed Craig as he used the sole of his wedge to tap in his par save.

Calls came out from the overserved parts of the gallery.

"Great shot, Craig."

"Nice, double C."

"Go get it, Craig."

Craig smiled and touched the brim of his cap as Waz took his wedge and cleaned it. As they watched Jordan size up his own par-saving putt, Craig murmured to Waz, "'Craig? Double C'? A few holes ago I was just Cantwell."

"Don't knock it," Waz whispered back.

Jordan got his own hand from the gallery when he got his par, then the group made their way to 10. Along the players' path to the next tee, ropes cordoned off the gallery. As they made their way, more than a few young and not-so-young patrons reached their hands over the ropes, hoping for a fist bump or a light palm slap. Craig was confused by this—he had resigned himself to being the guy galleries didn't much care for. He thumped his fist against a number of hands on his way to 10, then happened to notice a dad and daughter standing together watching him walk toward them. The girl was about fourteen, and her dad was saying something to her as they watched him approach.

"Good luck on the back 9, Craig!" the girl blurted out, reaching out with her hand.

Craig gave her a gentle fist bump and smiled at her, remembering another young girl she reminded him of.

"Thank you," he said and then looked at her dad. The man looked Craig in the eye and gave him a father-to-father nod.

Craig walked on to the tenth tee, energized by the crowd interaction and having no idea why it had shifted. Spieth and Greller had gotten to the tee ahead of him and were talking to each other in a way that was different than normal golf conversation. Jordan looked at Craig as he approached.

"You hear about Monroe?"

CHAPTER FIFTEEN

The tenth is one of the easier driving holes at Colorado Golf Club. The 463 yards is deceiving, as the drop-in elevation from tee to green is close to a hundred feet. A player can get a boost from the downhill and hit a drive that allows him to attack nearly any pin position on the green.

Craig felt a surge of energy as he approached the tenth tee. He attributed it to several factors. One, he had mostly survived an opening nine holes in which very little went his way. He knew he had played well and had the feeling that things were bound to turn in his favor. Plus, there is always a "clean slate" feeling about the back 9 of a round, a time to forget about the front 9 and produce a strong finish. The other part of Craig's positive shift was the buzz of Zeke Monroe's arrest. He could steer more easily away from what Kelly was enduring in her part of that because of the affection the gallery was showing him. It would not do to get caught up in it, yet the crowd's turn toward him felt good.

"New 9, bro," Waz said to him.

"Roger that," Craig said, taking the driver from his friend.

Craig focused on a distant peak on the mountain range twenty miles away and imagined sending his ball to the top of it. There is something about the certainty of a confident golf swing that produces a great result, and his drive flew long and straight and bounded down the right side of the fairway, finishing in perfect position, 120 yards from the flagstick.

"Nice shot, your eminence," Waz quipped, calling back their papal humor. Craig grinned and shook his head, grateful that he not only had a top caddy but also had an accomplished smartass on his bag.

What awaited them when they reached Craig's drive was one of the only straightforward shots Craig had that day. A level, clean lie, an accessible flag, and a perfect distance for his gap wedge. Even the breeze, which had been variable all day, had disappeared.

Waz checked the yardage again, then handed his man the gap wedge. "This green with this club will hold. Play the distance."

Craig's swing of his wedge produced a hit that was like a match being struck. The sound was like that also, the spin sizzling. After its initial velocity, the spin took over, and the ball seemed to rapidly float toward the target. This shot tracked toward the flag as if it were magnetic, hitting the putting surface two feet in front of the hole and bouncing to four feet behind. The inertia of the spin then took over and the ball backed up two feet.

Craig enjoyed the 120-yard walk to the green, his putter in his hand and the crowd's affirmation ringing in his ears. When he finished the formality of his two-foot birdie putt, he was only one shot back of the lead. The crowd was behind him, his game was on, and he literally felt bulletproof.

CHAPTER SIXTEEN

Southland Bank

The morning that the Southland Bank in Atlanta was robbed, Rachelle Keys was in a relaxed and pensive mood. Recently, things were somewhat of a mixed bag for her. First, the good stuff: Craig and Rachelle had rekindled their romance. While they were not at the point of total commitment, things were moving in a positive direction.

There were moments when Rachelle felt calm and happy when she was with Craig; relaxed in a way she had not previously thought possible. Her therapist had been very encouraged by this and cautioned Rachelle to take things one step at a time. The good doctor had explained that Rachelle was working through the baggage of a long career where she had experienced times of extreme stress and even trauma that would take a while to work through. Part of the process was that she had pulled back a bit from her work, not in an official capacity, but her supervisors had noticed that she might be losing the "edge" needed for the intense fieldwork she had always done. While Rachelle was a bit resistant to letting go completely, she saw an end game now. That was good.

She would feel even better about this if not for the fact that she was worried about her daughter. Kelly had left the Golf Channel abruptly, a job that Rachelle had thought she was passionate about. She had been somewhat idle since and, frankly, a little wild. Her daughter had never been one to drink and party, and that was going on despite the denials she offered Rachelle. When pushed on the subject, Kelly was emphatic that everything was all right. She just needed a bit of time to figure out what she wanted to do next. Rachelle's instincts told her something was wrong, but she did not know what it was or how to get Kelly to talk about it.

Thinking like this made her wonder if it was time to tell her about Craig. Rachelle wondered if the lack of a father might be contributing to Kelly's present mind-set. A part of Rachelle's hesitation about telling Kelly about Craig was that she still felt guilty over the secret and was not quite ready to own up to it. *Ah, well,* she thought this morning, *we have time. Maybe I can talk to Craig about . . .*

Her cell phone rang and interrupted her thoughts. A call this time of the morning immediately shoved her from relaxed reflection into K & R mode.

"Keys."

"Agent Keys, hold for Agent Hauptman."

Rick Hauptman was head of SWAT at the local FBI office. Not good. So much for the career winding down. She held her breath as Rick came on.

"Keys, it's Rick. We got one for you. Perp is holed up in a bank, multiple hostages. Southland National, downtown branch."

"Anyone talking to him or is it them?"

"Not yet."

"Okay, I'm about thirty out. Patch through any contact to me on my cell."

"Roger that. See you when you get here."

Despite her movement toward stepping back from frontline work, Rachelle's training and instincts took over. She did not hesitate. She looked in her trunk to make sure her bag was there and started her car.

CHAPTER SEVENTEEN

As straightforward as the tenth hole was, the eleventh hole at CGC tips the scales back to diabolical. Playing today as a 221-yard par 3, the green looks puzzling from the tee. It has three distinct tiers (or levels), giving it almost a stairstep look. The sadistic officials of the USGA planted the flagstick on the very back left of the green, on top of a bluff above one of the deepest sand bunkers in golf. The top and side borders of the bunker were left to grow wild, the natural prairie grass there roughly a foot tall.

Given all the trouble left, the natural tendency is for a player to bail out to the right. After all, the green is quite large, so there is plenty of room to the right. However, doing that meant a player had to putt up and over the severe mounds on the green, which presented a whole different challenge. The scoring average for the tournament field this day was just over four strokes, the second hardest hole on the course.

Craig and Waz understood and appreciated the challenge the eleventh presented and wanted to get through here with no worse than par. Given the toughness of the hole, 3 would put them one up on the field. Craig had the honor on 11, and he and his caddy went to work on the shot.

"I actually like a 4-iron," Waz said. "The miss is longer."

Craig was not sure. "I don't know, missing deep is a pretty tough up and down. As firm as it's getting, I like a 5 to the middle. It's likely to run to the back anyway." Craig made the call: 5 iron it would be. What was not spoken was the need to avoid the cavernous left bunker. That it was the worst spot to end up was obvious. It was just never a good idea to put any negative image in a player's mind. Craig and Waz both knew that negative instructions, such as "don't hit it there," put the wrong picture in the golfer's head. Neither of them had thought of the left bunker on the tee.

Craig took the 5 iron and went through his normal pre-shot routine. To any observer—even a knowledgeable one like his caddy—he looked present and intentional and ready to execute the shot he and Waz had planned out. What could not be seen was the seed of disaster that planted itself in Craig's mind. For a moment, somewhere in his downswing, a vision of that disastrous left bunker took hold. Another part of Craig's system knew the image was wrong and resisted it, but just for a brief moment, his internal tussle caused the wrong tension in the physical act of making this swing.

The shot started out left of Craig's intended target, the middle of the green. He had hit it solidly but pulled it. A pull tends to make a shot fly farther, and the initial line at that left flag caused a thrill in the gallery around the tee. Was Craig throwing caution to the wind and going straight at that tiny target? Craig knew he had pulled the shot, and his initial alarm at the error was briefly delayed by the hope that he would get away with it, that this would turn out to be a "good miss." The actual result squashed that notion.

The ball started at the flag and curved even further left. It hit flag high in the left fringe only ten feet left. It took a hop forward and even farther left and disappeared in a patch of long turf on the far side of the left bunker. The grass—a combination of a strain planted on the golf course and the natural prairie grass—was almost a foot deep.

A course marshal was standing to the side of the eleventh green when Craig and Waz walked up, and they knew he was there to mark where Craig's ball had come to rest. Course marshals are volunteers for the event, and Craig and his fellow pros know they could not have a golf tournament without them. Craig smiled at the man when he walked up.

"I am hoping you can find that shot in this mess," Craig said lightly.

"Yes and no. I saw it, and I know it's right here. I just can't see it."

Craig and Waz and the marshal began a careful search in a patch of gnarly grass, not eight feet square. The growth's thickness was hiding his ball. Several hundred people had seen exactly where his ball landed, including the group and the gallery, but after several minutes the three men had yet to find it.

The rules stipulated that if they could not find the ball in five minutes, Craig would have to declare it lost and return to the tee. From there, he would hit his third shot. As time ticked on, a small seed of panic started in Craig. A rules official had joined the search, and had there been room where they were looking, Jordan Spieth and his caddy would have helped as well. Right at the five-minute mark, when the official was going to call for Craig to go back to the tee, Waz spoke up.

"I think I got it," he said. Waz was on his knees and using his hands to carefully pick through the deep grass. He comically put his face almost to the ground, his entire head surrounded by the deep grass, then looked up at Craig and nodded. "This is it. I see your initials on the ball." He wasn't smiling.

Craig and the rules official stepped over and looked down, each with his hands on his knees. This photo, with Craig and the official peering straight into a grassy abyss and Craig's caddy on his hands and knees, would get wide circulation in the press. It might mark the end of Cantwell's chances in this Open.

Craig identified the ball as his, then stood up. He briefly removed his cap and ran a hand over his hair. He looked over at Jordan and Michael and with a wry look said, "Be right with you, boys."

Jordan, empathetic to his playing partner, looked away from Craig's plight as if he'd seen something disgusting.

"Anybody have a Weedwhacker I can borrow?" Craig said loud enough for the gallery to hear. There was real laughter from the two hundred people there, and Craig and Waz settled down to play this shot.

Craig knew he could only chop down at the thick grass with a wedge to move his ball out of it. The question was just how hard that swing needed to be. He knew that he and the club could get the ball out, but he was only twelve feet from the hole. Chopping down with his wedge as if he were splitting a log would send the ball sailing over the green; he had to swing hard enough to extricate the ball from the grass, and not so hard as to create a new disaster.

After numerous practice swings, as an attempt to estimate the grass's thickness, Craig stepped to his nearly buried ball. His effort was only partially effective; after the downward swing got the clubhead through the vegetation, the ball lifted off. It only flew three feet, and when it stopped it was still in the tall grass. It was now very visible, sitting right on top of a large tangled mass. It looked as though a soft breeze would cause it to settle deeper, but there it sat, defying gravity on top of ten inches of lush growth.

Craig's next effort required even more finesse than the last. He judged that he had to clip the top part of the grass holding up his ball with a soft swing, and he did just that. The grass had other ideas, and as his wedge disturbed it, the long turf recoiled and batted the soft flight of the ball backward. It landed just back of where it previously was and slowly made its way through the patch of deep grass and into the bunker. The ball stopped about six feet below Craig's feet in the sand.

If he could forget the fact that he now lay 3 in the depths of the bunker, Craig could notice that the clean lie in the sand was a much easier position to play from than his prior two shots. He had practiced and executed sand shots thousands of times, unlike the attempts he had just made to get out of calf-deep grass. The "easy" sand shot was really anything but, up over a six-foot lip, stop it quick on a super-fast surface. Executed well, his fourth shot still lay twelve feet from the hole.

When he barely missed that putt, Craig walked away from the eleventh with a triple-bogey 6.

Chapter Eighteen

Southland Bank

Rachelle Keys walked into the on-site command post located in an office across the street from the bank, about thirty minutes after her phone call with Rick Hauptman. She could see that the situation was serious; downtown streets were cordoned off, and the surrounding buildings had been evacuated. Hauptman and his staff briefed her.

"He or they went in last night. Kidnapped two bank employees after closing, before the timers and alarms were set. Local PD got an alarm at 1:45 a.m., showed up on-site and saw a man with a gun pointed at one of the bankers. They set up a perimeter but have not had any contact with the perps—just one of the bankers. It hasn't been a conversation. He's under duress and reading scripted messages."

"I'll need text on the messages," Rachelle said. "What else?"

"They have explosives. What kind and how much, we don't know."

"Demands?"

"None yet. Just a whole lot of extremist anti-government, anti-American bullshit. And again, it's been through the bank manager, not the perps. We haven't laid eyes on them yet."

An agent handed her the transcription of the messages. They were nearly gibberish, and she initially agreed that there was not much substance to them. She then listened to two recordings of the banker reading the perp's scripted messages.

Rachelle Keys brought twenty years of experience to this scene. Rick Hauptman and many other agents who knew her were always amazed that Agent Keys was completely cool, courageous, and shrewd all the while looking like she could sit for a photo-shoot for the cover of *Vogue*.

Rachelle read the messages again and stood deep in thought. Then she looked directly at Hauptman.

"These are bullshit, some sort of smokescreen. They want us to think they are idiot fanatics, but that doesn't fit the situation. They've been in that bank all night, they have barricaded themselves, and moved in whatever they needed. There is alley access to the bank, so that was easy last night. They cased well. They . . . and it is 'they.' This is too big for one guy . . . they are very slick. Get some analysis on bank security cameras, run profiles on terrorist suspects with hostages and explosive MOs."

"We're on the profiles, but looking at security footage will take some time."

"Cross-reference both searches; see if facial recognition software can scan the camera footage," Agent Keys instructed.

She jerked her head at Rick, and the two of them stepped away a few feet and spoke in low tones.

"This is bad, Rick. No demands, they could have robbed and run or killed and run by now. They want us here for whatever they're gonna do. This smells like terrorists to me."

"Me too, but why not just blow a bomb on a busy street at early rush hour?" It wasn't adding up.

She nodded. "Two priorities from me: the type of explosive and get me a profile. Trust me, these are not virgins. They've been heard from before."

Ninety minutes went by with nothing but tension. Rachelle had attempted numerous calls into the bank with no response. Then a tech ran in with a phone and handed it to Rachelle.

"Keys."

"Keys, it's Baker at the Barn." Barn was agent speak for the Hoover Building. "We've got three sightings on security footage of a terrorist suspect. Backtracking his movements, he came through Hartfield three weeks ago with an American alias."

"Give me a name."

"I'll go you one better. His alias is Enrico Panetta, real name Siad Alfah—Egyptian, by way of Saudi Arabia. Believe it or not, I have a cell number for Enrico."

"Okay, that's something," Rachelle said, though she doubted that "Enrico" would answer his phone.

When they had set up technology to trace the call and locate the phone, Rachelle dialed. To her surprise, an accented male voice answered.

"Yes?"

"Oh, um, hi. I'm not sure I have the right number." Eyebrows raised all over the room; Rachelle had sounded like a barfly calling the number of a hunk she had met the previous evening. Her voice was so sexy only a eunuch would have hung up.

"Who is this?"

"Well, who is *this?* You first." The purely female act was to buy time to locate the phone, which in a moment was not necessary.

"Is it possible that you are with the FBI? In the building across the street from the Southland Bank in downtown Atlanta?"

Her blood ran cold. This guy had expected this call?

Her voice changed. "Well, geez, here I thought I could buy a little time by flirting, and you want to get right down to business. This is Agent Rachelle Keys of the FBI, Mr. Alfah. Nice to meet you."

"Really? You are pleased to meet me?"

"Well, I'm just so damned bored over here it's nice to talk to anybody. I mean, I love the Bureau, but most of these SWAT guys are downright dull. Nice to look at though."

He chuckled lightly. "I did not expect chitchat this morning from the Federal Bureau of Investigation."

"What did you expect?"

"Suppose I had expectations? Is it you who could meet them? Or should I talk to your boss?"

Rachelle smiled inwardly at the slight. It wasn't new for men on the other end of the phone to ask to speak to her superior. The smart ones did it just to get a rise out of her. She made a quick decision not to play along.

"No, I'm afraid you're stuck with me. But I can't really get you what you want if you haven't asked me for it." Again, a hint of sexiness. She was playing a hunch that maybe, just maybe, Siad Alfah would want to meet the woman behind the voice.

"I will get back to you." The phone went dead.

"Well, that was interesting," Rick said. "Did you get a date?"

"This guy knows a little about how the game is played. He wasn't fazed by the presence of SWAT or FBI. He expected the call. Maybe he didn't expect a woman. This is just as serious as I thought at first, maybe more serious." She had been talking as much to herself as Rick, and now she looked at him. "No date, not yet. But I think maybe he is a bit thrown by the fact that a woman called. I have half a hunch that he's a bit of a horndog, so maybe he'll let me in there."

"Is there value in that? Why give him another hostage?"

"The value is that maybe I can get some intel before we breach." She looked at Rick. They both had held out the hope that a breach could be avoided. Rachelle was now giving him her expert opinion that a breach was inevitable.

"You really think he likes you that much?"

"I don't know, Rick. My hunch is that he's got the thought that if he's about to die in Jihad and go get his seventy virgins, that maybe he wants a threesome first with a forbidden American blonde."

Hauptman remembered that the devout Muslim martyrs of 9/11 had run up huge tabs at strip clubs in the nights leading up to their deaths. Maybe Keys was right.

The wheels and works of the FBI turned and churned. Information on Alfah, his affiliation, his movements, and his motives were all digested. Command-level decisions were being made; local strategies were being formed and approved. In the center of it all was Rachelle Keys. All of this, as well as her subsequent conversations with Alfah, led to her walking across the street three hours later with her hands extended outward, as had been agreed, and into the open door of the bank lobby.

The lobby was empty when she got there, but she knew she was being watched. She stood in the middle of the lobby with her hands still outstretched and waited. She was about to speak when she heard a voice.

"Put your hands on the back of your head and turn to face the street."

Rough hands moving over her body searched for wires and weapons and anything that had not been agreed upon. These were the conditions on which she had been allowed into the bank. With some effort, the man took off her blue FBI jacket, then undid the Velcro straps on her Kevlar vest, removing it roughly.

Her companion moved in front of her. He was dark-haired with very dark eyes that bore into hers for a second. Then, ever so briefly, his eyes moved down her body, and Rachelle sensed a small trace of shame in the man for noticing her figure.

"You can put your hands down now and follow me." She followed him past the deserted teller line and into an area of safety deposit boxes, in a room separate from the lobby. Just off this room was the large vault, the door open. As she stood in the room, Siad Alfah casually walked out of the vault, appraising her with an icy smile.

"Agent Keys, are you happy to meet me now?"

"Always good to put a face with a voice," she said with a slight smile she didn't feel. The tension here was palpable, and while she did not panic, she was inwardly scared by it. This was not going as she had hoped. Her experience told her that these men were ready to die, convinced that their deaths would be noble, and that they would be rewarded in the afterlife. There was still a tension though. A vestige of doubt that their faith in the result of this holocaust would be true to their vision. As she and her colleagues had already surmised, these men were not going to negotiate. She shuffled her feet just slightly.

"So, I am curious, why did you allow me to be here?" she asked Alfah.

"I want you to know before all the others. I want to see your face, your pretty blue eyes when you see what is coming. I want to look at you when you realize that there is nothing you can do to prevent it."

Rachelle could see that she had been wrong about Siad Alfah. There was no twisted amorous intention toward her. He hated women in general, and her particularly. It was immediately evident. What she wanted to know was how to gain just a little more time.

At least I'm here, she thought. She moved her feet just a little more again.

"What do you want me to see?" she asked him, looking right at the eyes that gushed hate.

He smiled a mirthless smile and pushed open a half door to one of the small rooms used by people opening their safety deposit boxes. On the floor was a metal case with the top half lifted off. She noted the metal casing, the attached trigger, and the wiring. While she was not an expert, she had been briefed on explosives of all kinds.

Agent Rachelle Keys realized that she was looking at a nuclear bomb.

She moved her feet again, just a side-to-side shift. This was good because the trackers in the heels of her shoes would tell the agents outside where they were. She tried to silently reconcile how long she had been in the bank. She could not, although she knew that the breach could not be long in coming. She longed for her Kevlar.

She noticed one of the bankers sitting on the floor next to the vault door. He was gagged and bound and did not move. He was wide-eyed and looking directly at her. She nodded slightly, and his eyes slowly shifted to the vault.

For some reason, her feet tingled. Despite her training and experience, since she had been shown the bomb, her body was doing strange things. She was beyond fear; the impact of what she had just seen was manifesting in untold ways. She had to at least attempt to draw things out, to buy time.

"How long?" she managed to get out of her dry mouth.

"Not long," Alfah replied. "It was not enough for me to have you wait outside to be incinerated. I have known enough American women to want to watch you die."

With that, he pulled a pistol from behind his back. As she faced her own death, Rachelle's perception slowed down. She heard a click as Alfah pulled back the hammer of his weapon. An instant later, she heard a flash-bang grenade detonate somewhere behind her. Then she saw the pistol muzzle flash before the sledgehammer blow from the bullet pierced her chest. She felt her body propelled backward as a cacophony of weapons erupted. As she lay on her back, she noted multiple bullets striking Siad Alfah, sending him to either his seventy virgins or to hell.

Then there were many feet in the room, many shouts, and many voices.

"CLEAR!" "MAN DOWN!" "MEDIC UP!" "BOMB TECH UP!"

Rick Hauptman was suddenly standing over her.

"Shit! Keys is down!" he hollered.

"Hang in there, kid," he said to her in a calm, quiet voice. "Medic's coming."

She nodded slightly, the movement excruciating. She knew she had to lie still. Then she knew that being still felt better. She relaxed, not because her job was done, but because she saw the beginnings of another place. A loving place to which a growing part of her wanted to go.

She shifted her gaze and again saw the banker on the floor next to the vault. His eyes were still wide, still looking into the vault, but he was anything but peaceful. There was a bullet hole in the center of his forehead. He had gone but had left her a message.

A mortal notion took hold in her. This was not training, but rather something undefined and undefinable that made her fight just once more for just a short time. She became conscious again and noticed the voice of Danny Feld, the bomb expert now focused on the device in the small closet.

"I'm glad these turkeys didn't know bombs very well. This trigger is bad. I already bypassed it. The nitrogen fog will put this thing to bed."

Hauptman's face again. "Looks like Danny has the bomb disarmed, Keys. Hang in there."

Suddenly, it was clear. How much time?

"Mmm," she managed, though it cost her more agony.

Hauptman had not heard. She moved her right hand again, more pain, to his foot. Mike looked at her and could see her distress. He knelt again.

"Keys, don't try to talk. Stay still. Medic's on the way . . . "

"Vau . . . Vau . . . " She barely got out. Now Hauptman knew she needed to talk.

"What, Keys?" He put his face an inch from hers.

He could see her desperation, her hope that she had enough strength and just enough time. Her hand was suddenly on his face, and with a final push, she spoke:

"The vault—get in the fucking vault."

Hauptman's eyes went wide with comprehension.

"Danny! The vault! Get in the vault!"

Feld had to step over the body of the banker, moving the heavy vault door with his left hand as he entered. He immediately saw the device on the table. The real bomb.

"Oh, let's dance." He had this job because he could detach his task from the consequences of it, and he did so now.

He started with the trigger, remembering clearly the course he retook every ninety days. He recognized the configuration and acted quickly. Four fasteners on the trigger device were first removed, then he used a canister of liquid nitrogen to freeze the mechanism. Once that was done, wires were stripped, then deactivated. As Mike Hauptman watched, Danny Feld expertly disarmed what would come to be known in the Bureau as the "Keys' bomb."

Danny looked at Hauptman as he picked up the trigger that he had removed. It had a digital timer on the bottom, the face of which showed seven seconds. He now went into a comic mode, bleeding the stress off with a running monologue:

"Shit, man. I had seven whole seconds. I could have taken a leak, had a nap, a sandwich. What else could you do in seven seconds, Rick? I coulda called my mom, sent a text. Hell, if I had known I had seven whole seconds, I woulda had *you* disarm this sucker. I coulda used one hand if I had known that shit, man."

Rick Hauptman looked at this crazy motherfucker as his heart started beating again. He shook his head even as his body began to shake, bleeding off the stress. *Well, we can still laugh, so we might as well,* he thought. The full impact of how close to death they had been would come with time; meanwhile, he would smile.

He left the vault. "Keys, this guy is totally insane. I mean, nuts, certifiably—"

He stopped when he stepped out of the vault and saw the tactical medic kneeling next to Keys. Troy Matson had worked with Hauptman for ten years and had known Rachelle longer than that. He could not maintain a professional mien. His eyes met Hauptman's, and he slowly shook his head. Danny Feld's crazy, stress-bleeding monologue was interrupted when he exited the vault.

Rachelle Keys' beautiful blue eyes were open and fixed. They were still magnetic, even though the light of her life was gone from them.

Just then, Hauptman's uniform microphone squawked. "Hauptman, do you copy? Report." He realized that less than four minutes had gone by since the breach. He grabbed his mike and keyed it, but his voice failed him.

"Are we clear?" Command asked again.

Rick cleared his throat. "Affirmative," he managed to get out.

"Tell Keys she's lucky. If this hadn't worked, she would lead the line to the shithouse."

Rick broke in. They had to know, and soon. "Keys is . . . " His voice failed again. A veteran of eighteen years in FBI SWAT, he still had to take a minute with this. All that Rachelle Keys was would have made this hard if she had died randomly. The fact that she had saved thousands of lives with her dying words was more than he could bear.

"Say again?"

He keyed the mike again. "Ah . . . " *Again, nothing. Why wouldn't his voice work?*

Danny Feld, the maniac bomb tech, bailed him out. Danny stepped over to Rick Hauptman and gently put his hand on the SWAT man's shoulder. He keyed the mike and spoke the words his friend could not:

"Keys is down."

CHAPTER NINETEEN

There is a statistic in championship golf called the "bounce back" stat. This is the frequency with which a player shows resiliency in following a bad hole—a double or a triple bogey—with a birdie. Golf pros are golf pros precisely because they are better than amateurs at dealing with adversity and recovering from mistakes quickly. This mental and emotional discipline can figuratively be described as the "heavy lifting" of a competitive round of golf.

There is a wide and varied methodology in bouncing back among Tour pros. Some purge the bad memory with a brief tantrum, slamming, or even breaking a club. (Tiger Woods, for example, was known for explosive outbursts in his day—as was Bobby Jones.) Others used deep breaths or other physical tools. Even distracting themselves with food or, in the time of the original Scottish golfers, a shot of whiskey, could be a method. Craig and Waz used humor.

As they walked to the twelfth tee, Waz offered up a solution. "Hey, if you want, I can kick you in the balls."

"That might actually make me feel better."

"I am here for you, buddy," Waz said, glad his man could engage after the gutshot on 11.

"I guess now is a good time to remember the Chinese," Craig said as he drained his water bottle.

"No doubt." The two men shared a smile, each grateful that he had a friend. The shift in perspective was easier because of the personal gauntlet Craig had run the last several years.

The shift was needed, as Colorado Golf Club was not about to let up; they had now reached the twelfth hole. A 531-yard, par 4. As if the length alone was not difficult enough, the green on the twelfth was an elevated, tiny surface, where the players needed to judge the distance on their lengthy second shots perfectly to hold the green.

Craig stepped to his tee shot, visualizing a gradual right to left flight. He again hit the drive superbly, and 325 yards later had a midiron left to the green. He struck a five iron from there and, from the pure feel of it, was sure he would have a chance at the bounce-back birdie. On a day where most shots were bounding off the firm ground, this one hit just short of the elevated green. Instead of the move forward it needed, this one was stopped by the hill and slowly rolled backward twelve feet—leaving a delicate chip up the hill.

Craig had a superb short game, and he struck this chip precisely. The contact made a crisp solid sound, and the ball hit the exact spot on the green he had picked. His vision was of the ball hitting that spot briskly, checking slightly from the spin, and then releasing to the hole. The deviation from his vision came from excess spin combining with the uncharacteristic softness of the green that caused the ball to stop quickly—much sooner than Craig envisioned. He left himself nearly 8 feet for par, and when this putt barely slid by on the low side, Craig had carded another bogey on twelve.

"Maybe I should have taken you up on that kick in the balls," he said quietly to Waz as they walked toward the thirteenth tee.

"Hey, my offer is still good." Neither man smiled this time. The gravity of being four over par the last two holes was palpable.

Waz handed Craig an energy bar. "We're still okay. Focus on the tee shot." His job now was simple but not easy: reinforce to Craig that they could only focus on the present.

CHAPTER TWENTY

Zeke Monroe sat in the cold sparse interview room in the Denver Field Office of the FBI. The restraints on both his wrists and lower legs were more than a little uncomfortable as he sat with his hands on the table in front of him and avoided looking at a large mirror opposite his seat. He was sure there were people observing him from the other side of that mirror, and that made him uncomfortable. Seeing his reflection staring back at him was even more unnerving.

Zeke was still staring at his reflection when the door to the room flew open and Rachel Burris walked in. She was followed by a man who Monroe assumed was there to make sure that he behaved himself. Agent Burris set a leather case on the table and sat across from Monroe, leaning slightly forward and looking at him. She said nothing.

After roughly thirty seconds of silence, Monroe spoke.

"All right, can I say something now?"

Burris looked mildly pleased that he had chosen to speak first, and so quickly. She gave a single nod as if to say, "please do."

"There has been some sort of a huge mistake. I don't know what this is about. A person in my position is a target for a lot of people, as you must know. I don't know what anyone else has told you, but I have not sexually assaulted anyone."

Agent Burris's expression did not change. She simply opened the leather case on the table and pulled out a file.

"Do you remember meeting a woman named Amanda Cox?" she asked Monroe.

Monroe did his best to look exasperated. "I meet a lot of people. I may have met her, I don't remember."

"I have both a video of Ms. Cox and a sworn statement and complaint from her that on the night of January 15th of last year, she was with you. And also, that she was drugged and sexually assaulted by you that night. This took place in Pebble Beach, California, during a golf tournament."

"This is an old story, Agent Burris. This is a woman I met who wants attention or money by claiming that I hurt her. As I said, a person such as myself is a target——"

Agent Burris put a photo in front of him, stopping Monroe's speech in mid-sentence. It was an old polaroid photo, the kind taken with a camera that spits out the picture as it is taken.

"This photo was found in your house, along with nineteen others very similar to it. The camera was also found in your home. Your fingerprints are on both the camera and the photos."

The picture was of a drugged Amanda Cox. She was naked, and the end of a golf club had been inserted into her vagina. A hand was visible on the golf club, and a ring was visible on the hand.

"This woman has been identified as Amanda Cox. That's your hand in the photo; we identified the ring as the same one you took off when we booked you into custody."

Monroe sat silent, his eyes open and looking at Agent Burris. It was good that she was in front of him, between him and the mirror.

"I have the sworn statements of seven women, all of whom tell the same story. I have a supply of Rufalin found in your home. I have the statement of a Rufalin dealer, one Mr. Carter Travis in Houston, who on numerous occasions sold you Rufalin. I have these photos, your finger-prints all over them," Burris told him in an even, matter-of-fact tone.

The color slowly drained from Monroe's face. His body reacted physically as the truth he wanted to deny was laid out in front of him.

"I have your DNA on a piece of clothing worn by one of the victims," Burris went on. She was still talking in an even, flat tone with her eyes directly on Monroe.

She saw his reaction as he realized what she knew. He shivered as if the temperature of the room had dropped. His hands trembled and his breathing elevated.

As head of Behavioral Sciences at the FBI, Agent Rachel Burris had met and talked with many serial offenders, so she knew that she was seated in front of yet another one. Although she was satisfied to have caught a predator like Monroe, on a clinical level, she knew that serial offenders were not born but were created by years of their own abuse. Stopping short of compassion, this awareness allowed her to be objective in her work.

"Are you enjoying this?" Monroe said to her. Her reaction surprised him.

"No, I'm not. Stopping someone who does what you have done is a relief, but it's not something I celebrate."

"Your job, I guess," Monroe said, still visibly shaking.

"Yes. Well, strangely enough, my job is to facilitate people healing from bad things. Your victims can start to heal now that you have been stopped. They at least have that chance, though it can be a long process."

"I didn't hurt them that badly," Monroe said defensively.

"Maybe you didn't hurt them that bad physically, but if you want proof of the damage you did to them, just examine your own past."

This statement from her brought a physical reaction from Monroe, as he literally recoiled from her. She had not made a move toward him, nor raised her voice, yet he reacted like a frightened animal.

For her part, Rachel Burris recognized that an instinct she had about Monroe was accurate. She did not know the details, of course. But Monroe just proved to her that his own abuse had made him the monster he now was.

She continued to look at Monroe and spoke frankly.

"You're going to have a lot of time to think, Zeke. You will not be granted bail; you're wealthy, the charges you are facing are violent, and you're a flight risk. With the evidence we have, you are not going to be released. So while you're thinking, think about this: How quickly do you want to get on with things? You are going away for a long time, and waiting is not going to make it any easier. Even in prison, you can start to heal. Even in prison, you can start to become better than what the past has made you. You can start to lay down this burden you've carried for such a long time. You can start to live a better life."

She put the evidence she had shown Monroe back into the briefcase on the table and stood up. Then she looked at the man sitting in front of her one last time and said,

"While you're thinking, think about when you want to start to become human again."

And just as suddenly as she had entered the room, she exited, the man silently following behind her.

CHAPTER TWENTY-ONE

Craig executed an easy tee shot on the thirteenth hole, a relatively short par four. He stroked an average three wood to the middle of the fairway, leaving a wedge to the small green. The shot itself was something of a breather amid the tough nine back at CGC. Hitting a driver to this fairway could be tricky, as it sloped off a spine in the middle. Since the hole was short, Craig took the easier (and popular) choice of laying up with a fairway wood.

Walking up the thirteenth fairway, Craig felt the suffocating U.S. Open pressure ease a bit. He had been in the pressure cooker since the tournament began on Thursday, and fatigue was a factor by now. He was three over par for the round, and as a result was five shots behind the leader, his playing partner, Jordan Spieth. All in all, he was having a superb tournament, coming back from virtual oblivion to lead the Open after three days. As golf commentators and fans were now well aware, he had accomplished a great deal in this Open. Even more than that, the day's events had brought about a public redemption for Craig. The world's perception of him had swung from highly negative to warm and empathetic. As a result of this week, he could rightly expect to resume his place in professional golf. He could reap rewards and go back to doing what he loved.

So, with most of six holes remaining in this U.S. Open golf championship, Craig Cantwell began to feel resigned to a "good finish."

His second shot to the thirteenth green was 132 yards, and he played a good pitching wedge that found the green twenty feet from the hole. Walking up to the green, Craig got a nice ovation from the gallery. He marked his ball and noted quickly that he had a very tough putt, one that he had to be cautious in two-putting. Jordan had missed the green and was setting up his third shot, then needed to consult a rule official about his lie on the border of the gallery. It looked like he was getting a drop away from a trash basket, so Craig would wait a bit longer.

"Might as well make ourselves comfortable," he said lightly to Waz.

Waz looked at Craig hard when he heard those casual words. Having known Roy Wasson for years, no words were needed for Craig to read the look. In an instant, Craig knew what he had slipped into.

He had begun to feel comfortable, satisfied that he had given this final round a good "try" and that "everyone could see he had done his best" and made a good showing.

In the several minutes that Jordan Spieth took to chip onto the green, Craig reflected soberly on the memory of Seth Reede, on a special day at SGZ.

"There are only two stages of development: growth and decay," Seth had said. "So often we seek out stability and comfort, and these are illusions. We are either growing or decaying. I can tell you with certainty that I am familiar with both growth and decay, and that both are uncomfortable."

Craig remembered vividly that Seth had then paused and smiled that smile of his. The smile that reminded him of a sunbeam shining through dark storm clouds.

"It's just that growth is a hell of a lot more interesting."

Craig realized he was slipping into being comfortable, as a result of Waz's look and the memory of Seth that it evoked. Comfortable being an "also-ran" in a major championship, as he had been many times before. Satisfied that he had a place among the golfing elite, making a lot of money, and living a "good" life—that's what he'd settled for. Comfortable being a "good enough" father. Satisfied by the gallery's affection for his emergence on the other side of victimhood. Satisfied that he was the guy good for a laugh and a fifth-place finish before he caught his NetJets flight home.

There are crossroads in life, and there are crossroads in a round of golf. Craig Cantwell had reached one here, and against his prior experience, he made a choice to turn the wheel and take the unknown route.

After Craig had two-putted for par on the thirteenth, he handed his putter to Waz, and they started toward 14. As they moved, Waz spoke. "You comfortable now?"

Craig looked back at him with a stare that would have backed up a charging gorilla, then smiled like a daredevil.

"Fuck comfortable, let's go cause some trouble."

Chapter Twenty-two

Craig and Waz walked to the tee at the fourteenth hole at Colorado Golf Club knowing where Craig stood. That is, he knew where he stood in the tournament and knew where he stood in his life. As for this current U.S. Open, Craig Cantwell was five shots behind the leaders with five holes to play. He could dwell on how he lost the two-shot lead he had at the start of this final round, but that would do no good. He could think about the near future and how he wanted to be viewed by himself and others after this round concluded—but that was equally irrelevant.

What was far more essential was Craig's immersion into being here right now.

Craig took a minute to draw a parallel between where he was in this golf tournament and where he was in his life. As was natural for him, he could imagine how he was viewed by others. At this point, he was still in a bright spotlight. Would that drive him, sustain him, satisfy him? He had returned to this crucible, by looking inward and assessing what he wanted from himself. As many distractions as now existed outside of him, going inward was now the only thing that would do.

This inward look was still tainted by the falseness of his prior beliefs. Like his time earlier in this golf round, self-doubt and self-pity still abided and wanted to assert themselves. These were the products of his own experiences, bags of refuse that sat in his subconscious. Below even this was the truth. Not lies he had told himself, as Seth Reede taught him, but the stubborn truth that he could find through faith in himself.

Craig could feel his abdominal muscles contracting. He took a deep breath and squared off against one piece of solid truth. Whatever else had happened before in his life, or in this round, he would expend everything in this last stretch. Beginning right now, he would be present in his best.

The fourteenth at CGC is a diabolical tease of a par 4. At 320 yards today, it urged a golfer to swing hard at a driver and bring a chance for eagle. The hole bent right to left, and a spot in the approach to the green would kick a ball that was hit to perfection downhill and to the left onto the putting surface. That was only the initial challenge; from there it had to avoid a deep pot bunker that the green wrapped around in the front. This shot also had to stop on the lightning-fast green before it rolled over and down a steep slope into a gully. The fourteenth epitomized risk and reward.

For the golfer close to the lead, or one protecting a lead, the shot at the fourteenth presented choice and dilemma. For Craig Cantwell, five shots back, the choice was clear.

"I think we need a home run here, yeah?" Craig asked Waz.

"You could also rightfully think the Pope shits in the woods," Waz said back, low enough to not be heard by the gallery.

Craig smiled wide at his own line being thrown back at him. *Truth is truth.* That line is funny, and I am driving this green.

The gallery stirred and reacted when Craig pulled his driver out of the bag. Many of them stayed on this hole all day, wanting their golfing idols to throw caution to the wind and hammer a drive that would reach the green. The crowd was two or three deep all the way up to the green, and the reaction rippled that way when they saw Craig with the driver in his hands.

He teed his ball and stood behind it, looking toward his target. He narrowed his focus away from the pines and people lining the hole, away from the obstacles in the way, the many distractions, and toward the smallest target that was the edge of a mower strip in the fairway, three hundred yards ahead. Craig beat back thoughts of technique, of physical methods to hit this crucial shot. He knew how. He had done this many times before; he had only to trust himself fully. His mind's eye looked for the shot, the one he needed now. Not the good one that fell short, not the push to the right or the bullet that would not hold the green. His golfer's intelligence sorted through all the available outcomes to pick the ideal one, the one that was in him that wanted to be brought to life. The sublime effort that was now in his imagination and wanted to be a physical reality.

Craig addressed this drive and settled into position in the middle of the heavy silence that a thousand people produce. Almost in slow motion, he started to swing the club back.

It is strange that a single man hitting a small white ball with a golf club should hold the interest of so many. One thought that the gremlins in Craig Cantwell's subconscious would bring to the surface is "what does this matter?" In the realm of the world, why would a silly thing like a golf shot amount to anything? In the scope of just one man's life, this would seem trivial, of little consequence.

What Craig had decided—of his own accord—was that this moment did matter. The truth that he had come to, not just in this moment, but also as a result of all his searching, was that what was in his heart was important. The total of his choices, his passion to practice and strive at this silly game, the energy and joy and intent he brought to golf, dwarfed the physical. Like a wild animal in the wild, this was Craig Cantwell expressing himself fully without a thought for approval, reward, or judgment.

This shot mattered for no other reason than that Craig had decided it did.

Pundits and commentators would ask what this shot, and this tournament, meant in the grand scheme of things. They would want to label it, as though doing so would make the thing more valuable because it was put on a shelf for sale. The very desire to label this experience for others was futile, as their own experience of it was undefined and undefinable, ranging from nothing to the most impactful moment of their lives and all points in between.

Craig Cantwell and all the artists in the world cannot busy themselves with how the world will judge them. They can only create from their best selves with the knowledge that it is all they were made to do. Being focused on the art of the moment with love, trust, and faith is the simple truth of the artist—whether she paints with a brush or a 45-inch driver.

Craig struck the drive on fourteen with his strength and his heart and soul. The ball left the clubface at 160 mph, and the sound of its rapid movement through the air echoed off the pines and the galleries on either side of its flight. The inane cries of the gallery idiots followed its flight, which Craig watched knowing his best was delivered—the physical tingle of the great golf shot flowing through his limbs. The ball drew just slightly, hit the very mow strip Craig had focused on, took a high bounce, and rolled toward the green.

The hole this day was positioned on the back, close to the top of a slope that sped away to purgatory in the back of the green. Even putting toward that hole from below was treacherous —being overaggressive would put the ball in a deep swale that ended in the scrub oak. Craig's ball narrowly missed the front bunker and looked for all like it had too much steam to stop on the green. At the last moment, it trekked through the border of deeper grass left of the bunker. That piece of turf acted as a brake for the ball's momentum. It emerged from the other side of the grass at a slower pace, and the crowd noise built as it rolled toward the hole. This gallery had watched very good shots go too far here; they collectively wondered if this one would stop or go on to oblivion.

From the tee, Craig and Waz saw most of this. After a certain point in the ball's journey, they could only listen. The throat of the gallery would tell them the result of Craig's effort. The crowd's cry rose to a crescendo, one that would abruptly cut off if his shot missed its mark.

As they started walking off the tee, the crowd's noise maintained its high pitch, and the applause rippled back from the green to where they were like an echo off a canyon wall. When they turned the bend in the fairway, Craig's ball sat three feet below the hole.

CHAPTER TWENTY-THREE

Spiritual Ground Zero

Craig stood off to the side watching the other SGZ attendees say their good-byes to Seth Reede before boarding the bus that would take them back to their various destinations. While he was exhilarated by his time at camp, he was also a little reluctant to leave because he truly felt something magical about the place. He had also formed an unexpected bond with nearly everyone, especially Seth Reede, the man who had impacted him the most. He continued to watch and wait as most of the forty-five people stopped to personally say goodbye to Seth. He patiently waited his turn; he had driven to camp and was in no particular hurry.

After about an hour, the bus filled up and drove off, leaving Craig alone with Seth and the man everyone had referred to as "Seth's Man Friday." The man had shadowed Seth all week and, although he was always only a step away from Seth, was neither friendly nor warm. There had been lots of speculation among the camp attendees about the man's role at the seminar. Was he an assistant, administrator, or bodyguard? Nobody could quite figure it out.

"Hey, I'm hoping you can help me, sir," Seth said to Craig as Craig approached him now.

Craig played along. "Well, I'll do my best."

"We seem to have misplaced one of our seminar attendees. He closely matches your description, but there are some key differences. When he showed up here, he was sullen, angry, withdrawn, and frankly a pain in the ass."

By now Craig was laughing. "Yeah?"

"Do you have any idea where the fuck he went?"

Both men laughed and smiled into each other's eyes. Craig thought how strange it was that he now craved Seth's company. A week ago, he could barely stand it.

"It's been an amazing week," Craig said. "I don't know how I could ever thank you. I did have something I wanted to leave here though. This is something I bought here that I no longer need."

Seth recognized the gravity of Craig's tone. "What's that?"

Craig nodded toward his car, which was a few steps away. He walked that way and Seth followed. Craig took out his key and unlocked the doors, walking over to the passenger door. He sat in the seat and opened the glove box. In it was his handgun, the one that seemed to call to him at various times before, most significantly a week before as he sat by Clear Lake. Craig was aware that a gun was only as good or bad as the person holding it, but this one represented the feelings that he never wanted to feel again.

"I don't need this anymore," he said to Seth. "I was thinking that I'd like to leave it here with you."

Seth's face and eyes darkened on seeing the weapon, then it quickly passed. Seth nodded to Craig and slowly turned to his right toward the man with an unknown purpose. The man's eyes were trained intently on Seth, but Craig failed to notice the man's right hand inside his light jacket. Seth smiled with an understanding the man did not expect as he slowly stepped back, neither toward the man nor directly away.

"Dale, do you think you could take care of that?" Seth said.

There was a real surprise in the man's eyes as he relaxed. He smiled slightly, looking a bit surprised that Seth knew his name. Dale nodded, stepping to the car and taking Craig Cantwell's handgun.

Seth took a couple more steps away from the car as a slightly bewildered Craig followed him. Seth looked at him and smiled. However, Craig was struck by the contrast in the compassion in Seth's eyes and the dark look he had seen only moments before.

"How—how did you come to be here?" Craig asked.

"What do you mean?" Seth responded, quizzically.

"Did you always do work like this?"

"Um, no. Why do you ask? What stories have you made up about me?"

Craig chuckled lightly. "I don't know, that you are clair-voyant? That you are the business genius who taught Tony Robbins all he knows?"

Seth laughed. "No, not quite."

"I just see you as a master, someone who has always been a success, and now you teach others."

"I always find it mystifying that someone comes here, starts to find their own answers, and then falsely elevates me to the oracle's pedestal. A master? No, my friend. I'm a student, just like you. Just trying to find my way."

At this point, Dale had walked back over to them and was standing a few steps away. Craig's curiosity won out, and he finally asked a question the class had speculated on for the last week. He turned to Dale and said, "Okay, I just have to ask, who are you? Solve the mystery for me; nobody seems to know."

Dale remained silent.

"He's with me. He's . . . well, Dale is my handler," Seth said, filling the silence.

"What's a handler?" Craig asked.

Seth bent down and pulled up his pant leg and showed it to Craig. On his ankle was a device Craig recognized as the kind of tracker put on bonded criminals.

"What the . . . ?"

"This item is unique. It has a GPS tracker that will tell my handlers exactly where I am. If I exceed the boundaries here at SGZ, a series of reactions begin. It starts with a low level of electrical current and builds to a higher level that is eventually capable of rendering me unconscious. It is the only way I can be here to do what I do."

"I don't understand."

"I am serving three consecutive life sentences. When this group leaves, my handlers will take me back to San Quentin or, as we affectionately refer to it—*the Q.*"

Craig's mouth was hanging open. He wondered if Seth was playing a joke on him. There was just no way this man was a criminal. He had demonstrated more wisdom, instinct, and compassion in the last week than Craig had seen in a lifetime.

Seth chuckled. "Now, I know this is not something you read in our brochure. We kinda figured it might be a tough sell for people wanting to find themselves."

Craig shook his head. "Come on, this is bullshit."

"Oh, Craig, think back a bit. Have you ever seen me alone here?" Seth looked over his shoulder and nodded at Dale, who nodded back.

The realization raised more questions for Craig. A lot of old programming kicked in, such as, how could they allow a convict to run a personal development retreat? Things like doubting the truths he had discovered about himself in the last few days. He caught himself and looked again at Seth.

He could see that Seth knew just what was going through his mind, and like so many other things, Seth understood.

"Few people know my story, Craig, for obvious reasons, but somehow I think you should know it. So, if you will indulge me, I'll tell you my story, and you can judge for yourself whether your time here has been of value to you."

Craig knew he would listen to anything that Seth had to say. He had come too far with this man to do anything else. In a way, he felt honored to know the story of Seth Reede. So, he listened intently as Seth began to tell the story only a few knew about.

"Like so many inmates at San Quentin, I grew up without a father. My mother never told me about him, and I guess I was angry about not knowing my dad—maybe it was the first of many things I was angry about. When I was fourteen, I met a man who I thought cared for me as a father does for a son. He was the first strong man I had met who treated me with respect, who took the time to teach me what he knew. I suppose the thing that appealed to me was that I got his attention, that he found me worth spending time with. I didn't really give much thought to what he wanted to teach me or why. I was starved for a father figure. He was there and that was enough for me.

"This man was a thief, a professional thief. Not a con man or a swindler, he was the kind of thief who would assume any risk if the payoff was big enough. He would kill if he had to and had killed before. He was smart—even gifted—and when he had to be, completely ruthless. My emotional hunger drew me to him; he was what I thought I needed and had been looking for all my life. He taught me well, and when we had 'success,' the monetary rewards enthralled me even more. I was not a gangster in the classic sense. No, I was part of a crew that pulled off high-dollar heists. We had information systems and access to whatever technology and weapons we needed. If someone got in our way, they got hurt or killed.

"What I did not realize at the time was that that life was the perfect outlet for my rage. I had formed the belief that I had been denied in normal life, that I was not worthy of having a father to guide me or a mother who cared enough to keep me from a thief's life. I was an angry young man and thought that the more I could steal or bully or kill, the more I could prove the world wrong. *I'll show the world for shorting me. I'll teach the world a lesson.*

"As it always is, I found more and more evidence to support my beliefs as my career as a criminal unfolded. Friends were not really friends; they would betray me for money. Women only wanted what I could buy them. Even my mentor betrayed me, leaving me behind or for dead when he was in danger. This all reinforced, without question, what I thought I already knew—that the only one I could depend on was me. That I did not have nor want the capacity for love or forgiveness. That the idea of God or true love was a sick, common, stupid joke.

"So I lived my life taking my revenge. Revenge for the crimes and slights I imagined had been perpetrated against me. I stole. I killed if I had to. I would have told you that I had no soul.

"I told you that I had a teacher. I met him at a very unlikely place, in a very unlikely way. For nearly six months, I had planned a bank robbery. A young member of my crew was hired on at the bank, and through him I knew when a large shipment of cash was coming in. Unlike a typical takedown, we went in at the end of the day. Eight employees were still in the bank. We took them as hostages and had them make calls to their loved ones with excuses about why they were working late. As the evening started, my young accomplice made a mistake. He allowed a banker to get his gun, and the banker held it on him, demanding that I give up my weapon too. I remember smiling at how absurd that was. I told him once to put the gun down. When he didn't, I shot him between the eyes. When my young accomplice apologized to me for his mistake, I just shook my head and shot him as well.

"These events were really not that far from the norm for me. I still had just over 1.5 million dollars in cash that I now no longer had to share. I could pack up and leave with it. My preference was to leave the remaining bankers there, tied up and alive. I was still okay and could score and go on taking my revenge.

"What I didn't know was that the banker I shot had activated an alarm. Looking out the front door of the bank, I saw the first squad car pull up and knew I wasn't going anywhere.

"Craig, it's still hard for me to describe what I felt right then. I was thirty-one years old and had been a thief for more than half of my life. I had spent my life in pain, inflicting pain on others, in a futile attempt to relieve my own. What I saw in those cop cars was death, and I welcomed it.

"A hostage situation ensued. I was barricaded in with seven live hostages. I knew the police would not trade their lives for mine. I also knew my chances for survival (let alone escape) were zero. Surrender was never an option.

"After an hour, I told the police to get me an armored car; I would leave four hostages and take three with me that I would later release. We set a time, a deadline that the police missed. When that happened, I executed one of the bankers with the police listening on the phone. 'Get me the fucking car, or I will do the same thing again in one hour,' I told them over the phone.

"Over the next three hours, I killed two more of the bankers. The first one had been defiant, cursing me, condemning and dismissing me. He acted brave and had tried to intimidate me. He judged me or tried to. What he did not know is that my judgment of myself was harsher than any he could offer.

"The third banker cried and pled for his life. He was authentically terrified and pitiful. All he did was disgust me. At least the other guy had shown some balls. Neither one of their lives was hard for me to end.

"Time dragged on; my demands went unmet. It was time to execute another of the bankers. They and I had begun to understand that I wanted to die, that I had decided that this was it for me. I could see their terror, their helplessness, and in my state of anger and ultimate revenge, I took pleasure in it. It was perverse, this feeling, and yet I clung to it because it was familiar to me. I selected a man to be next, for reasons I will never know.

"That selection turned out to be the choice of my life.

"He was nondescript, nothing notable about him. He was maybe thirty-five and looked like you would picture a banker. He was neither thin nor fat, handsome nor homely. I sat in front of him and smiled my Satan's smile, brandishing my weapon, perversely wanting to see his terror or defiance. Either of those emotions would have been fine, would strangely have sustained me.

"But he looked up at me with neither terror nor defiance. This was totally unexpected. I was inwardly confused, as he looked directly at me, even into me, without a trace of fear. He wasn't smiling and was certainly not acting. I knew instinctively that his look and his emotion were real, authentic. In retrospect, the emotion and feeling from him was something I had never experienced before, not once in my entire violent life.

"This man, whom I had taken prisoner, and now planned to murder, was looking into my eyes with compassion.

"He was not deluded or crazy or manipulative. There was a clarity in his eyes; he knew exactly where he was and exactly what was about to happen. There was no question he felt fear, but something else in him overrode the fear—a force more powerful than his fear. This was the kind of situation, Craig, that you know is unique at a deeper level. Even at the time, in my violent state of mind, it hit me all at once. The pressure of terrified hostages, corpses lying about that I had killed, police outside who I knew would kill me, all that was trumped by the presence of something in the eyes of my next victim that I could not define.

"'*Back to business,*' I told myself.

"'Are you ready?" I asked.

"He nodded. 'It's all right. I forgive you.'

"I nearly laughed. I started to, then my mouth dropped open. *Forgive me?* I knew this to be utter bullshit, yet he still looked at me with compassion. Well, I knew how to end that. I pointed my gun at a spot just between his eyes, the muzzle not six inches from his forehead. 'Let's see if you can forgive this, motherfucker,' I said coldly.

"He continued to look directly at me or rather into me. It was so strange, Craig, this look. It was comprehension, as though he totally understood me. It was kindness, though not pity—that would have just enraged me. It was empathy, almost as if he understood the pain that I had felt all my life. Finally, there was no trace of disagreement or judgment since he himself had felt pain and had wanted to lash out. No, rather there was a vestige of hope, I guess. A knowing in his eyes that there was another way, a better way, to respond to the world's cruelty. This was just the slightest challenge to me to do something different for once.

"All of this he communicated with his eyes, in a flash, and with a loaded handgun pointed at his head.

"While I sensed all of this, the worst part of me declared that I was not man enough for this, that there was no turning back for me. I was so programmed to inflict pain to relieve my own anguish that I could do nothing else. Again, I decided to pull the trigger.

"Seconds went by. I looked at my hand, my gun, in literal confusion. Why had it not gone off? I checked the safety, even looked in the chamber. There was a round in there. I pointed my gun again, this time putting the muzzle against

297

his forehead. One of the bankers cried out, knowing the inevitable, fearing the crack of the gun and the mess it would make.

"I was suddenly breathing hard, panting as though pulling the trigger required more strength than I had. I just couldn't do it.

"My mind began arguing with my body. *This is ridiculous. What is one more life?* I had already killed four people; police were probably planning the breach of the bank that would drop me. A welcome thing that would end my pain in a hail of bullets. *Why can I not pull the trigger and kill this man?* I wondered.

"He continued to look at me, his gaze and all the feelings he emoted remained constant. Even more, his look said he felt my conflict.

"'What's happening?' I asked.

"'I don't know,' he replied honestly. 'It was easy for you before.' He nodded toward the dead bodies. 'What is different now?'

"'You're different,' I answered, not even recognizing the sound of my own voice. 'Who are you?'

"'I am nobody,' he said with a small smile. 'Or maybe I am everyone. Maybe I am you.'

"'What do you mean?' I asked, my anger temporarily gone, my curiosity piqued. 'You can't know me.'

"'I know you are in pain.'

"'What the fuck do you know about me?' I asked scornfully. 'You know nothing about my pain.'

"A small shrug. 'True, I don't know your pain. But I do know pain. All of us do.'

"This shook me out of confusion and back into anger. I pointed my weapon again. 'Do you know this kind of pain?'

I hissed, feeling I had been conned and wanting him to know—wanting to see his terror—now that I understood his game.

"He just nodded slightly. 'It's all right. As I said before, I forgive you.'

"Again, there was something wrong with my trigger finger—it would not pull. Comically, I reached for another pistol, pulled it, released the safety. Pointed it at his head. Again, nothing.

"He looked again at me. 'I even love you. I always will.'

"The fact that these words did not send me into a cynical rage was remarkable. Understand, Craig, to this point in my life, I had never seen love, never felt it. I had only experienced brief imitations of love, only to find that they were imposters. All these cheap imitations of love had made me sure that love was a myth. A ridiculous, impossible notion, like Santa Claus or the Easter bunny. The man there that day in the bank holding a loaded 9-millimeter had given up on the idea that love existed. That my next victim would profess love for me should have made me collapse in laughter—right before I blew his brains out.

"But my reaction was different. This declaration from him had unbelievable power. His words were like a mountain—immovable, unquestionable, undisputed. The words had a power that dwarfed my weapons, even dwarfed my hate.

"'Who are you?' I asked him again.

"'Maybe I am just the one man that you don't want to kill.'

"This again was a truth that I could not deny—but there was more. There was something divine in his words, in his presence. It was not so much that I did not want to kill this man; it was that I did not want to kill the divinity that I felt from him. Something in me desperately wanted to believe that this divinity existed—that it wasn't a sham or a con. I did not want to be the one to kill that.

"When I told him this, he again surprised me. He smiled. 'That's why I am not afraid. That which you are unwilling to kill is impossible to kill.'

"This was a truth that defeated me, that trumped my hatred, my anger, my greed. I stood with my gun hanging limply, pointed at the floor, suddenly weary with the weight of all the terrible things I had done. I could not move my eyes from this man as he continued to look into mine with his limitless compassion.

"What now? Every bit of my experience would have dictated a shrewd and probably violent path, but I was suddenly tired of violence. I looked at the gun in my hand and thought about taking my own life. Again, part of me asked, 'What's one more life?' The pain would end.

"As I raised the gun, the look on the banker's face changed. While still comprehending, there was disapproval. For some reason, I looked at him questioning.

"He shook his head slowly. 'Why be selfish? It hasn't worked so far.'

"In an instant, I understood what he meant. I saw my selfishness, which was how I had lived my life. There was no denying that it had not worked for me, not at all. It had brought me here, enraged and in pain.

"'You can still give.'

"Impossible. I hadn't ever given anything, not in all my life. I had taken; this was what I had learned and what I knew. When I considered his words, I saw the act of giving as I saw the act of climbing Mt. Everest naked. I had no idea where to even begin.

"'Give what?' I croaked, dismayed, believing I could never do this, even though I had begun to want to.

"'Give this,' he replied, pointing to my chest. He meant my heart, or he would have if I had one. 'You DO have one and you can give from it. It's a better way. That's how you fill it up.'

"I walked out of the bank, leaving my weapons inside. I knelt on the sidewalk, crossing my feet over each other and lacing my hands behind my head. I surrendered. I surrendered to the police, I surrendered to our system of justice, and mainly, I surrendered to the truths that my teacher in that bank had shown me with his bravery and his compassion.

"After my arrest, I later agreed to confess to my crimes. The only condition I wanted was to live. As it happened, the death penalty was not an option in California. My confession was not given in negotiation; there was no way for me to avoid spending the rest of my life behind bars. I did want to live, however. I did not yet know how, but I was going to find a way to give.

"I began to study in prison. All manner of things but primarily psychology and human behavior. I earned two college degrees in two years, then a master's degree, and finally a doctorate. As impressive as that may sound, it was nothing compared to my real education. That began when I came here for the first time.

"All the intellectual learning had value, of course, but only when I tied that to the power of emotion did I really begin to learn. It was at that point that I knew to lecture people was a far inferior way to reach people. I helped found Spiritual Ground Zero as an experiential way of self-learning. I did this to finally break my own cycle of revenge.

Facilitating others to find their own answers—the answers inside of them—was how I finally began to give.

"I went to prison fifteen years ago, Craig. SGZ began ten years after that. Coming here and meeting and working with people like you is a gift I hardly deserve. This is what sustains me, what keeps me alive. I thank God every day for meeting my teacher that day in that bank."

CHAPTER TWENTY-FOUR

On the fifteenth tee, Craig hit a driver that looked to the gallery like it might leave Earth and go into orbit. His swing had a slow and deliberate start, then a shockingly explosive move into the ball, sending it streaking down the center of the fairway. The whoops and cheers of the gallery followed this shot, which came to earth again 315 yards down-range, hitting the fast-narrow fairway and bounding farther. It finally came to rest nearly 345 yards from the tee box.

Craig's eagle at 14 moved him closer to the lead; more than that, it energized him. Both he and Waz knew that their only thought now was catching the leaders and overtaking them. There was a freedom in this realization, like a warrior who had accepted his own death and marched toward it without concern for his own mortality. Craig was a golf warrior who was formidable now, free of any concern or consideration of failure, committed to the best within himself. The eagle at 14 provided the jumpstart to this approach. Craig had surrendered to where he was now, any thoughts of victimhood forgotten. He walked the fifteenth fairway with purpose and focus and energy.

Craig and Waz needed little discussion or deliberation on the second shot to the par 5 15th. The ball lay 261 yards from the front flag position, and Craig knew as soon as he saw his drive he would be going for the green in 2. There was a freedom in needing to make up ground in a short time; any indecision is gone.

A slight breeze was quartering into them from the right, and if Craig had been anything but focused on the flag, he would have noticed the shot had to carry a water hazard in front of the green. As on the fourteenth tee, he saw in his mind's eye the 3 wood shot needed. He stepped to the shot with a knowing that produced the impact that matched the image in his head.

The speed of Craig's swing transferred to the ball as it rushed out and up. The velocity and spin took it to a height that gave the illusion of orbit—a shot like this looks initially like it will soar over the target never to be seen again. Craig watched the flight from his finished position, his eyes moving from the ball to the target. Internally calculating, reconciling the feeling of impact with the target.

The ball landed on the front tier of the two-tiered green where the hole was located. Because of the high flight, the landing was softer as a result. There was still a substantial bounce, and the ball rolled up the slope toward the back tier. The slope was killing its forward momentum. If it went too far and up that back plateau, the putt back down would be impossible to stop. The gallery, as well as Craig, knew this, and they both willed the ball to stay on the lower level. It climbed up to the top of the slope, and a foot from the top slowly started back down the hill. The crowd started cheering, thinking Craig would have another great chance at eagle.

The hill had a different plan.

The U.S. Open green was fast enough and the slope of the green severe enough that the ball would not stop on the lower tier. Gallery cheers turned to groans as the ball kept rolling down and did not stop until it had found a bunker in front of the green.

Most golf fans and even experienced pros would often recognize that the golf course had punished Craig's excellent effort. After all, he hit a 3 wood off the deck, flew it 260 yards to a small target, and the green spat it back to the deep bunker. The choice to feel victimized was attractive to a golfer and those pulling for him.

At this point, Craig's resolve did not allow for thoughts of anything other than the present moment. The choice he had on the fourteenth tee—that he surrendered to—was to be totally present. For him, in the present moment, there could be no celebration or disappointment in the past, no anticipation of the future. It was a childlike feeling. Strange because it was born of long experience that dwelling on a past event was ineffective.

Craig sized up his bunker shot and felt a thrill as the solution lay before him. He had a clean lie, and a common tendency would be to splash the ball out conventionally, taking great care to leave it below the hole. Craig wasn't looking at the hole though; he was looking further uphill to the slope that confounded his second shot.

After sinking his feet in the sand, Craig swung his sand wedge down to a solid *thump* two inches behind the ball. This produced a small shovel full of sand that the ball rode out of the bunker. It landed left of the flag, and it looked to Craig initially like he had hit it too hard. The swing had produced the right amount of spin, and the ball hopped once, then the spin briefly grabbed the grass before the ball's forward momentum released it. It tracked up the same slope to the back tier, only this time it slowed a good two steps earlier than Craig's colossal second shot. It slowly moved right and then worked back down. It crept slowly toward the hole and then stopped six inches from Craig's second straight eagle.

As the gallery continued its applause, Craig exited the bunker and tapped the sand off his shoes with his wedge. He traded the wedge for his putter that Waz handed him, allowing a smile and a wave to the crowd. He tapped in his birdie and noted that Jordan Spieth had made the same score on the hole. The realization that he had needed birdie just to stay three shots behind the leaders made it easier to snap back to the present on the walk to the sixteenth tee.

As good as Craig had played the hole, he wanted to be better still.

CHAPTER TWENTY-FIVE

A unique aspect of Colorado Golf Club is the back-to-back par 5s at 15 and 16. Two holes late in the round that offers either scoring opportunities or disaster, depending on the day. The sixteenth at CGC is a hole unlike any other. A small creek meanders down the center of the fairway for nearly three hundred yards, creating a dual fairway. The wider side is to the left; it's a far easier shot from the tee to a wide landing area. However, because the hole doglegs left to right, the left side leaves a substantially farther second shot. Hitting a tee shot to the right side of the creek is far more demanding; the landing area is half the width of the left fairway, and the fairway ends in scrub oak after three hundred yards. Taking this risk off the tee cuts off fifty yards to the green, making an eagle a real possibility.

A great golf hole presents the player with choices—exactly what hole 16 did.

Since Craig was still three shots behind with three holes to play, he had the advantage of being unburdened by dilemma. He stepped up to his ball and laced a 3-wood down the center of the right fairway, his ball stopping several paces short of the end of the fairway in perfect position. Craig was still flushed with purpose, a warrior knowing he had to give it all. It was his certainty that made this shot simple.

On the tee, Jordan Spieth showed hesitation for the first time in the round. Craig watched as Jordan and his caddy pointed and analyzed and discussed out of earshot how to approach this hole and Jordan's strategy against Craig. One part of Jordan seemed to want to be aggressive down the right side and pad his lead even more. On the other hand, he only needed par for the last three holes to pick up his second U.S. Open win. Craig suspected this was the counsel offered by Jordan's caddy, Michael Greller, as they huddled together. The conservative route was to play defense, but Craig sensed Jordan was feeling Craig's energy at the moment. Craig was hot. He appeared to have put the disaster at 11 behind him and was rolling now. Playing defense might just not work for Jordan.

"Let's go 3-wood down the right," Craig heard him say to Greller. The caddy handed over the club, knowing that decisiveness was key now. Jordan made his usual solid swing and hit the shot well. The ball curved just slightly more than his usual draw, and as it flew, both he and Michael urged it right. Craig suspected there was just enough indecision in Jordan's mind as he swung to pull the shot toward the safer haven on the left, just enough inner conflict to put the shot in between the two targets, the narrow one right and the safe one left. The result was Jordan's ball splashing in the narrow creek between the two fairways.

"Ah, Jordan!" Spieth wailed. He was semi-famous for venting at himself out loud.

The crowd of several thousand around the tee and down the fairway murmured audibly on observing the first chink in Spieth's armor. This development was impossible for Craig and Waz to ignore, but right away, they both knew that any thoughts on this had to be banished. As before, Craig had to focus only on his own game.

The second half of the sixteenth at CGC continued to present multiple options to the golfers. The entire hole plays downhill until it rises roughly twenty yards from the edge of the green. After that rise, the hill slopes even more dramatically down to the green, which continues to run downhill to the back right. The firm conditions that day dictated that a long second shot would not hold if hit to land on the putting surface. Any attempt to reach the green in two had to be hit short and left and allowed to run down the slope to the green. The variable was just how far the ball would roll once it cleared the rise in front of the green. The course architects and Mother Nature have combined to require both power and a high degree of finesse to reach the target in two shots.

Spieth's errant tee shot had left Craig an opening; far more prevalent in his mind was the challenge this second shot presented. The yardage to the front pin was deceptive; he knew flying a shot that far would result in his ball rolling well over.

He and Waz decided on a target to land the shot just short of the rise in front of the green. Having achieved that, the shape and trajectory of the shot were still key. A high shot with backspin would likely stop and not crawl over the rise and roll down to the green. The shot had to be low both on altitude and spin.

Craig recalled a time in his early development as a golfer in which he learned to hit low, running shots. Punch shots they were called. He had gotten so good at this shot that at nineteen he had relied on this strategy almost exclusively. So much so that his first teacher Hank christened him . . .

"Punch."

Craig took his 3-iron from Waz and played the ball back in his stance. He made a three-quarter swing and cut off his follow-through such that the clubhead never went more than waist-high. The ball shot forward like a bullet, staying much lower than a normal shot. At its APEX, the shot was no higher than twenty feet off the ground. It hit the fairway short of the rise in front of the green, then hopped a couple of times, and began to slow as it crested the hill. Then it picked up speed as gravity took over, rolling down the front approach area and onto the putting surface. The pin was positioned on the front left of the green for this final and most difficult round. The slope and firmness of the green would not allow it to stop close. It trickled on, finally stopping thirty feet below the hole, in the middle of the green.

Like the approaching conclusion of any high-level sporting event, the charge in the air as Craig and Waz walked to 16 green was tangible. Craig focused on his breathing and noticed his surroundings in an enhanced way. There was a shimmer in the air around the trees, the green, the gallery that Craig was somehow more aware of. It was as if he could objectively notice the essence of his immediate world, able to take note and apply what was essential. He could hear the gallery, the gentle rush of the creek, even the distant *thrum* of traffic several miles away. He could smell the grass, and as he passed it, the sand in the front bunker. He felt as if he could close his eyes, as he continued walking, and tell the exact moment he first stepped on the closely mowed green by the subtle change of grass under his feet.

He was conscious of his breathing, his beating heart, the feeling in his arms and legs. He could recall with fondness and wonder his meditation on the hill at Spiritual Ground

Zero and know that the practice of being truly present was a wondrous tool he could use.

Craig's awareness was peaked, and he had never felt more alive.

As Craig began to line up his putt for eagle, everything outside that thirty-foot path to the hole dropped away. He saw the path the ball would take to the hole as clearly as a well-worn trail in a thick forest. His mind's eye saw what he desired, and his spirit harmonized with it almost like an introduction of two people who have long wanted to meet.

He felt the grip of his putter in his hands, knowing this was the exact implement for this moment—this alignment of his being with the living grass in front of him. There was vibrant silence all around him, matching the stillness in his spirit as his finely disciplined talent moved the putter back and hit the waiting ball. He watched the ball roll over the living surface of this green, not with hope but with the faith of knowing the harmony he had demonstrated through his stroke. He observed the ball's movement with a smile, as he might witness a young hawk soaring. He experienced joy in witnessing his certainty demonstrated as the ball moved closer and closer to the hole.

Craig was literally jolted as the crowd exploded. As his eagle putt rolled into the center of the hole, they erupted. They were on his side now, and the energy that his brilliant putt had generated literally crackled through the air. He high-fived Waz as they walked off the green, and Craig half expected to see sparks as their hands met. They walked onto 17 only one shot back of the U.S. Open lead.

CHAPTER TWENTY-SIX

Golfers and other athletes talk about being in "the zone," a state of mind and body that yields peak performance. Some consider this a happy accident, a coincidental aligning of the stars that put the player in optimal mode. Sports psychologists and coaches have for years worked on the formula for intentionally producing this magical state of mind. Most agree that the formula is largely elusive.

In whichever way this is brought about, Craig Cantwell walked to the 209-yard, par 3 17th hole on Sunday of the U.S. Open feeling in "the zone." Completely aware of his situation and surroundings, Craig appeared unflappable, possessed of a heightened level of focus that enabled clarity and creativity. He was for this short time aware of and yet unconcerned about his desires, fully conscious that his process was the path to them. Craig could pick out any and all details of his thoughts and the world around him and focus on that which served his purpose. Even though he could acknowledge nerves and pressure, this heightened awareness allowed him to use that energy positively.

His mind and heart were still here in the eye of the storm that was Sunday at the U.S. Open.

The seventeenth at CGC is a natural beauty, a mid-iron shot to a green bordered on the front and left by a deep barranca. The green slopes sharply from right to left, and it was extra firm as a result of the sun and the lack of any man-made hydration. The pin was set back and left, in a risky position to hit to. Again, since Craig was a shot back, the choice was easy; there was only one target, and that was the flag.

Craig factored in all these variables, not like a computer but more like an animal hunting to survive. After a minute of instinctive reflection, he voiced his decision to Waz.

"Six iron. Let it land in the middle and release left."

Speaking almost to himself, he never took his eyes off the target. For his part, Waz simply handed Craig the requested club, having an expert's knowledge that nothing else was needed. The caddy could read his man's energy as clearly as a green light at an intersection.

As Craig teed his ball and physically rehearsed the shot that was vivid in his mind, the crowd around the hole went quiet. The five thousand spectators around the green were silent, but their attention moved an energetic needle to red. In this vibrating stillness, Craig took his stance.

With nothing else in his mind except the shot he wanted to produce, Craig swung. The sound of the club's strike of the ball was similar to the amplified sound of a match being struck—the ball's resulting spin and velocity like the sizzle of burning sulfur. The sound seemed to bounce off the trees around the tee releasing the silent energy of the gallery as they watched. After feeling the transfer of his intention to the ball, Craig did not even need to watch its flight. He did, however.

The ball landed on the putting surface some twenty-five feet right of the flag and hopped forward. Then the spin imparted by Craig's six-iron slowed it. Without the severe right to left slope, this shot would stop twenty feet right of the hole. The slope would not allow that today, and the ball began a slow roll left toward the flag. As it moved, the gallery noise grew, the voices leading the ball closer. As Craig watched the physical manifestation of his clear vision, his ball trickled to a stop just six inches from the hole.

Then Spieth stepped to the tee, having witnessed Craig's brilliant shot and feeling every ounce of its effect. Jordan had been playing with the burden of the lead as well, knowing that his fellow competitors were intent on chasing him down. He had to match Craig's brilliance here on 17 or go to the last hole tied.

Jordan hit what was a superb shot, his ball finishing only fifteen feet from the hole, leaving him an uphill effort at birdie. His putt had to be precise, however, and the break of the green and the pressure of the moment left his ball above ground after a strong effort.

After each player tapped in, Spieth for par and Cantwell for birdie, they walked to the eighteenth hole tied for the lead.

CHAPTER TWENTY-SEVEN

The electric intensity at the Open ramped up even more as Craig and Jordan walked from the seventeenth green to the 464-yard, par 4 18th tee. They were the last group on the course, so the gallery collectively descended on the eighteenth hole. The presence of scoreboards and online, real-time scoring reports informed all the patrons of the situation.

After four days of championship golf, the best players in the world on this magnificent stage had come down to this last hole, the last stretch, with Cantwell's rally creating an unreal buzz. This was a golfer who logically did not belong with the youthful elite of this game. At forty-seven, he would be the oldest U.S. Open champion in the history of the event, which began in the 1890s. If Craig's age and "on-paper" deficiency next to the young titans of golf were not amazing enough, his play on the last four holes was unprecedented. Golf fans worldwide would be in awe of a four-hole stretch played 6 under par by a Jordan Spieth or Dustin Johnson, but by a forty-seven-year-old, washed-up journeyman?

All of this created joyous disbelief in the golf world. An unfathomable scenario that was nonetheless real.

Added to all this was the off-the-course, outside-the-tournament bombshell that had exploded in the last few hours. The day began with the golf world seeing Craig as a man whose right to be here was questionable due to his past, but Zeke Monroe's arrest and the revelations by Kelly Keys brought a full, new understanding of Craig Cantwell to the world far beyond the world of golf. Craig's attack on Monroe was not excused, just well understood. He had been silent about the event that ruined his career and reputation; he had done so to be true to his word to Kelly's heroic mother. Craig had made the choices for his daughter and had silently accepted the consequences. Then he had fought his way back to the U.S. Open.

Without a conscious effort toward this result, Craig Cantwell was now a hero.

Pressure—the pressure of the U.S. Open. The achievement of golf immortality. Anxiety—born of fear of failing thousands or maybe millions of people willing your victory. The vulnerable, naked feeling of so many people knowing so many personal things about you. The steel resolve of your worthy adversary, a young man who wears the braid of experience of winning this very event. Jordan Spieth was a grounded warrior, who was rising to the very pressure you feel. The nervous distraction of imagining, just a short time in the future, lifting a trophy that you have dreamed of winning since you were a boy. That idea was both wonderful and frightening at the same time. Winning would bring such changes—great ones maybe—but at what cost? Every achievement had its cost. What would this one be? Fame, money, more pressure? *Will I be worthy of that success? Will it ruin me? Will I lose myself? What if . . .*

Craig suddenly and unexpectedly felt a hand gently touching his. He looked to his right, initially startled. He relaxed when he looked into his daughter's blue eyes. Kelly was suddenly by his side. She was flushed with the excitement of the moment to be sure, and her look also showed relief over finishing her day's disclosure. With that now in the past, she would join him here in the crucible of the final part of this journey.

Kelly's presence meant more to Craig than anyone else could know. He was a man who, through his own actions and struggle, had come to feel alone. Even the crowd's acceptance today, though gratifying, reinforced his loneliness. On a public pedestal even if he were worshipped, Craig must still be clothed in the respectable. He was excited by his new acceptance, yet still found it uncomfortable and intimidating. He had seen firsthand what a public persona gone wrong can do to his self-worth. Craig knew that finding himself in the view of others was fickle and false, and wanted now to be able to stand on a stronger foundation of who he was.

He could now find that foundation in his daughter's eyes, in her gentle and brief touch of his hand. In looking at her, he could be reminded of the best part of himself. Far more than seeing his own heritage passed down, she had been the catalyst toward his recovery. She had offered him a vehicle, a process that he accepted and that led him out of the dark abyss that had been his life. She did that with no plan or agenda, expecting nothing in return. Kelly had offered him a rope out of love, and he had accepted it. He could see this now for what it was—a prize far greater and more lasting than the earthly one he was in pursuit of. This was a rock he could stand on to reach higher.

On a deeper level, Kelly saw their combined strength as well. The love in her eyes was mixed with a competitive passion that was a mirror to Craig. He borrowed that steel and added it to his own resolve as he left Kelly and climbed to the eighteenth tee.

The eighteenth hole at CGC is fittingly one of the most challenging in golf. At 464 yards, it plays uphill, which adds an additional thirty yards. In a casual round of golf, the fairway looks narrow; in the oppressive energy Craig and Jordan Spieth were now in, it was a narrow ribbon of grass surrounded by calamity. Fairway bunkers left and right, and three-inch-deep rough bordering the entire hole to the green. If that were not enough, the putting surface was one of the most severely sloped on the course. It slanted hard from back left, and the stern masters of the U.S. GA had placed the hole just above a tier on the back portion of the green. Getting an approach shot close meant flirting with the back of the green, and playing a shot from there was like trying to stop a golf ball on tempered glass.

Craig and Jordan both felt the full weight of U.S. Open pressure as they stood on the tee box. For Craig, catching Jordan from behind as he had done intruded on his fearless approach in a way that all competitive golfers know. The pursuer has more aggression and less fear than a golfer playing with the lead. Despite the conscious effort of putting aside where he stands relative to an opponent, the reality of being tied leaks into the golfers' thinking. A bit of caution—something Craig had not played with since the thirteenth hole—is present regardless of whether a player wants it or not.

Playing first, Craig visualized this crucial last drive. He picked the exact spot in the center of the fairway he wanted and knew that a miss just left was preferable to the right side. That knowledge, secondary to thoughts of his target, resulted in Craig guiding his drive, unlike the previous four holes in which he let the shot go more freely. The contact was solid, yet more mechanical than before, and his shot drifted left. On seeing this, he and Waz wished for a lie in the long and shallow bunker to the left rather than the three-inch rough. His ball landed in the left edge of the fairway and bounded straight, then kicked just a little right and wound up in the first cut of rough. It was a manageable lie just left of the fairway.

Feeling the same pressure, Spieth was just a bit too anxious in his swing, seeing his drive just left of Craig's. Jordan's ball hit the left part of the firm fairway and bounced further left, ending up in the left bunker.

Craig and Waz realized that this was the first real favorable bounce they had had in the round.

As the pair walked up the eighteenth fairway, they continued to feel the weight of the situation. There had been several light moments between the players and their caddies throughout the round, but now there was silence. Craig and Jordan both had their own thoughts, and both were immersed in the weighty task of focusing on the one shot that they now had to play. It was a task akin to that of a tight rope walker—simple if he could only detach from the consequences of failure.

Jordan was away and played first from the bunker. His shot had to clear the bunker's front lip of about four feet and travel nearly two hundred yards to reach the green. A tough shot in casual circumstances made brutal by U.S.

Open pressure. He caught the ball cleanly and solidly, clearing the bunker lip by a foot and flying nearly to the front of the green. The ball hit fifteen yards short and took a brisk hop forward off the firm fairway. The steep slope slowed the shot, and the ball barely rolled on the front, settling some thirty-five feet below the hole.

Jordan's shot was superb under the circumstances, and now Craig had to answer. He had exact yardage—184 yards—and a good lie. He and Waz chose a 6 iron, the same club he hit to six inches on the last hole—a great image for his confidence now. Craig rehearsed the swing several times, then stood to the ball and swung.

This swing was every bit as technically sound as his shot on seventeen, the difference was the shallow grass he hit from. The blades interfered minutely with the club's contact with the ball, and it jumped slightly left of his intended line. The ball also had less spin and as a result "knuckled" slightly, hitting the green just short of flag high and releasing against the hill. As Craig and Waz and eight thousand people around the green watched, Craig's ball found the rough long and left of the eighteenth green, sitting there like an Easter egg left for a child to find.

As he and Waz started walking and he saw this latest challenge before him, Craig felt the fatigue of the final round in full. They had started this round four and a half hours ago, yet it suddenly seemed as though they had been playing for days. His mouth was dry, despite the six bottles of water he had consumed over the day. He suddenly felt as though his feet were heavy; he had to be conscious of putting one foot in front of the other. His experience told him the physical fatigue was not real; it was a result of his mind's reaction to where he was and his desire to prevail. As Craig drank more water, he wondered briefly if Jordan had the same symptoms.

He then heard the PA announcer from the last grandstand. "Please welcome the final group of the day. From Dallas, Texas Jordan Spieth!" The crowd erupted as Spieth took off his cap and acknowledged them. They applauded Jordan not only for the U.S. Open champion that he was but also for the man they knew him to be.

"And from Joplin, Missouri, please welcome Craig Cantwell!" To Craig's surprise, the crowd's acknowledgment of him was several octaves louder than that of Jordan. He removed his cap and nodded to them as he walked, and the ovation continued. As Craig walked, Waz dropped back a few steps, following his man while letting him have this moment. Waz had always known the man and was now finally glad the crowd did as well. As he watched, he saw the patrons stand and applaud, which they had not done for Jordan. The ovation continued for Craig until they had reached his ball in the rough just off back left of the green.

While Craig's ball lay off the putting surface, it was closer to the hole than Jordan's. Spieth had a daunting putt from the front part of the green, thirty-five feet that had to climb up a steep shelf in front of the hole and yet had to stop before it went too far past. Going long of the hole with this putt would leave a lighting fast second putt downhill, one that if it missed might roll all the way back to where he started.

Jordan Spieth had gotten to his lofty status as a Tour champion by being one of the best putters in the world. He lined up his putt, not with the thought of getting it close. His only vision was to make it.

There were now some twenty thousand people surrounding the eighteenth green. Tournament officials had allowed the galleries to crowd onto the fairway after the golfers passed so that the green was an island surrounded by humanity. Millions more watched on television as no fewer than ten cameras around the spectacle reported and recorded it. Despite their large number, the gallery fell silent as Jordan stood over his putt. Though there was silence, the crowd's collective energy fairly crackled like the hum of an electrified fence.

Using his familiar grip, Jordan rolled his putt up the slope toward the hole. There was a very little break in the putt; the challenge was to gauge the distance precisely. One experienced and witty commentator compared the putt to rolling the ball up the hood of a car, up the windshield, and stopping it on the car's roof. That analogy was accurate. After he stroked this putt, Jordan watched its progress wide-eyed, knowing his best was delivered.

The ball appeared to have too much speed as it ran toward the steep shelf in front of the hole. As the ball reached the incline, it slowed and crept over the crest, still rolling. As it slid further toward the hole, the crowd found its voice and an involuntary high-volume tone from witnessing the amazing. It was right on the line if it only reached the front edge of the hole. Jordan raised his putter in his left hand, his right ready to assault the air in exhalation, his breathed sucked away by the crowd's awe.

The pitch of the rising sound the crowd made changed abruptly as the ball stopped four inches short. Jordan dropped his putter to the ground and his hands went to his knees, the only thing that kept him on his feet. The shock of so much change in just a few seconds all over his face.

Supreme focus, apparent ecstasy, then abrupt disappointment. All a matter of perspective, his was an amazing effort, one that was a fraction of a fraction short of the mark.

The crowd's amazement gave way to applause for Jordan's amazing putt. They clapped and cheered this splendid warrior as he numbly walked up and tapped in, his work for now done.

Craig and Waz were participant spectators in Jordan's effort. Both had thought for more than a few seconds that their opponent had made his impossible putt—which would have most likely ended Craig's bid for the title. The good news was that Jordan had not done the impossible. The bad news was this; the challenge facing Craig to get his ball in the hole in two more shots was as daunting as any he had ever faced on a golf course.

Craig's ball lay twenty-five feet from the hole in 31/2 inches of lush grass. It was visible, and looking at it from right above gave the impression of an egg that was lying in a nest of grass. The ball was an unknown distance above the solid ground beneath it, tangled well-fertilized grass making up that uncertain margin. A scientific device to measure the depth and density of the turf Craig had to assess had not been invented; this was purely something he had to feel—he had only his experience and the information vaguely transmitted from his feet as he walked and through the club to his hands as he made practice swings through the thick grass.

Gauging the thickness of the turf Craig's ball lay in was essential to knowing how hard to hit it, which was in turn crucial to getting the shot to stop close to the hole. Looking toward the hole from behind the ball, Craig saw about six feet of thick grass, then the closely mown surface of the green sloping down and to the right. This shot would traverse across the slope and down, on a surface that was super firm under only ¼-inch of green grass. In order to get his ball in the hole in four shots and remain tied, Craig had to negotiate this slick slope exactly. To be too timid and leave the shot above the hole meant a lightning-fast putt for 4; being just a fraction too firm meant the ball would pass the hole and catch the downslope on the other side that had slowed Jordan's putt from below. This was almost like chipping down a staircase, needing to stop the golf ball halfway down.

This shot would have been dauntingly difficult if Cantwell and Spieth had been concluding a casual match for a post-round beer. Add to the situation the electrified silence of twenty thousand golf fans surrounding the scene and numerous cameras broadcasting the event to millions around the world. Throw in the redemptive possibilities to Craig's life of winning and the return to the abyss of his life should he fail.

All these external factors pressed on Craig like deep water, as though he were fathoms down in an ocean of expectation. He could see his desires in one result, and his failure in another. He could feel the weight of fame, which would judge him incompletely no matter what the results. These factors manifested physically in him, feeling his pulse in his temples and fingertips.

Without a conscious desire to do so, Craig took a slow and deliberate inhale through his nose. As he slowly released his breath, he noticed the smell of the grass and pines back of the eighteenth green. He breathed slowly in again as he remembered the peace of breathing on a Northern California mountainside. In the stillness he created there, he had experienced a sunset. At this moment, his breath had facilitated an even more wondrous experience.

On the mountainside at SGC, Craig had begun to strip away the false ideas of his life to reveal who and what he really was. His breakdowns to that point were vital to his discovery that he was not his failure nor his success. He was not the events and experiences of his life, good or bad, but the product of his choices through those times. Like a sculpture with a chisel, Craig Cantwell could chip all the falsehoods away and reveal his authentic nature.

He had scaled up the rock face of his life, and of this golf tournament, and as he climbed higher felt the fear of falling more and more acutely. The knee-trembling fear of looking down was now replaced by the exhilaration of being higher and more alive than ever. Self-aware, he knew he could not fly, but he also knew that he could climb higher. Above the noise, the expectation, the pressure—above the earthbound limitations of all who watched him in the arena.

Most golfers will acknowledge that the most difficult adversary is not the golf course, the opponent, or the wind and rain and rough. The toughest opponent is oneself—all the untruths and distractions uttered by the cowardly, yammering version of the golfer. Craig had quieted that inner critic, and now that limiting character was transformed. He joined Craig now, not as an adversary but as his greatest ally.

From this precipice of pressure, Craig saw the result. It was a result he willed, but it formed outside of his thoughts. The vision now in his mind drew energy from the emotion of successfully bringing it to reality. This thought was audacious, it was daring, and he may have been the only one in the world to dare think it.

I'm not going to get this close. I'm going to make it.

The event took shape and texture in his imagination, with the ethereal instructions now coming clear. His will created the vision, and he now trusted his body—with all its training and experience—to bring the vision to life. Everything aligned in Craig—the years of practice, the lessons learned from failure, the resulting trust in his own instincts, and most importantly his intention to rise higher than he had ever been.

Intuitively, he knew. He knew the exact pace and force with which to swing his wedge; he knew how the ball would react to his strike out of its nest in the deep grass. He knew how it would bounce and roll on the unpredictable surface of the green, and he knew how to measure the mix of slope and gravity that would take the ball to the hole.

At that moment, he was certain.

Craig took his stance next to the ball, his eyes fixed on the exact spot on the green to land his ball, and with the image of the shot from start to finish in his mind. The loop of the next few moments ran in his mind, not just the visual, but also the sound, feel, texture, and even smell of this shot repeating over and over until it was ingrained in his mind. Immersed in this present moment without a memory of before or a thought to after, Craig swung his club.

The club swished through the deep rough and popped the ball free. In his heightened state of awareness, Craig saw it rise out of the grass with the exact motion he had seen in his mind's eye. The ball hit lightly on the putting surface at the exact point he intended and began to roll down and to the right. The steep slope took it, and the crowd noise rose; they at first took the certainty of the ball's roll as a mistake. It would surely roll past the hole and even off the front of the eighteenth green. For those first few instants, only Craig knew where the ball was going. Unimpeded, the ball would not stop. However, Craig's certainty was precisely delivered, and the ball's path followed his intent unerringly.

As the ball hit the base of the flagstick and dropped in, the crowd erupted in spontaneous wonderment. The collective shout that arose could be heard for several miles. To them, this was nothing short of a miracle. They were all riveted in the hope that Cantwell could summon the skill and courage to get this effort close, and thus manage a tie with the splendid Spieth, and he had the audacity to succeed in bringing the impossible to reality. The crowd's collective roar was the result of twenty thousand souls expressing, *"Did that just really happen?"* The verification would come through countless replays.

The impact of the moment slowed Craig's conscious awareness down, like witnessing an accident in slow motion. The power of witnessing his vivid intention being born into reality seemed to slow time. As the moment passed, the crowd's eruption assaulted his ears. The adrenaline thrill lifted him as he levitated, the club falling from his hands as he looked around for Waz, who abandoned all professional control in running in jubilation to his boss and friend. Both men's eyes and mouths were open as the release of joy and tension ran out of both. They embraced, player and caddy, as only two men who truly know the feeling of triumph can. Both had witnessed it before, but being close to it and being IN it are vastly different. This victory, both powerful and sweet, could only be truly known to them.

Craig broke away from Waz as the crowd continued to exult him and took steps toward the hole without feeling the ground. This level of euphoria was foreign enough for him to need confirmation that it was real. As the crowd continued to roar and applaud, Craig stopped at the final flag and looked down to see his ball in the hole. At this moment, he truly lost control.

He dropped his hands to his knees and bent down as the tears flowed freely. He moved his hands to his face, knocking off his cap; now there was nothing in the way of his emotions. The collective barrage of emotions was too much to deny, and Craig Cantwell released it in front of twenty thousand live witnesses and millions more on television. His body shook with sobs of joyful exhaustion, as the crowd's voice rose even higher.

Roy Wasson walked to his friend, and through his own tears put his hand on Craig's back. The caddy's eyes, however, were up and scanning a section of the gallery off the green, seeking the only person to adequately celebrate with the new U.S. Open champion.

Kelly Keys stepped out of the gallery, moving from a part of the crowd to be the first in a long line of those who would honor Craig. She covered the twenty steps to her father quickly, her own tear-streaked smile immediately recognized by the crowd. Craig and Kelly hugged each other in celebration as the world watched, affirming their history and launching their future.

GLOSSARY

While this story is about a golfer and is set in and around golf, it is not meant to be *about* golf. The intention is that this book will be entertaining and inspirational to both golfers and non-golfers alike. So, for those readers not afflicted with the golf disease, this glossary of golf terms is provided. (Who knows, maybe some of you may be compelled to take up this silly game!)

GOLF COURSE: There are 18 holes (catchy title, huh?) each of varying length, that length measured in yards in the United States (meters in Europe and abroad). There are **PAR 3's**, **PAR 4's**, and **PAR 5's**.

The **TEE BOX** or **TEEING AREA** starts a hole. There are markers that show the allowed area where a player may place their ball on a TEE for their first shot on a hole, also called their **DRIVE**.

The **FAIRWAY** is the closely mowed area between the **TEE** and the **GREEN** that is the most conventional path to the **GREEN**. **ROUGH** is the area off the fairway, consisting of deeper grass that is harder to hit a ball out of.

HAZARDS can consist of **SAND BUNKERS**, **WATER HAZARDS**, **WASTE AREAS**. They are known as **HAZARDS** because it is more difficult to hit a ball from them than the fairway or green.

OUT OF BOUNDS means an area beyond the course boundary.

The **GREEN (AKA PUTTING SURFACE)** is a contoured area of closely manicured grass, and the **HOLE (AKA CUP)** is located someplace on the green.

GOLF SCORING: PAR is a benchmark score for each hole. A PAR on a PAR 3 is 3, meaning that the golfer who hits his/her ball into the hole in three shots has made PAR. (Naturally, a score of PAR on a par 4 is 4, etc.)

A BIRDIE is a score of one under par on a hole (a score of 3 on a par 4, a score of 2 on a par 3, etc.)

An EAGLE is a score of two under par for a hole (a score of 3 on a Par 5, for example). A double eagle is a score of three under par for a hole. A BOGEY is a score of one over par for a hole (a score of 5 on a par 4). A double bogey is a score of two over par for a hole (a score of 7 on a par 5.)

One can also make **TRIPLE BOGEY** (three over par) **AND QUADRUPLE BOGEY** (four over par) on a hole.

A tournament like the U.S. Open (and most professional golf tournaments) consists of four rounds of 18 holes. The scoring is shown for each player in relation to par on a cumulative basis. For example, in the beginning of the last round of the U.S. Open, our hero Craig Cantwell was a cumulative 4 under par, two shots ahead of Jordan Speith who was at 2 under par.

GOLF EQUIPMENT: A golfer carries up to 14 clubs in his bag, per golf rules. **WOODS** are actually metal in modern times and consist of a **DRIVER** (used to hit **TEE SHOTS** of a tee box to start holes), a **THREE WOOD**, a **FOUR WOOD, FIVE WOOD**, etc.

IRONS are so named because they are made of metal. Most pro golfers carry irons from #2 or #3 up to a 9 iron and several **WEDGES. HYBRIDS** are a cross between an iron and a wood and are often substituted for the lower numbered irons. The lower the number, the longer distance the club is designed to hit a ball. (A 3 IRON will hit a long-distance shot than a 9 IRON.) A professional golfer will know how far each club will hit the ball in yards on a consistent basis.

A PUTTER is used to **PUTT** the ball on the green or hit low rolling shots of a short distance.

CADDY: This person carries the golfer's bag (which holds his clubs, balls, extra clothing, snacks, water, etc.) and during a tournament is the only one allowed to give the golfer advice. Caddies are great at knowing distances, judging the wind and other variable conditions, and also maintaining the golfer's equipment (cleaning clubs and balls, etc.). A caddy may also judge the surface of a green for his player (called **"READING THE GREEN"**). A caddy also occasionally acts as a therapist to a golfer during the pressure of a competitive round.

Made in United States
Orlando, FL
30 August 2022

21790364R00189